Ghosts of Valhalla

Haunting the Route: A Prequel Novella
Choosing the Slain
Calling the Blood*
Waking the Fire*
Raising the Dead*
Seeking the Frost*
Breaking the World*
Drawing the Blade*
Burning the Gods*
Riding the Storm*

*forthcoming

CHOOSING THE SLAIN

GHOSTS OF VALHALLA
BOOK ONE

AMY CISSELL

CHOOSING THE SLAIN
Amy Cissell

A Broken World Publication
13820 NE Airport Way, Suite K395495
Portland, OR 97251-1158
Choosing the Slain
Copyright © 2023 by Amy Cissell
ISBN 978-1-960766-02-1 (ebook)
ISBN 978-1-960766-03-8 (paperback)

Cover Design: Damonza
Edited by Two Birds Author Service
Proofread by Christopher Barnes, Cissell Ink

for the strongest people out there: those of us who go head to head (heh)
with our brains to survive (and everyone who loves us)

ONE

I bounced on the balls of my feet. My pulse accelerated and heat rose in my cheeks. I knew I was walking on dangerous ground, but I was a risk taker, and danger was my middle name.

I laughed at my ridiculous joke and took another swig from the tumbler on my nightstand.

The front door slammed.

Fuck. She was home early.

I looked around our bedroom frantically, but there was no way to hide the evidence in time. The room was small—our king-sized bed took up most of the space, and our shared dresser used up what little floor space remained. Gwen hated "stuff," and the only surface that had anything not utilitarian on it was my nightstand. My nightstand that didn't even have a drawer to hold my mess. She was going to see all the things I'd meant to clean up before she got home. Unless I could keep her downstairs.

I pulled on a T-shirt, spritzed the perfume Gwen had given me for our last anniversary, and popped a breath mint.

I ran my fingers through my tangled, black hair—already

showing two inches of blonde roots, even though I'd had it cut and dyed less than a week ago.

"Gwen," I called down the stairs. "Is that you?"

The *thunk* of a heavy bag hitting the hardwood was my answer.

I ran down the stairs and skidded to a stop at the bottom, willing my pulse to slow. I took a deep breath and walked into the entryway.

Gwen was standing in the doorway, several stacks of boxes surrounding her.

"What the fuck, Frankie?" Her honey-brown eyes moved from the delivery boxes on the front steps I hadn't heard arrive to the ones in the front hall that'd shown up yesterday and I hadn't had a chance to hide yet.

She was wearing blue jeans that hugged her slight curves enhanced by her muscular frame, a red T-shirt with her fire station's logo on it that complemented her lightly tanned skin, and had shoved her sunglasses up on top of her head. Her shoulders looked tense—a sure sign she was angry.

I grabbed at and discarded a dozen excuses before I came up with something plausible.

"Greg's not home," I blurted. "So I'm accepting his packages for him. I'll take them over as soon as he gets back."

Gwen bowed her head, and her long, blonde hair that she usually kept tightly braided fell in a wave over her face.

"Frankie, all these packages have your name on them," she said, exhaustion riding her voice.

I recognized that tone, but I also knew how to override it.

"I'll send them back," I promised. I took the last couple steps to close the distance between us, wrapped my arms around her waist, and tugged her close.

I kissed her, tracing her lips with my tongue.

For a moment, she leaned into me, and a surge of triumph welled inside me.

Then she reared back and pushed my arms off her.

"You've been drinking and your mouth tastes like a minty-fresh ashtray."

I bit the inside of my cheek. "I went out with Ash for happy hour and had one cigarette and one drink," I said finally.

"It's nine o'clock in the morning, and your hair smells worse than mine does when I get back from a fire." Her voice was flat.

I wrinkled my nose in confusion. "No. It's nine p.m. I just got home—Ash dropped me off like an hour ago."

Gwen pushed past me and headed upstairs. I chased after her. She walked into our bedroom, dropped her bag, and pulled open a dresser drawer. "Have you been taking your meds?"

My eyes darted to my nightstand. It held a half-empty bottle of Wild Turkey, my condensation-coated glass, empty but for the melting ice, and a baggie of white powder. What wasn't there was my bottle of lithium. I followed her gaze down to the floor. Pills were scattered everywhere, and one bottle was half-visible from where it'd rolled under the bed.

"You promised." She turned her back to me and grabbed a black T-shirt and black cargo pants that were not as fitted as her jeans, but still not baggy on her slim form.

"Are you going to work?" I asked. "You came home two days early from your conference just to go to work?"

"I'm home two hours early—I caught an earlier flight. And yes, I'm going to work. There's been a series of fires that look like arson, and I'm heading into the station to meet with a fire investigator. Ash better not be as messed up as you are. He's been called in, too." Gwen changed clothes swiftly, not glancing my way even once.

"You hate Ash," I pointed out.

"I do. I hate that you two are friends. He's a crap person and every time you hang out, he gets you into trouble. But he's the best firefighter on my team, and his abilities to find the source of a fire and know the best way to put it out before any of the rest of us do makes him invaluable."

She turned around and looked at me, unshed tears in her eyes.

My stomach clenched. I clasped my hands in front of my body, twisting them together so she wouldn't see them trembling.

"This was your last second chance," Gwen said.

I couldn't let her catch my gaze. I was afraid of what I'd see there. My throat closed up, and my breaths started coming in short, shallow gasps. This couldn't be happening.

"I'm sorry, Gwen. I really am. I'll be better. I'll take my meds. I'll go back to my psychiatrist. I'll go back to therapy. I'll stop drinking." The desperation in my voice was a pale reflection of the panic coursing through my veins.

"You're not going to therapy anymore? You quit your shrink? That's the third one in six months." Gwen grabbed a belt and laced it around her waist and braided her hair, wrapping it into a tight bun at the base of her neck. She stuck pins in it to ensure it wouldn't escape and become a fire hazard. She was the only firefighter I knew with long hair.

"Look at me," she commanded when she'd finished.

I forced myself to meet her eyes and searched her face, looking for any hope at all.

"You and I are through. I'll sleep at the station tonight and tomorrow. Find a place to stay by Thursday, and make sure your stuff is gone in two weeks, or I'll donate it." She held out her hand. "Give me the ring."

I looked at the diamond on the fourth finger of my left hand. I heard the echo of my ecstatic *Yes!* and saw the happiness and love glowing in her eyes. We'd been engaged for only three months, and now it was over.

Things were always ending.

"Frankie, the ring."

I pulled it off my finger and handed it to her. She tucked it into her pocket.

"I'm surprised you haven't pawned it yet." She stared at me. I couldn't read what was in her eyes. It didn't look like the heartbreak that was washing over me and pulling me under.

I couldn't breathe.

"Please, Gwen. I can be better. I love you."

She walked forward and cupped my cheek with her hand. "I love you, too, Frankie. And maybe you can be better, but I can't watch you try anymore. Take care of yourself, please. Stay strong and stay alive. Call your parents if you need to, but don't call me." She brushed a kiss against my lips. "Goodbye."

I trailed after Gwen as she went downstairs and watched her grab the duffle bag she'd brought home, then walk out.

The front door closed so softly I barely heard it through my tears.

I trudged back upstairs and collapsed heavily on the bed. Then, I filled my glass with Wild Turkey and dumped the bag of powder onto the top of my nightstand, then retrieved the razor blade and straw from the floor.

I cut the coke with the razor, forming it into straight lines. I picked up the straw and snorted the first line. Then the second. My pulse picked up, but instead of the feeling-numbing euphoria I was expecting, panic rode my chest.

I did the third line. After all, it no longer mattered, did it?

Without Gwen, without a place to live, what was the point of being strong? What was the point of anything?

What was the point of me?

TWO

My cellphone ringing pierced my brain and reverberated in my skull. I pulled my pillow over my head, but it did nothing to block the sound.

I pried open my eyes. They were stuck together with a thick, crusty paste, and I had to scrape my fingers against my eyelids to release them.

The phone stopped ringing, then immediately started again.

I stared at the bedside stand and reached for my phone. It wasn't there.

My head pounded until it felt as though it might roll off my shoulders and bounce down the hall. I pushed down on it to keep it in place and tried to focus.

On the top of my nightstand was an empty whiskey bottle, shards of glass that looked like they'd piece together into the tumbler I'd been drinking from, smudges of white powder, and no phone.

There was a pause in the ringing, then it started again.

I followed the sound. My phone was under my pillow. Smears of mascara stained the rose-colored sheets. The screen said it was Ash.

"What do you want?"

"Hey babe." Ash's voice, which always sounded a little sarcastic, echoed too loudly in my already-throbbing head.

I pulled the phone away from my ear. "'Hey babe' isn't an answer." I knew I was being bitchy, but I couldn't find it in my hungover body to care.

"I heard Gwen dumped you, and I wanted to know if I could take you out for sympathy drinks."

The thought of drinks roiled my stomach, and I gagged. "Not right now."

"I didn't mean now." Ash laughed. "It's like ten o'clock in the morning."

"What day is it?" I croaked. I stumbled into the bathroom and filled the water glass that was sitting next to the sink.

"Thursday?" he said, making it a question. "Are you okay?"

"Shit," I said. "What time does Gwen's shift end?"

Rustling papers on the other end of the call gave me time to put the phone on speaker and grab a washcloth. I ran cold water on it and swiped it over my face, removing most of the clumps of mascara and crud. The running water woke up other parts of my body, and the pressure on my bladder became insistent.

"I have to pee," I announced. "I'll call you back in a minute."

I hung up, peed, washed my hands, and stared at myself in the mirror. My eyes were bloodshot—you could barely tell they were light brown—and my lightly tanned white skin was flushed. My hair looked two inches longer than it had the last time I'd noticed it. Ugh. Of all the superpowers to get, why did mine have to be too-fast hair growth?

I called Ash back. "Did you find out yet?"

"Her shift is over at two."

I walked back into the bedroom and looked around. "She said I had to be out before she gets home. What am I going to do? I'm broke as fuck and don't have anywhere to stay." I held my breath and crossed my fingers, hoping he'd offer to let me stay with him. I'd only been to his place once when we'd stopped by so he could grab his jacket, and I hadn't gone inside.

He lived in a huge, sprawling house, and from what I knew, he lived alone.

"Wow, that sucks." Sympathy oozed from his voice and coated me with insincerity.

I knew should just ask, but I wasn't sure I could handle being rejected after everything else. "I need to shower, clean up my—*her*—room, and pack before she gets home."

"I'll pick you up at one," Ash said. "I'll take you out for drinks, my treat, and we'll figure out what you're going to do next."

I huffed out a sigh. "Tomorrow's payday. Maybe it'll be enough to get a motel room for a couple nights." If I could just stay out till midnight, the money would hit my account and I could grab a room at the Western Scene. It was the cheapest, crappiest motel in Santa Fe and was an especial favorite of sex workers. It rented by the hour if you knew how to ask, and the lack of Wi-Fi, cable, and regular maid service that would've kept the rooms in clean, bedbug-free sheets meant even I should be able to afford it.

"See you later, babe," Ash said. "And don't worry, you can leave your shit in my car for a few days."

The line went silent.

I swiped through my phone and brought up my music app. I had a lot of playlists for just about every mood, but had never created one for "super hungover, newly single, and suddenly homeless." I found the next best thing and started the Scandinavian folk metal playlist that buoyed me whenever I wanted something loud to hide my feelings.

Once I'd turned the volume up as loud as my pounding head could stand, I stripped out of Gwen's favorite T-shirt and my rattiest boxer shorts and turned on the water.

I stepped into the shower—the water was hot enough to redden my skin immediately—and let the heat push every emotion, every last fear, into the dead space where I kept such things.

When I was void of all emotions again, hollow and clean, I turned off the shower, turned down the music, and packed up my life.

I STOOD by the front door waiting for Ash to buzz up so I could let him in and con him into helping me carry my life down to his car.

I had one backpack, two suitcases, my sword, and three boxes of books. I had survived with so little for long enough that even when I'd moved in with Gwen and found stability for the first time since leaving home, I hadn't accumulated much.

Still, knowing how little I had to show for my thirty-five years was almost enough to pull regret and grief out of the walled-off corner of my mind. Almost.

I opened all the Amazon boxes in the entryway and left the printed return codes on all but one so Gwen could return them and get her money back. The last box had things I actually needed. A new sports bra, running shoes, shorts to replace the ones that were too worn and baggy to wear, and the kate spade purse I hadn't been able to say no to when Amazon suggested I'd love it.

I shoved the new clothes and shoes in my backpack, moved my wallet and phone into my new purse, and waited.

When my phone rang, I jumped.

"Ash, I thought you were picking me up here. I've got all my things ready for you to carry down to your car."

He laughed. "Leave it. I don't want anyone to break into my car and steal your junk before you have a place to put it. Gwen's meeting with the arson investigator at two, so as long as you don't leave your keys behind, we can grab it tomorrow. Just shove your shit in the corner and text Gwen that you'll get it later."

I huffed out a breath. It made sense to leave my things here until I had a place to stash them. "Fine. I'll be out in a couple minutes."

"I'll be waiting for you!"

I pushed my suitcase and three boxes into the corner of the living room, sent a message to Gwen letting her know I'd be back to grab my stuff and leave the keys, and taped the note to the top box.

I eyed my backpack and sword. I couldn't take the sword into the bar. I leaned it against the wall next to my suitcase. I didn't want to leave the backpack behind—it had my change of clothes and all the meds I'd been able to salvage from the bedroom floor—but it'd be ridiculously unwieldy to carry around. When my phone started buzzing with incoming text messages, no doubt from the eternally impatient Ash, I tucked my purse into my backpack, slung it over my shoulder, and went downstairs to Ash's waiting Aston Martin.

THREE

Ash dropped me off in the parking lot of the Western Scene motel and sped off almost before I'd closed the car door. The building was a faded tan that looked anemic under the blinking neon sign advertising color TV and the few security lights that weren't burned out. All the doors had strips of red paint hanging off them. The buzz of bug-killing lights drowned out the sound of distant traffic. Barred windows on the office and the cage around the soda machine completed the look and lent verisimilitude to the right-on-the-money depiction of a seedy motel.

I wove unsteadily into the motel office. A scuffed wooden desk with white paint peeling off the work surface was centered under a swinging, naked light bulb.

I slapped my bank card on the desk and looked at the person behind the counter. "I need a room for two nights."

The white man with wispy brown hair that showed more scalp than it concealed picked up my card, peered at me with hazy blue eyes over wire-rimmed glasses, and pushed a clipboard toward me. "Write your name and phone number here. You'll be in room seven. It's seventy-five dollars for two nights. No drugs. No solicitation. No noise." His voice was monotone as he repeated the words he must've said a hundred times.

He swiped my card through the card reader. It beeped twice. His eyebrows drew together in a vee. He swiped the card again. Two beeps.

He handed my card back and pulled the clipboard away from me. "Your card's been declined. Either pay cash or hand me a different card."

"That's impossible," I protested. "It's payday."

He didn't answer, just pulled a pack of cigarettes out of a drawer and tapped them against the desk. After sliding a cig out of the pack, he crossed his arms over his stained white T-shirt and leaned back.

"Pay up or get out."

"How much is one night? Can you run my card for that?"

He took the card back, tapped a few buttons on the computer, and ran it again. *Beep beep*. Declined again.

"A couple hours?" I knew my desperation was clear in my voice, but I didn't care. It was two in the morning, and if I didn't have enough to stay here, I didn't have enough to stay anywhere else. I didn't have anything warmer than the jeans, T-shirt, and light jacket I'd left the house in, so sleeping outside would be uncomfortable.

"We don't rent by the hour. Don't let the door hit you." He stood and walked out the front door, lit his cigarette, and watched me with suspicious eyes until I followed him out.

I pulled out my phone and opened my banking app. There had to be a mistake. Had the paycheck just not gone through yet? It usually hit around midnight on payday.

A deposit showed, but it was more than fifty percent smaller than the five hundred dollars I was expecting. There were also three overdraft fees and a current balance of fifteen dollars.

I put my phone back in my purse. It jingled my keychain. I wrapped my hand around the three keys. I had one for Gwen's condo, one for her car, and one for the animal shelter where I worked part time.

I didn't think Gwen would feel sorry enough for me to let me stay with her, even if the alternative was sleeping on the street. Her car was off-limits, too, then. That left the animal shelter.

They'd stiffed me on my paycheck, but I was willing to overlook it and let them make it up to me by providing me a place to stay.

I looked around to get my bearings. The streetlights were far apart in this part of town; the small circles of light barely making a dent against the dark. The animal shelter was about a mile up Cerrillos Road. I could be there in twenty minutes.

I LET MYSELF IN, closed and locked the door behind me, and crept through the halls to the locked janitor's closet. I grabbed some extra blankets and bedding we had set out for our rescues, made myself a little nest in the back corner of the closet, and curled up in a ball. I remembered to set my alarm—I needed to be out before my boss showed up in the morning—then closed my eyes and tried to will myself to sleep.

Usually I didn't have any trouble falling asleep when I was drunk, but the humiliation at the motel and the walk had woken me up too much. I opened my eyes and stared at the ceiling. I couldn't make out anything more than vague shapes in the light that made it through the cracks in the door, and the longer I stared, the more they took on the shape of monsters in the dark.

I closed my eyes. There was no such thing as monsters—at least not any that I hadn't created with my mind. I tried to find my happy place, the one I'd built when I'd been trying to manage my bipolar with mindfulness and meds instead of Jack and cocaine. The vision of a soft wildflower-filled meadow in the shadow of soaring mountains and overlooking jagged fjords refused to come, but my eyes grew heavier, nonetheless.

Something soft brushed against my ankle.

I shrieked and bolted to my feet. I hopped the two steps toward the door and flipped on the light.

An orange tabby cat sat in the middle of the floor looking up at me.

My pulse slowed, and the sweat that had broken out on my forehead cooled.

"How the hell did you escape, kitty?" I squatted down beside the cat and held my hand out. The cat made no move to sniff it. Instead, it stared at me in a very uncatlike manner. "You must be new; I don't recognize you, and there's no way I'd forget such a handsome young man."

The cat stood and stretched, turned around, then lay down, looking slightly less annoyed now that I'd complimented him.

I rolled my eyes. Now I was anthropomorphizing animals. I dropped to the ground next to the cat. "I should put you back in your cage, you know."

The cat shuffled over until it was leaning against me. Its mass was much heavier than a cat's should be, even one this hefty. I reached out slowly and let my hand rest on his back, just behind his neck. When he didn't move, I slid my hand up and scratched between his ears.

He tilted his head until he found the ultimate position, then purred.

Something about the subtle vibrations in my hand popped open the door I'd determinedly closed that morning, and tears streamed down my face. The cat climbed into my lap, flopped down heavily, and let me pull him close to my chest while I sobbed.

FOUR

Something cold touched my nose. I don't know if that's woke me, or if it was the pressure on my bladder, but whatever it was, it wasn't pleasant.

I cracked opened my eyes, bracing for the hangover I deserved.

When the headache and nausea didn't immediately make itself known, I opened my eyes all the way and stared directly at a furry, orange face.

"Jesus Christ!" I sat up and scooted backward until my back hit a shelf full of janitorial supplies. "Personal space, dude!"

"It's about time you woke up." The cat sat back on his haunches, lifted one paw, licked it, and rubbed it over the top of his head and one ear.

This explained the lack of hangover. I was either still drunk and high, or I was full-on in some kind of altered state of mind due to the bipolar. Possibly a combination of the two. I'd finally done what everyone had been expecting me to do for the last decade—I'd lost my goddamn mind.

I smiled tightly at the talking cat, who was regarding me with the steady gaze of all cats everywhere when they wanted something.

"You probably need a litter box or food or something. Sorry, I thought you talked to me." I closed my eyes and shook my head.

"I can take care of myself, thank you very much." He sounded affronted, which was what I always assumed a cat would sound like. Definitely hallucinating.

"You're not hallucinating." He let out a sigh that sounded nearly human.

I pulled my phone out of my pocket. It was four in the morning; I'd only been asleep for an hour. "I shouldn't be awake. No matter how uncomfortable my makeshift bed was, I should be passed out." Why was I still talking out loud? I did not want to have a conversation with the cat. The cat who could not have a conversation. Because he was a cat.

"Check your texts," he said.

I unlocked my phone. I had four unread texts, all from Ash.

Just got called in to work. Four alarm. Is Gwen there?

Nvm. She's at the scene already. This fire is a monster.

Dude. Lady dude. Whatever. This. Is. Crazy. Crazier even than you.

I grimaced. I hated it when people called me crazy, but Ash never seemed to remember, and every time I called him on it, he rolled his eyes and told me I was being too sensitive. I took a deep, cleansing breath and read the last message.

Shit, babe. This building's about to collapse, and Gwen's inside. I'm going in after her. Peace out.

My pulse accelerated and panic clogged my throat. I had to get there. Wherever there was. And I had to do it without a car.

I let myself out of the room and barely noticed that the cat had snuck out with me until he brushed against my ankles. "What am I doing? Where am I going?"

He looked up at me. "Where would Gwen think you were if you weren't at home? What's the one burning building she'd run into against all protocols?"

I went cold. "The Western Scene?"

"Got it in one." The cat sounded bored, but his pose belied that attitude.

"Okay, that's not a long walk. She needs to know I'm okay and that she should get the fuck out of the burning building." I slipped my shoes back on and beat feet for the back door. The cat kept pace with me.

I was nearly hyperventilating by the time I got outside. The air was thick with smoke, and the flames that were more than a mile away lit the street with their flickering orange glow.

I HITCHED my backpack over my shoulders and took off at a light jog. In two blocks I was out of breath, which was humbling since I'd been an avid runner until a few months earlier when I'd replaced morning runs with brunches with Ash.

I slowed to a walk and tried to keep from wheezing.

"You're a mess," the cat said. Despite his housecat size, he'd had no trouble keeping up with me, and to add insult to the weirdness of a talking cat, didn't even sound out of breath. "Pick me up or we'll never get there."

"That makes no sense," I said, trying to speed up and even my breathing at the same time.

The cat flopped to the ground in front of me. "Do you argue about everything? Just pick me up. You're wasting time."

My heart was beating a choppy staccato in my chest from exertion and fear, and I didn't have any energy left to keep arguing. I crouched and scooped up the cat, grunting a little with the effort.

"Good. Now walk toward the fire."

I did as commanded. I figured toting my new friend would still give me forward movement and allow me to catch my breath, even if there was little other benefit to carrying a cat to a fire.

I stumbled and looked down at the uneven sidewalk as I caught my balance. When I looked up again, the motel was in front of me, and fire engines choked the streets.

"How..." I shook my head. I must have blacked out. It wouldn't be the first time that'd happened in the last few months. I clutched the cat to my chest and started toward the flames consuming the ramshackle two-story motel.

"Ma'am, you can't go past this line," said a firefighter who looked vaguely familiar but whose name I couldn't come up with.

I pushed past him and took three steps before his arm wrapped around my chest and pulled me to a halt. I tripped over my feet and dropped the cat, who darted away without a backward glance.

"Let me go," I said, struggling to wiggle out of the firefighter's hold.

Heat seared my skin, and the air was almost too thick to breathe. Dark, oily smoke roiled through the shattered windows, and streams of water continued to shoot from the hoses into the building. I wasn't a firefighter—in fact, fire had always terrified me—but even I could tell this building would be a total loss.

"Terry, that's Gwen's girlfriend," someone near me said. I don't know if they were whispering or shouting. Everything paled in contrast to the roar of the fire.

"Someone radio her and Ash, tell them to get out now. There's no one left in the building—at least no one we can save," Terry said. His grip on me loosened, and I broke free.

I dropped my backpack on the ground and ran toward the motel. The stamina I'd lacked on my way to the fire returned with a wave of adrenaline.

If Gwen died in there, I'd never be able to forgive myself. She didn't deserve to die because of me. I had to get her out, no matter the cost.

The lobby where I'd been so soundly rejected a couple hours ago was barely recognizable. Between the ravaging flames that hadn't yet fully consumed the room, the darkness and smoke, and the ashes swirling through the air, the place resembled a horror film set more than a flophouse.

I ran back out of the lobby. They wouldn't be looking for me there. They'd think I had a room. Gwen probably assumed I'd blacked out and hadn't woken up.

"Frankie!" Ash's voice cut through the roar of the fire and echoed in my head. I pivoted toward him.

He was standing in a doorway seven rooms away from where I was. I stared at him for a moment.

"Get down here!" he yelled frantically. "Gwen won't come out until she finds you. You have to show her you're okay!"

All hesitation ceased, and I sprinted. I careened into him, and it took both of his gloved hands to steady me.

"Where is she?" I asked.

He spun me around to face the room behind him. There was nothing visible beyond the curtain of smoke. "She's in there. She won't listen to me."

"I'll get her." Determination hardened my voice.

Ash put a hand on my arm. "Don't be ridiculous. You don't have any experience, and you don't have the gear."

"I'll just be a second. It'll be fine." It was stupid, but that'd never stopped me before. I'd done so many stupid things and always come out on the other side just fine. I shed my jacket, tied it over my mouth and nose, and pushed my way through the smoke.

A CRACK like a gunshot reverberated through the room as a beam collapsed. An echoing scream followed it.

I could barely breathe through my panic and the smoke, but I could see two figures trapped under the beam. One wasn't moving at all, and the second was struggling to lift it.

I dashed forward, dodging sparks and falling pieces of ceiling, and dropped to my knees.

Neither of the faces were visible through their protective gear, but I didn't need to see them to know that the one on the ground, bleeding and still, was Gwen.

"What the fuck are you doing, Frankie?" a voice I recognized as Zach Keene's asked. "Get the fuck out of here."

"Not without Gw..." My words dissolved into a fit of coughing. Shit. Was I dying now?

The walls, the fire, and everything else faded into transparency. The battle against the fire raged all around me, but it was like watching a scene through a greasy window. Zach and Gwen struggled in front of me, the latter fighting for her life now, and the rest of the crew outside trying to contain the flames before they could spread to nearby businesses.

I looked down at Gwen. Her spirit wasn't fighting. It was leaving, and if it got away, she would die. Even though I knew this was a smoke-induced hallucination and a sign of my imminent death, I couldn't watch her die. I couldn't let that happen.

"You are going to live!!" I screamed. I grabbed her spirit with both hands and shoved it back into her body. But it wouldn't stay. Every time I let go, it started to drift away with the smoke.

My eyes darted around, trying to find something, anything, to glue her back together with, to keep her whole.

Zach's spirit was strongly attached to his body and pulsed gently with his heartbeat. I could see where it resided and how it was attached. If I could just use a little of that, of his soul-glue, I could keep Gwen's spirit from floating away.

I pushed Gwen's soul down with one hand and used the other to reach into Zach's chest and grab his spirit where it attached to his body. It was sticky, and I had to yank to pull some away. I took my eyes off him and turned my attention back to Gwen. She was slipping through my fingers. I had to get this done now.

I tugged harder without looking at Zach, and a handful of ether came away in my hand. I pulled it down to Gwen and used it to attach her spirit to her body. The edges of her spirit were ragged—they didn't have the same smoothness as Zach's—but it worked. I anchored her spirit to her body, and she coughed weakly.

Gwen was alive.

Now that she was okay, I could work with Zach to get the beam off them both and get them out of there.

I pivoted back toward him. I couldn't see his spirit, the soul stuff. There were a few threads hanging from where it had been attached to him, where I'd pulled from it, but nothing else. His spirit was gone.

His body was unmoving, his chest no longer rising and falling.

Shit shit shit. Where was his spirit?

The ridiculousness of my panic hit me, and I laughed. It didn't matter. None of this was real. I was dying, or maybe I was already dead. There was no way I could see souls, much less move them around and glue them back in.

I'd come to show Gwen I was alive to save her, and we were all going to die, all because of my selfish stupidity.

"Oh, shut up," a voice said next to me. "You're not dead. You're finally awake, and you have already screwed up. Stay on the floor. You'll all be rescued in a moment."

I turned toward the voice, and as I did, the glow that'd permeated the smoke and flames disappeared, leaving me once again shrouded in the inferno. The cat was sitting beside me, his expression filled with so much contempt and disappointment that I leaned away from him.

Before I could ask him what he meant, silhouettes appeared through the smoke and the cat disappeared.

"We've got 'em!" someone shouted. I was lifted and carted out of the building and handed over to a pair of EMTs.

They asked me questions about insurance, but my eyes were drooping and it hurt to talk and breathe. I knew I was fading fast and would be unconscious in moments but needed to know two things.

"Gwen? Zach?" I rasped.

The EMTs exchanged a look. "There's no final word," one of them said. "Close your eyes now, and we'll get you to the hospital."

Coolness enveloped me as they loaded me into the ambulance, and I let myself drift away.

FIVE

The world faded back into view, and I started coughing. My lungs ached, and my throat was so dry I wasn't sure I'd ever be able to swallow again.

"How are you feeling?" a calm voice asked.

I couldn't answer, so I did my best to shrug and figure out where I'd woken up this time.

The bright lights and antiseptic smell gave away the mystery almost immediately. I hated hospitals.

I struggled for a moment to sit up before the nurse pushed a button on a hand-held controller, and the bed raised my upper body higher. I stank of smoke, and my arms were an angry red.

"You're lucky," the nurse said. "You don't have any serious injuries and no signs of smoke damage to your lungs, which seems nearly impossible to believe."

"Drink?" I rasped.

"Of course." She noted something in the chart hanging at the foot of my bed and grabbed a small glass of water sitting on a nearby shelf. "Drink slowly."

I sipped at the water, even though I wanted to chug it. When the cup was empty, the nurse handed me another.

"Thank you," I said. My voice was still rough, but it didn't hurt to talk anymore.

"You're welcome." She removed my IV and handed me a cotton ball to press against the pinprick of blood that appeared. "A doctor will be through to see you in a bit, and then you'll probably be cleared to go." She smiled, refilled my cup one last time, and exited through the curtains drawn around my bed before I could ask about Gwen and Zach.

Seconds later, I was done with my water. I was still thirsty as fuck, but even more urgent was the need to pee. I slid out of the bed, wobbled a bit, and pushed through the curtains to find a bathroom.

A breeze hit my backside at the same time I realized I was no longer wearing the clothes I'd fallen asleep in the night before.

"Nice ass, babe," Ash said from behind me.

I reached behind myself to clasp the edges of the hospital gown together. Ignoring Ash, at least for the moment, I motioned for the attention of the next person who walked by and got directions for the bathroom.

Once that immediate need was taken care of, I padded back to my little enclosure. Ash was perched on the foot of the bed, my backpack on the floor next to him. His nearly porcelain white skin and blond hair were unmarred by any of the ash that caked my more bronzed complexion, and his androgynously elfin features looked more amused than concerned.

"I thought you'd want this." He nodded toward my pack. "It's a good thing I found it, or you'd be walking out of her stark naked."

"Where are my clothes?" I asked.

He wrinkled his nose. "What was left of them was probably too gross to keep. When you came out of the fire, they were practically falling off. That was a really stupid thing to do, Frankie. Brave, but stupid."

"I had to go after her. I had to. If she died because she was looking for me, I would never forgive myself." The memories of everything that'd happened while waiting for someone to come in and save us hit me.

"I had the weirdest experience. I must have been hallucinating or something, but I could've sworn that Gwen almost died, and I saved her by sticking her spirit back into her body." Even though it had been a hallucination, I didn't want to admit that I'd used some of Zach's soul-glue to keep Gwen's in place.

Ash laughed. "That's wild. Fire can do weird stuff to a person. Every one of us who's been caught in an inferno with no obvious way out has had some kind of mental trip."

"Is she okay?" I knew she was. She had to be.

"Gwen's going to be fine, but she'll probably be in the hospital for a few days."

Relief coursed through me, and the grin widening across my face threatened to crack the layer of ash and soot coating my skin.

"But Zach didn't make it," Ash added quietly. "He must have had a heart attack or something. There wasn't a mark on him—even that beam that fell didn't give him so much as a bruise, and he showed no signs of smoke inhalation. He just...died."

It had to be a coincidence. I didn't kill him. That's not how things worked. "That's terrible. He seemed okay when I first went in."

Ash narrowed his eyes at me but didn't say anything further. "I stopped by to see if you needed a ride somewhere."

"I'm supposed to get out of here in a few minutes. Once I get changed, if you could take me back to Gwen's, that'd be great. I need a shower more than I've ever needed anything. I'll stay there tonight, then figure the rest out tomorrow."

Ash nodded. "I'll be waiting in the lobby. Don't take too long."

He exited the room, leaving a pile of guilt and dread behind.

"I didn't kill him," I said aloud. "I couldn't have. It wasn't real. None of it was real."

I paced nervously in front of the door to Gwen's hospital room. I wasn't sure if she'd want to see me, but I needed to see her to reassure myself she was still alive. But now that I was here, I was having second thoughts.

The hallway felt crowded, even though there was no one else visible. Every once in a while, I'd catch a flash of a figure, but whenever I tried to focus on it, it disappeared.

I hadn't had any alcohol since Ash had dropped me off at the motel twelve hours earlier, and I didn't feel the effects of the many things I'd consumed last night coursing through me, but there must have been something lingering.

Before I could talk myself out of it, I darted forward and knocked on the door. The worst had already happened. She'd kicked me out of her home and out of her life.

"Come in," she called. Her voice was gravelly but strong.

I pushed open the door and walked in, running my eyes over her body to reassure myself she was okay.

"Frankie." Her voice was flat and betrayed no emotion.

"How are you?" I asked, then mentally kicked myself. She was in the hospital after nearly dying in a fire trying to save me. Obviously, she wasn't great.

"Better than I should be," she said.

"I'm sorry. I—"

Gwen held up a hand, an IV line hanging from it. "Stop. It was my choice to go into the motel. It was my guilt that made me stupid. But at least I backed my stupidity with training and protective gear. Yours wasn't. Thank you for coming in after me. But I don't know if I can thank you for anything else that happened."

I froze. I had no idea what she was talking about, but she couldn't be referring to my hallucination. "What do you mean?" I asked cautiously.

"You held me together and wouldn't let me die."

I laughed airily, but it sounded false to my ears. "That's ridiculous. I sat by you and held your hand until help came, but I didn't hold you together."

Gwen's eyes narrowed. "I know what I saw. You did something to me and something to Zach. Now I'm alive, and he's not. I don't know what happened, and I am never going to talk about it or even think about it again. I'm going to be here for a couple more days. You can stay at the house until then."

"Ash is giving me a ride back home. Back to your home," I corrected. "I can bring your car if you want me to leave it here for you when you get out."

Gwen shook her head and closed her eyes. "You should be at work, and I should be asleep. Don't visit me again, Frankie."

"I love you." I stared at her, willing her to open her eyes, to look at me, to tell me she loved me, too.

The world shifted in front of me, and everything solid faded, leaving nothing but ghostly outlines. Gwen's spirit burned brightly, but it wasn't attached to her. It was wrapped around Zach's spirit, and his was tethered to Gwen.

My mouth fell open. What had I done?

"Goodbye, Frankie."

The spirit world disappeared. I took a deep breath and turned around. The cat had been right. I had fucked up, and I had no idea how to make it right.

SIX

The clock above the reception desk in the cat rescue office showed I was only twenty minutes late for work, which was better than usual. Considering everything I'd been through in the last couple days, it was practically early. It was a good thing Ash had waited for me to shower then dropped me off.

"Frankie, is that you?" my boss called from his office. "Can you come in here?"

I dropped my backpack and jacket in the small breakroom and headed into David's office. He was a big white man with a shock of brown hair that stuck out in all directions and a wispy mustache that gave me the wig every time I saw it. He was wearing, as always, khaki pants and a striped polo shirt that strained over his belly. "What's up, David?"

He pointed at the clock. "What time were you supposed to be at work today?"

My spine straightened. He'd never bugged me before about when I showed up—at least not seriously. And he had a lot of room to talk since he'd shorted me on my paycheck. "Gwen almost died in a fire overnight," I said, a touch more acid in my voice than necessary. "I've just left her hospital bedside."

David's expression softened for a moment. "I'm really sorry to hear that. Is she going to be okay? Will you be getting back together?"

I wrinkled my nose. "What do you mean, are we getting back together? What makes you think we were apart?"

David spun his laptop around so I could see it and pressed a button. The security camera feed came up on the screen. I watched myself enter the building, grab the blankets, and lock myself in the janitor's closet. He hit a button, and the tape skipped forward a bit. The next scene was me leaving the closet with my backpack in hand and the cat at my feet.

"You can't break in and sleep here," he said. "This isn't your crash pad."

Anger, hotter than the fire I'd been through in the middle of the night, burned at my chest. "I wouldn't have had to sleep here if you hadn't shorted me on my paycheck. All my automatic payments bounced because there wasn't enough money to cover them, and I couldn't even afford a room at the Western Scene. Which is good, actually, since it burned down."

He sighed and folded his hands on his stomach. "I didn't short you. You shorted yourself by only showing up to half of your scheduled shifts, and none of those on time. Frankie, I have given you so many chances the last couple years. You are bright and so gifted with the animals. It's not often a veterinarian wants to work at a cat rescue, and I hate to lose you, but you are not the reliable employee we need, and I can't afford to hire someone else to take up your slack and keep paying you."

The room swam in front of me, and I backed up toward the wall. "What are you saying?"

"I'm sorry, Frankie, but you're fired. Take whatever you left in the janitor's closet and anything else that's in the break room." He stood and held out his hand. "The key."

My hand trembled as I fished my keyring out of my pocket. I broke a nail pulling the wires of the ring apart enough to slide the key off, and I dropped it on the floor twice before putting it in David's hand.

"I can do better." My voice sounded like it was far away as the echo of the words I'd said to Gwen three days ago leapt into this conversation.

"I know you *can*," he said. "But I don't think you will." He dropped the key into his desk and pulled out an envelope. "Here's your final paycheck for the hours you worked last week. Good luck finding a new job. And give my best to Gwen. She's a wonderful woman."

The words "unlike you" hung in the air while I stared at him.

Then I shook myself into action. Arguing with David wouldn't yield any better results than arguing with Gwen had.

I ran my fingers through my hair and got them stuck in my braid. *Fuck.*

I shook them free, tearing out a few strands as I did so.

"Fuck!" I screamed. I kicked the break room door open, grabbed my jacket, and stormed out of the building.

I sat on the curb and pulled my phone out of my pocket. In less than a week, I'd lost everything.

I dialed Ash's number, but it went straight to voicemail. I hung up. He never listened to his messages, so it wouldn't do any good to leave one.

I texted instead. *Are you free? Can you pick me up at my job and take me back to Gwen's?*

His answer was immediate. *No can do, babe. I've got a hot date with a hotter person, and I'm still trying to get the smoke smells out of my car after giving you a ride this morning. Try one of your other friends.*

"Fuck," I muttered. Then I stood, hitched my backpack a little higher, and started on the five-mile walk back to Gwen's.

CHAPTER

SEVEN

I watched the sun come up from the small, shared courtyard of our—of *Gwen's*—condo complex with a cup of coffee pressed into my hands. A Santa Fe sunrise was something magical, but it'd been ages since I'd seen it from the right side of the morning.

I took a sip of the coffee and did my usual morning review of how I felt. Nothing hurt, I wasn't bleary-eyed and tired, and the thought of food didn't make me want to vomit.

In other words, I felt weird.

I'd gone days without drinking or drugs in the past. I never had more than a couple glasses of wine when I was out with Gwen and never even thought of visiting my dealer—aka Ash—when she was home. But a four-day International Association of Fire Chiefs conference in Baltimore that Gwen had bookended with vacation time to see her family in D.C. meant I'd been mostly on my own for almost three weeks. It'd only taken two days before I'd found myself closing down the bars, then closing down the bars no one was supposed to know about.

I'd nearly forgotten what it felt like to wake without a hangover.

I'd always been a morning person, and a chipper one at that. But a few months off my meds and a couple weeks of trying to destroy my body had not only robbed me of my relationship and my job, but I'd lost my sunrises, too.

I took a long drink of my coffee and checked the time on my phone. My favorite coffeeshop wouldn't be opening for another hour, and I didn't feel like messing up Gwen's kitchen by making breakfast.

I slipped back inside and found my running clothes. Panting for breath on a one-mile jog to the fire in the way-too-early morning hours the day before—god, yesterday had been the longest day— had been just one more wake-up call.

If I was going to make good on my promise to Gwen to shape up, I needed to take action.

Once I'd glared at my hair—the dye had faded out, and it was almost completely blonde again—pulled it back into a ponytail, and donned my sports bra, running tights, and shirt (all black, as were most of my clothes), I slipped on my neon pink sneakers and matching hat. I strapped on my fitness tracker, grabbed my water bottle, and hit the pavement.

I took off on my regular easy route, a meandering loop of five miles through some of the nicer neighborhoods in town. I made it about half a mile before I started gasping. I slowed to a walk and breathed through the stitch in my side by switching my inhale to when my left foot hit the ground instead of my right.

A couple minutes later, I was breathing smoother again. I sped up but didn't try for my usual eight-minute-mile pace.

I knew I was out of fuel before I was two miles in, but I would not give up, no matter how high my heart rate trended and how much my quads burned. I was a "five miles is my short distance" runner, and by all the gods, I was not quitting now.

My run took me by a cemetery where I'd probably fit in with the zombie population if my shambling gait was the only thing needed to qualify me. I slowed down to a walk and gazed in. I'd always loved cemeteries. Looking at the headstones had been a favorite hobby growing up. Maybe it was because seeing the bookends of people's lives left such a sweetly painful lump in my chest. All we were in the end was a set of dates with no memory of what happened between them.

Or maybe it was because my mother was the funeral parlor director in my hometown, and my earliest memories were of accompanying her to work.

I stopped in my tracks and shook my head. I hadn't thought of my mother in ages, other than fleeting recollections that I had one. I had an entire family, in fact, but I had neither seen nor spoken to them in ten years. My parents would be in their late sixties now. My sisters were adults. They might have husbands. And children. I could be an aunt.

I closed my eyes. I couldn't think about this now. I'd resolutely refused to talk about my family with every therapist I'd ever seen, and every single one of them had told me that if I didn't fix my relationship with my parents, I'd never manage to fix myself.

Eight deep breaths later, and I was ready to continue. I had just under two miles to go, then I'd be home. I could shower, dress, and get coffee and breakfast.

I opened my eyes to find myself looking directly into the translucent gaze of someone who hadn't been there a moment ago.

I was no Hollywood scream queen, and my shriek of surprise and terror dwindled into a choked-sounding wheeze in seconds.

The figure in front of me didn't move.

When I finished coughing and took a sip from my water bottle, he took a step forward.

I took ten steps back and held up my hands. "Stop."

He stopped and tilted his head.

Now that my initial startlement had subsided and my pulse had returned to its regular, although elevated from exercise rhythm, I could take in the form in front of me.

He was translucent but clearly human. He was taller than me, but only by an inch or so, making him five-five or five-six. It was hard to tell, but he looked Black. He was wearing jeans, a T-shirt, and sneakers and couldn't have been more than twenty years old.

He opened his mouth as if speaking, but if he was talking, I couldn't hear it.

He didn't look like Gwen's or Zach's spirits. Theirs had been amorphous shapes that didn't resemble the people they belonged to at all. This one looked like what I'd always imagined a ghost to look like, if I'd spent any amount of time thinking about ghosts in the past few years.

But more than being able to tick my "I'm being haunted" boxes, I wanted to help him. Sadness emanated from him, and I ached to change that.

"I'm sorry, I can't hear you. Maybe if you talk slower, I could read your lips?" I offered.

The ghost—I'd decided that was definitely the right word—grimaced. Then he spoke again. The translucency of his mouth made it difficult for me to figure out what he was saying, not that I'd been a particularly gifted lip reader to begin with.

I growled in frustration.

"You're trying too hard," said an acerbic voice at my feet.

I looked down toward the voice, already knowing what I would see.

"Cat."

"Person." He sat, curling his tail around him.

The ghost looked at the cat for a second, then returned his attention to me.

"What do you mean I'm trying too hard? How would trying less hard enable me to hear him?" Everything about this conversation was insane. Was I really asking a talking cat for advice on how to hear dead people?

But this felt real. And last night, when I'd anchored Gwen's soul to her body, inadvertently grabbing Zach's...that had felt real, too.

But how could any of this be real? Nothing made any sense.

"There are more things on heaven and earth," the cat murmured.

"You're trying, but you don't believe you'll succeed, and that's what's blocking you. If you don't think about the sheer madness of this situation, if you accept it as what *is* instead of what shouldn't be, you will be open to him."

I looked between the ghost and my talking cat. This was not okay, which meant I was not okay. I needed help, and since Gwen had taken herself out of the picture, that left only one person.

I took off at a run, too fast for my current exhaustion and fitness levels, and let adrenaline carry me the last two miles in under fifteen minutes.

My legs were trembling by the time I got to Gwen's and let myself in.

I stood in the kitchen gulping water until I stopped sweating enough that I could get in the shower without ruining the cleansing effects.

As I stood under the spray, I reviewed the last few days. I didn't know when the mental break had happened. Had it been when Gwen broke up with me, the night I couldn't remember and the entire day I'd lost, or was it the night I'd gone out with Ash and continued my grief-fueled bender?

It didn't matter. What mattered was that I recognized it now. Hallucinations and delusions were often tied to bipolar disorder, and although I'd never suffered from either before, it didn't take a genius who'd read everything she could find on her mental illness to make the connection.

When I was clean and dressed, I pulled out my cell phone and scrolled through my contacts until I found my last therapist's number.

"Hello, this is Mary Diaz."

I opened my mouth to start the word vomit of everything that was going on, everything that'd happened the last few weeks with complete and total honesty, something I'd never tried with any of the mental health professionals I'd seen over the years. But before I could start talking, she continued.

"If this is a medical emergency, call 911. I'm unable to take your call right now. I'm either with a patient or out of the office. Please leave a detailed message with your name, date of birth, phone number, and reason for calling, and I will get back to you at my earliest convenience."

There was a moment to center myself before the beep announcing I could leave my message. "Dr. Diaz, this is Frankie Ström. Frances Ström. Um... Birth date is April 8th. I think I'm having a psychotic break. Do we even call it that? I don't know. Anyway, I'm hallucinating, and I don't know what to do. I don't think I need to go to the hospital. I don't feel like hurting myself or anyone else, but I'm a little scared. Call me back. Please."

I hung up. "Dammit!" I hadn't left my phone number or the year of my birth. I debated calling back, but she knew who I was. There certainly wouldn't be another Frances Ström in her patient list, and she had my phone number on record.

I didn't know how long it would take her to call back, but there was no point in waiting around dwelling on it, especially not when my stomach was wrapping around my spine and growling in protest of its empty state.

I checked my bank balance again, knowing that even after depositing my final paycheck, it wouldn't magically be overflowing, but hoping something had changed.

Now there was just over a hundred dollars. Not enough to live on for more than a day, but it was enough for breakfast.

I pocketed the keys and my wallet and walked out into the sunshine.

EIGHT

I'd had one latte, one green chili breakfast burrito, and three cups of drip coffee before the phone rang. I pushed the talk button before looking at the caller ID.

"Dr. Diaz?"

"You know I love to play doctor, but I don't think you'd want to play patient," Ash said.

My shoulders slumped. I loved Ash—he was my best friend, after all—but he was not who I needed right now. I had more fun with him than with anyone else, but that kind of fun might lead to more delusions. "Hey Ash. How was your hot date last night?"

"A complete dud. She didn't want to play nice with me and walked out after a few minutes." Genuine frustration tinged with anger floated through the airwaves.

I pulled the phone away from my ear for a second and stared at it. Ash had never expressed any feelings about a person he'd dated, either positive or negative, beyond surface-level descriptions of their relative attractiveness and sex potential.

"And you care because?" I asked.

"Why wouldn't I care? Who likes being rejected? She was

different from the people I usually take to bed. It could've been amazing; she could have changed the world." Wistfulness coated his words. "Ha! Just kidding! Bet I had you going for a moment though, right?"

I rolled my eyes. "Yeah, for a moment I almost believed you were a human with real human feelings. Just hurt pride then?"

"You wound me, Frankie. It wasn't *just* hurt pride. It was also terrible sexual frustration! Do you know how hard it was to find someone else to warm my bed last night?"

"Not at all?" I asked drily. I leaned forward and caught the eye of the server. I had to get out of the diner soon, or I'd spend the rest of my money on coffee. Besides, there was no way I wanted to take the call from my shrink in public. It was bad enough talking to Ash when there were potential eavesdroppers around.

"Where are you?" Ash asked. "It's my day off, and I want to brunch."

"I'm at Downtown Subscription. I just had breakfast and coffee and couldn't possibly brunch now. I'm heading home." I squeezed my eyes closed and took a deep breath. "Headed back to Gwen's, I mean. I'm waiting for a phone call and need to start looking for a new job."

"Boring," Ash said. "Why am I getting rejected by everyone now? Have I lost my charm?"

"You're just as charming as ever, but unless you're going to invite me to live with you and become my sugar daddy, I need to find a job." I crossed my fingers under the table. There was no way Ash would offer to be my sugar daddy, but maybe he'd invite me to stay with him until I found a job and had enough money to get a place to live.

"Ha. You know that kind of arrangement wouldn't work between us. First of all, you aren't into the kind of things I'd ask of my sugar baby, and second, I don't want to ruin our friendship by changing anything now. You'll have to find someone else to pay your bills now that Gwen's out of the picture."

I gritted my teeth. He hadn't said anything untrue. Gwen had paid all my bills, and there was no way I could've survived on my own without her, but the idea that I *needed* to find another provider or I'd be out on the streets grated on me. I wanted to be the strong independent woman my mother always told me I could be. Mother. I hadn't really thought about her for years, and here she was, showing up in my thoughts twice in one day.

"Maybe I can get my job back at the animal hospital," I suggested, trying to shove the memories of mother to the back of my head.

Ash laughed. "Do you think they'd actually give you your job back? After you went to work drunk three times in one month and didn't show up at all several other times?"

I winced, and the corners of my eyes burned with the tears. I had fucked that job up so royally. It was unfortunate it'd happened right after I'd met Ash. Not only did he know all about it, but he'd gotten to witness my downward spiral firsthand. He found it a lot more amusing than I did, and he seldom missed an opportunity to bring it up.

"You're right. And since I just got fired from another job, I don't think I have a lot of good references going for me." This job hunt was going to suck. "Maybe it's time to move on." I ran my hand over the semicolon tattoo on my forearm that I'd gotten when I was twenty-five, fresh out of the mental ward, and making a new start in a new city. The day after I'd moved to Santa Fe, I'd walked into the first tattoo parlor I'd seen and gotten the ink. It was a constant reminder that as bad as things were now, I'd survived so much worse, and there was no way I was going to give in to the ghosts of my past, even if the present seemed hopeless.

"Yeah, your time here is probably just about up. Better go now rather than let things get worse, right?" Ash's voice shifted from the sardonic light-heartedness he usually employed to deadly serious.

"What are you talking about?" Something about his tone twisted my stomach, but I couldn't put a finger on it. "I'm talking about getting out of Santa Fe and trying somewhere new."

"And so am I," Ash said, his usual tone back in place. "What else would I have meant? Did you think I was telling you to kill yourself or something? How big an asshole do you think I am?"

I gathered my stuff and took off toward the park, shifting my cell phone to my other ear. He'd asked that question more than once over the last couple years, and I always gave the expected reply. Of course he wasn't an asshole. He was my best friend and was always there for me when I felt the bottom dropping out of my world.

But he was always there just before the bottom dropped out of my world too.

"No answer?" Ash teased. "I'm a little hurt."

I forced a laugh. "Of course you're an asshole, Ash. But you're my favorite asshole."

"Then do me a solid and meet me for early afternoon brunch. I'm buying. We can drown your sorrows in whiskey drinks, and I probably have a few extra intoxicants lying around just for you, if you know what I mean. Wink."

"I don't think you can call it brunch if it's after lunch, and I don't want whiskey drinks or any of your 'extras' today. If you feel like buying me something, take me out for dinner tonight." I hoped he wouldn't push brunch any harder. I really, really wanted to meet him for whiskey and drugs, but that wasn't how I would prove to Gwen, prove to myself, that I could be better.

"Fine. Be boring. Meet me at 315 Bistro at seven-thirty. I'll buy you food, you can regale me with your sorrows, and we'll have a lovely time." Ash hung up without waiting for a reply, which was great, because I wasn't sure I had one.

NINE

I arrived at 315 at seven twenty-five, lightheaded and with a growling stomach. *Ash better not be fucking late*, I thought, *or I might pass out on the sidewalk.*

At a quarter to eight, he still hadn't showed. I walked into the restaurant and got a table for two. He was picking up the tab, and there was no reason I needed to wait for him to get there to order an appetizer. It wasn't like they were going to ask for cash up front.

I ordered the side salad from the appetizer menu and a glass of water. If Ash didn't show, I wanted to be able to afford my meal.

Ash breezed in a few minutes after eight and flopped into the chair across from me. "Babe, you would not believe the day I've had."

The server came over before he could elaborate, and Ash ordered a bottle of their best champagne.

When the server disappeared, Ash looked at me with his head tilted and his brows drawn in disapproval. "Water? And a side salad? What are you doing with your life, Frankie? Life's too short for salad and tap water. Although I commend your dedication to enhancing the effects of the alcohol by not filling up on food. You always know how to party."

"I was hungry, but I was waiting for you. I'm definitely planning on ordering some more food—and I don't really want any champagne. I think I've reached my limit on alcohol this month."

"It's the fifth of August," Ash said.

"Exactly. I hit my monthly quota four days ago. But that means you get an entire bottle of champagne for yourself. You know how much you love it." My shoulders were creeping up around my ears as the tension of refusing a drink took hold.

Fuck. I was a fucking alcoholic, wasn't I? Dammit. And what a time to figure it out.

Ash waved my words away. "You can't watch me drink a bottle of champagne myself and not have a single glass. That's rude. You wouldn't want to be rude, would you?"

I didn't, but also...

The champagne arrived, and the server poured two glasses. "Are you ready to order?"

I opened my mouth to ask for the chicken cordon bleu that I'd had my eye on for a half hour, but Ash shook his head.

"We're just drinking tonight. Food gets in the way, right?" He smiled at the young main waiting for our order, and I watched him melt under the force of Ash's smolder.

"I actually want something to eat." The firmness in my voice rocked me back in surprise, and it looked like Ash was equally taken aback. "Can I get the cordon bleu with mashed potatoes, please? And I'd like another glass of water."

The server nodded at me, barely taking his eyes off Ash. "Of course. Are you sure you don't want anything, sir?"

Ash shook his head and waved his fingers carelessly. "Nothing for me. I'll let you know when I need something from you." The look he raked over the man nearly set the entire restaurant on fire.

Once the server had departed with a flustered wave, Ash turned to me. "I hope you can afford the food, since I'm just buying the champagne."

Heat suffused my cheeks. "You know I can't, but you offered to take me out to dinner, and that generally includes food as well as unlimited booze."

He laughed. "I'm just teasing you. Why must you take everything so seriously? Of course I've got you covered. I'll even buy you dessert if you want that on top of everything else you're eating tonight. But now, a toast." He held up his champagne flute and looked expectantly at me.

I bit back a sigh and picked up the glass. I was getting my meal covered, and it was only one glass, right? No harm in one glass. "Are you making a toast?"

"Of course! To us, our friendship, and all the adventures that are coming our way." He gently tapped his glass against mine.

"To us," I repeated, then took a drink.

THE SERVER POPPED the cork on our third bottle of champagne as I polished off my lemon meringue tartlet.

My shrink hadn't called me back that day, and I was desperate to tell someone else what was going on with me. "Ash, I have something to tell you, but you have to promise not to make fun of me."

"Babe, when have I ever made fun of you?" Ash asked, placing his hand on his chest and leaning forward. "You know you can tell me anything."

He'd made fun of me plenty of times, but that wasn't where I wanted to steer the conversation right now. Right now, I felt good—more than good. I loved champagne almost as much as I loved whiskey, and the calm that was swirling through me made it seem possible that everything I'd experienced in the last few days had been real and not the product of my mental illness.

"I think I can see ghosts," I whispered.

Ash's burst of laughter was so loud, the neighboring diners looked over with raised eyebrows until he calmed down. He wiped the tears away from his eyes. "You can see dead people? This is the big secret you wanted to tell me?"

"You promised you wouldn't make fun of me," I reminded him. "And yes, I can see dead people. The first time was when I was in the fire with Gwen and Zach. I could see her spirit trying to get away from her body, so I grabbed it and stuck it back in." My words were slurring together a bit, which wasn't lending credence to my story. I wanted to tell him more, tell him what I'd done to Zach, but I wasn't ready to share that with anyone yet, even someone who wouldn't believe me.

"Babe, you were trapped in a fire, inhaling smoke, and watching the woman you love almost die. Anyone would hallucinate in that situation. But it's not real, and if you're blurring reality with hallucinations, then things are even worse with you than everyone suspected." He reached a hand across the table and squeezed my arm. His thumb dug into my forearm where scars running the length of my arm neatly bracketed my semi-colon tattoo. Then he let go of me and refilled my champagne glass.

"It wasn't a hallucination," I protested. "I saw another ghost this morning outside the cemetery. It wasn't part of anyone alive, I don't think. I mean, its body had already died, so it didn't need shoving back into anything. He wanted something, but I couldn't hear him to figure out what."

I debated telling Ash about the advice I'd received from the cat. Fuck it. In for a penny and all that, as people on the British shows I binge-watched on PBS when I was a kid said. "A cat told me I was trying too hard and that if I just relaxed and believed instead of trying to believe, I'd be able to hear the dead guy."

Ash grabbed my champagne flute and downed the contents. "Okay. No more bubbles for you. You are clearly rounding the corner to Crazy Town and picking up speed. I should take you to the hospital and get you checked in." He pulled out his wallet and dropped several hundred-dollar bills on the table. Then he walked up to the adjacent table. "We have to get out of here early. My friend is having a psychotic break or something. Do you want the rest of our champagne?"

When he returned, I crossed my arms over my chest. "I am not having a psychotic break, and even if I was, telling other people is an asshole move."

"Let's just get you out of here. Then we can figure out what to do next." His voice was soft and placating, and everything I hated.

He held my arm as we wound through the tables toward the restaurant entrance. I didn't speak again until we were out the door.

"Look, I know it sounds ridiculous," I said. "And to be honest, I'm not one hundred percent sure it was real, but..." The giant orange cat waiting in the middle of the sidewalk, perfectly lit by the glow of the nearby streetlight, stopped me in my tracks. "Ash, there's the cat."

"The cat that gave you advice on how to talk to ghosts?" he asked.

"Yes!" I crouched down by the cat. "Tell him. Tell him what you said."

"It doesn't matter what I say," the cat replied. "It won't make a difference."

"Of course it will! You already have." I stood and spun back to Ash. "See?"

"See what? I see a cat—that much is undebatable. But I don't see any proof that you got advice from the mangy creature."

The cat hissed softly, and I glared at Ash. "Don't insult him. He's not mangy, he's gorgeous. And he just spoke to me."

"Oh, he talks to you in your head," Ash said, nodding. "I've never had a cat—never could stand them. But I understand that lots of pet people have entire conversations with their animals. Why didn't you just say that?"

I looked between Ash and the cat who was now cleaning the top of his head with a paw. "Not in my head."

"I told you," the cat said. "Best to stop trying, or he'll get you to doubt your own sanity next."

"Can no one else hear you but me?" I asked. That sounded even more ridiculous than anything else I'd said until now.

The cat didn't reply, and the look of concern Ash leveled at me made tears spring to my eyes—a feeling I'd become way too familiar with over the last week.

"Babe, let's get you back to my place so you can sleep it off. If you're still hearing cats and seeing ghosts tomorrow, we'll get you some help, okay?" Ash's voice was softly solicitous, and my tears started to fall.

I let him help me to his car and spent the ride in silence, staring out the window at the desert city roads as we wound along the streets that led to the exclusive neighborhood where Ash lived. Either he was right, and I really was as crazy as I'd suspected earlier that day, or I was seeing and hearing things that no one else could. Either way, telling him—telling anyone—had been a mistake.

And not one I planned to repeat.

TEN

Coffee, toast, and a bloody Mary were waiting for me and my hangover on Ash's expansive back patio when I got up. I doctored my coffee with cream and sugar, buttered my toast, and, after ensuring Ash wasn't around to see me, dumped the cocktail into the nearest terracotta planter.

Ash's maid refilled my cup. I hadn't realized people who didn't live at Downton Abbey even had maids anymore, but that was beside the point. A middle-aged Latina woman in a neat, black, knee-length dress and sensible flats, wearing a dour expression that didn't invite questions or comments, served me coffee.

When I'd finished eating, I moved to a chair that afforded me a view of the carefully landscaped backyard and the mountains beyond it. Coffee in hand, I leaned back to enjoy the way the sun danced over the reds, tans, and browns of the desert, so different from the lush greenness of my home state of Oregon.

Something brushed against my leg, and I barely suppressed a shriek.

The cat was on the patio.

The cat that definitely couldn't talk. And if I could hear it, that meant I really had taken the fast track to Crazy Town, or whatever Ash had said the night before.

"Shoo!" I said quietly, flapping my hands.

He didn't move.

"Scat!" I tried more forcefully.

He just stared at me.

I looked around. Neither Ash nor his maid were anywhere to be seen. "I don't know how you found me, but you need to get out of here before Ash finds you. He hates cats, and he already knows I'm completely crackers."

"You're not crackers, or crazy, or any other derogatory words you might find to describe your mental state. In fact, when you were taking your meds regularly, you were as stable as anyone gifted with balanced brain chemistry from birth." The cat walked forward and lay in a patch of sunshine, closing his eyes and tilting his face toward the early morning sun.

"If I'm so sane, how come I'm talking to a cat that no one else can hear?" I whispered.

He opened his eyes and blinked lazily at me. "What makes you think no one else can hear me?"

"Ash, last night... He didn't hear you."

"How do you know?" The cat's eyes closed again, and he stretched out to his fullest length, which was impressively long.

"Because he said he didn't. And that is usually a pretty good indication."

The cat made a noise that sounded suspiciously like a human snort of derision. "And Ash is well known for his truthfulness, candor, and kindness? Or would you say he's the sort of person who might enjoy making a person feel off-kilter?"

I opened my mouth to defend Ash, but nothing came out. "He's my best friend," I said weakly.

"Don't confuse a best friend with an only companion. Now, gather your belongings and let's get out of here." He stood, arched his back in a stretch, and padded toward the sliding door leading back into the house.

"Where are we going?"

"Anywhere but here." He sneezed delicately. "I'm allergic to your best friend."

I laughed. "I went to vet school, and I was a practicing vet for seven years. I don't remember any cases of cats being allergic to humans. That's not a thing."

"How many cats did you survey?"

"You can't survey a cat. They can't talk. Now give me the real reason I should follow a cat out of this very nice home to an unknown location other than you don't like it here."

"I have a name, you know," the cat said. "You could use it."

My head, still a little fuzzy from my champagne hangover, whizzed with the change of conversational direction. "Of course you have a name, but I don't know it."

"You could've asked."

"My apologies, Mr. Cat. Please tell me your name." I crouched beside him and held out my hand. He'd been amenable to neck scratches the first time we'd met, but I wouldn't offend him by touching him again without consent.

The cat moved under my hand and wiggled about until he had my fingers in just the right spot behind his left ear. I obligingly began a gentle scratch.

"My name is Archibald T. Maelstrom. You will not call me Archie or any other variation of my name. It is acceptable to use just my first name, of course. No need to be overly formal."

I bit my cheek to keep from laughing. After spending the previous evening being laughed at by Ash, I had no desire to treat anyone else the same way. "Thank you for sharing your name with me, Archibald. I feel honored. You know me already, but my name is Frances Lenore Ström. You can call me Frankie."

"Did you just introduce yourself to a cat? A cat that is on my patio where it isn't welcome?" Ash asked scathingly from the doorway.

My heart stuttered in my chest as I took in the scene he must be seeing. Hopefully, he hadn't heard the earlier part of our conversation. I wasn't convinced any of it was real yet, but it was currently my reality, so I would roll with it. However, that didn't mean I had to let Ash know I thought it was real.

"He showed up a few minutes ago, and I thought it only polite to introduce myself since we keep running into each other." I'd stopped scratching Archibald's ears when Ash showed up, and he head butted me until I resumed my ministrations. "I don't know why he's here. It seems absurd that he could've followed us from the restaurant last night, but unless you got a wild hair up your ass to give me the same cat I tried to convince you could talk, that's what must have happened."

"Well, get him out of here. I am allergic to cats, and he cannot be here. If you want to stay, then you need to take that...thing...back to the shelter where you got him."

I froze. Had he just said I could stay? I looked at Archibald. I could stay in a nice home with a pool and a maid and air conditioning, and all I had to do was take the cat back to the rescue where I'd found him? A no-kill rescue where they'd treat him like the gorgeous creature he was until someone came to adopt him?

It wasn't a choice at all, was it?

Archibald met my eyes, and in them I saw so many more choices than staying with Ash, looking for another shit part-time job, drinking and drugging with him every night, and drifting farther and farther away from myself. And besides, how on earth could a person get rid of a cat named Archibald T. Maelstrom?

"Oh, hey!" I said, making the connection. "Our last names are almost the same!"

Ash wrinkled his nose at me. "What the actual fuck are you talking about, babe? My last name is Messinger, which is nothing like Ström."

"Never mind. I know you're allergic, but if I promise to vacuum your car, will you give me and Archibald a ride to the shelter so I can give him back?" I couldn't look at the cat. I didn't want to see anger —or worse, disappointment—at my decision.

"Sure. If you vacuum and detail my car, I'll give you a ride. We can stop by Gwen's place after for your things. I'm glad you decided to stay with me. We're going to have the best time." He stood and tossed his keys in the air, then caught them again and winked at me. "And if you admit you were making up all that ghost shit last night, I won't even tease you about naming a stray cat Archibald." He turned and walked into the house.

I scooped Archibald into my arms and stood. He weighed about fifty pounds more than he should've. Cats have a way of increasing their mass that's nearly supernatural. Although, in Archibald's case, it might be supernatural. Talking cats weren't what I'd call part of the natural world. I stifled a giggle.

Archibald swiped at me and left three angry scratches on my arm, neatly bisecting the scars from a previous suicide attempt. Blood welled at the edges, and I glared at him and put him back on the ground. "What was that for?"

"You know," Archibald said.

"Fine. I know. But you're a fucking magic talking cat, and this is a place to live. A *nice* place to live until I get a job and have enough money to get an apartment. What am I going to do if I walk away from this? I don't even have a car to sleep in. I don't have enough money to stay at a motel for one night, and I'll be broke and unable to buy food inside of three days, even if I have no other expenses. What do you want from me?" I was almost shouting by that point. I took a deep breath. The last thing I needed was for Ash to investigate and rescind his invitation because I was yelling at a stray cat.

"You have to have a little faith," Archibald said.

"Faith is all well and good when your other needs are met. I haven't fallen in with any of the 'we can save your eternal soul for only fifteen dollars a day' preachers, and I'm not about to fall into that trap because of a cat."

He rubbed against my ankles. "There's somewhere you could go, you know. And if you reached out, they'd provide for you and make sure you don't go hungry."

"I've never been a Christian, and I'm not about to jump into prodigal-daughter mode now. That's too far in the past. Too many bridges burned. They won't welcome me back with open arms, no matter how that parable ended."

"Are you coming or not, Frankie?" Ash yelled. "Let's get that cat out of here."

"I need more than faith and a phone call to my parents. I need shelter and food, and that's what Ash is offering." I heaved a sigh. Ash's home was great, and it would be lovely to live here, but the thought of home had been tugging at me more and more the last couple days. I'd love to see my mom again, to find out how my sisters were doing, to tease my dad about whatever his latest hobby was. When I'd left home, it was whittling. He was crap at whittling, but determined that it would be the craft he mastered.

"Call her. If she's not happy to hear from you, I'll drop it and walk out of your life. You can stay here with Ash. But ask yourself one question. How much will it cost you to stay?"

"He wouldn't charge me rent. He knows I don't have any money." Would he? No—at least not now. Once I had a job, maybe. I bit my lip.

"That's not the price I was talking about. Ash doesn't do anything for free, and eventually, he will make you pay." Archibald turned his back to me, stuck his tail straight up in the air, and walked into the house as if he owned it.

I watched him go, then looked around. It was perfect. A stone patio surrounded by native plants, the Olympic-sized swimming pool behind the fence to my right, the view of the mesas, and the sprawling adobe house with enough bedrooms that I could sleep in a different one every night and not have a repeat for a week. Not to mention I'd have my own bathroom. And Louise. And Tony the pool boy. It was a luxury I'd never dared dream of experiencing. Staying was the right decision.

I walked into the house. Ash was standing by the front door, jangling his keys. "It's about fucking time. Let's get out of here. Unless you want a bump before we go."

I shook my head. "No thanks. Maybe later."

This was the price. I'd never get my life together here. But at least I'd be a mess in style, right?

ELEVEN

I hadn't cried when I left Archibald with David.

I hadn't taken Ash up on his offer to help me forget my troubles and had gone to bed sober for the second time in three days.

And now that I was awake bright and very early Monday morning, I wasn't rehashing everything I'd ever done wrong over the last week.

Nope. I was rehashing everything I'd ever done wrong over the last ten years since I'd ended up as an inpatient in a psych ward after the last in a string of suicide attempts between the ages of nineteen and twenty-five.

I'd been so angry. At my sister Jackie, who found me and called the ambulance, and at my mother, who'd signed me into the psych ward against my wishes even though I was twenty-five and had just finished my internship and graduated from vet school. At my father and my other sister, who hadn't done anything at all to stop my mother.

I'd been so angry that when I could finally check myself out, I emptied my bank account, filled my backpack with a few clothes and belongings, and took a series of buses and rides from strangers until I landed in Santa Fe. My shiny new DVM degree and glowing references from my profs helped me get a job in no time.

The job came with insurance, and I found a good shrink and a great therapist. I ran, I practiced yoga, I took my meds, and I made friends. I met Gwen when she brought in a cat she'd found after a fire, and we hit it off immediately.

Things were good. Great even. Seven years of stability and happiness.

I'd never been able to pinpoint exactly when things went wrong, but it was about three years ago, right around the time I'd gone to my first firefighter shindig with Gwen and met the rest of the guys.

Ash was new to town and needed a friend. I'd been distancing myself from my own friends in favor of spending every second with Gwen.

Six months later, I was jobless. The only thing that saved me from being homeless was Gwen asking me to move in with her.

I couldn't blame Ash for the last three years. Everything I'd done was my choice. I just made a lot more bad ones when I was hanging out with him.

And now I was in the wrong place. Archibald was right. Whether I was one trip away from rock bottom because of self-sabotage and a series of bad choices didn't matter. I wouldn't be able to get my shit together at Ash's, and I didn't have the resources to straighten out my life in Santa Fe without him.

I wasn't going to ask Gwen, and I didn't have any other friends. What bridges that remained unscathed when I'd thrown myself into my relationship with Gwen, I'd burned when I started hanging out with Ash.

That really left me only one choice.

I retrieved my phone from my backpack and heard a slight rattle.

I dumped my stuff onto the bed. Two pill bottles landed neatly in the center of the small pile of clothes I'd been carrying around. Lithium and the five Xanax I was allowed to have at any given time.

I grabbed a glass of water and took my meds, then picked up my phone to make three calls.

The first was to my shrink to inform her I was leaving Santa Fe and to request a ninety-day refill on my meds. She readily agreed and directed me to get a new psychiatrist immediately upon landing wherever I was going next and to make sure they got my medical records from her. She didn't mention my rambling message I'd left for my therapist, which meant that info fortunately hadn't been passed on.

The second was to David to ask if I could formally adopt Archibald.

"I was a shit employee, but you know I'd never put an animal in danger. I only dropped him off because my friend I was staying with was allergic, but I'm moving on and that won't be an issue."

"Frankie, I would trust you to care for any of the animals and wouldn't hesitate to let you adopt one. But the cat you dropped off earlier today is gone."

"Someone already adopted Archibald?" My voice rose shrilly. Dammit! I never should've taken him back.

"No. I mean he's gone." David sounded pissed off and confused —a state he'd often been in with me. "I took him to the quarantine cage until he could be examined and deemed fine to hang out with the general population. And when I returned thirty minutes later, he was gone. Poof. Nowhere to be found."

My breath left my lungs in a *whoosh*. I wouldn't have to steal—er, liberate—him from another family after all. He'd freed himself and was probably stalking angrily about, cursing my name. He wasn't with me, but at least he wasn't having his tail pulled by a well-meaning but sticky child somewhere. "Okay. Okay. Sorry to bother you."

"I'll call you if he turns up," David said.

"Thanks. Talk to you later." I hung up and prepared for phone call number three.

Instead of digging through my contacts for the numbers I hadn't looked at in years, I put on my running gear. I knew I needed to make the call, but the shrink had promised my prescription would be ready in an hour. If I went for an hour-long run, or a fast walk, whatever the case might be, they'd be ready by the time I could get to the pharmacy.

I walked out the front door and planned my route. I was way the fuck away from the neighborhoods I usually ran through, but I had Santa Fe mentally mapped.

A five-mile loop that took me past the pharmacy could, if I wanted, also take me by the cemetery. I didn't know if the ghost would be there, but I felt bad that I'd ditched him yesterday without finding out what he needed.

A laugh escaped me. Apparently, I'd decided that my cat talked and ghosts were real sometime in the last twenty-four hours. I no longer felt crazy—well, not any more than usual—but I was diving all-in on the idea there were things out there that should not be real, and I was the special snowflake who was experiencing them.

It sounded even more out there when I put it like that, but I didn't feel delusional. Of course, a person probably didn't *feel* delusional. That's what made them delusions. But even if none of it was real, the least I could do was help the poor ghost out. Especially if I'd invented him.

Mind made up, I started a slow jog that would take me by the cemetery and hopefully allow me to provide him some closure.

CHAPTER
TWELVE

I slowed to a walk when I got to the cemetery and tried to control my wheezing. I went through the gate and looked around. I didn't see anyone waiting to talk to me, which made sense. There was no reason for a ghost to hang around hoping I'd show up again after I'd run away the first time. He probably had other things to do. I didn't know what ghosts got up to in their free time, but hopefully they had something more than lurking to occupy them.

I leaned against a mausoleum and scanned the area, trying to see ghosts. It made sense that if they existed, there'd be more than one in a cemetery, right? They'd come out at night and have ghost parties and talk about their lives, solve their own murders, and spook anyone bold enough to creep through a graveyard at midnight during a new moon.

But there was nothing. No one.

"Maybe they sleep during the day," I said.

"They're spirits, not vampires," Archibald said.

"Arghh!" I looked down to where the cat had appeared at my feet.

"Never ever, ever sneak up on someone looking for ghosts in a cemetery!"

He continued without acknowledging how my soul had nearly jumped out of my body to join those in the graveyard. "You won't see any ghosts. They're not nearly as common as most people want to believe. Only a handful of souls refuse to move on."

"Really? Because I would totally stay behind to haunt all the people who annoyed me while I was alive. And do a little light stalking, of course." I'd never really thought of life after death—or whatever happened when a person died—but had I known ghosting was a thing, I would've signed up for that post haste.

"Given the choice between a possible eternity of being incorporeal—unseen, unheard, and alone—or being taken to an afterlife where you won't be alone, which would you choose?" Archibald hopped to the top of a nearby headstone, balanced precariously, and stared at me until I answered.

"Solitude for a few years might be nice," I hedged, not wanting to give up my haunting dreams just yet.

"It's not a few years, though. If your escort shows up after you die and you don't go with them, there's no guarantee that you'll have another chance. A spirit can't move on without help. Most people are escorted by a reaper, but those connected to another belief system with other psychopomps usually get that experience instead."

I plopped down on the ground next to Archibald's perch. "What's that supposed to mean? And why am I talking about the afterlife with a cat?"

"You need to know. If you can see souls at the moment of death—and after—you need to know what happens, what's supposed to happen, and all the ways it can go wrong."

The image of shoving Zach's soul into Gwen to get hers to stick burned in my memory, and I hastily reburied it.

I was about to ask more questions to detract from the guilt that was stealing over me when goosebumps raced over my skin, and I shivered.

The sun blazed in the cloudless sky, and there wasn't even a hint of a breeze. There was no way I should be chilled right now.

"To your left," Archibald said softly.

I turned my head slowly. The ghost from the day before stood there, hands clasped in front of him and staring at me with large, pleading eyes.

"Hi," I said softly, climbing to my feet. "I'm sorry I freaked out and ran away yesterday. You're the first ghost I've seen, and I was scared."

He didn't open his mouth, and I wracked my brains to figure out what to say next.

"I know I couldn't hear you yesterday, but maybe I can today? I believe I can, just as sure as I believe you're standing in front of me and you need my help." I crossed my fingers that I really could hear him and wasn't just blowing smoke up his ghostly ass.

"I want to go."

I jumped a step back and hit the mausoleum I'd forgotten was behind me. His voice sounded far away and garbled, like it was coming to me from underwater or through a bad phone connection, but it was audible.

"Okay. You don't have to stay here and talk to me."

"No." He shook his head in obvious frustration. "I'm tired. I want to go. Please."

I looked at Archibald, who was busy cleaning his whiskers and not giving me the time of day.

"You mean you want to stop being a ghost and move on to the afterlife?" I hazarded. It was a damn good thing I'd gotten the cliffiest of CliffsNotes from Archibald before the ghost showed up.

He nodded, and the corners of his lips turned up a little.

I grimaced. He might be smiling now, but I was about to flip that smile upside down. "I don't know how to help. I can see you, but that's the limit of my powers."

"STOP LYING TO ME, REAPER!" he screamed.

Wind whipped around me, and a few tendrils of hair broke loose from my ponytail and smacked me in the face. I tried to take another step back, but the increasingly inconsiderate mausoleum still blocked my path.

"This is another reason it's bad to stay behind," Archibald observed placidly. "Centuries of solitude, of seeing the world move on but being unable to interact with it, can deteriorate even the strongest of minds. And for most, it doesn't take centuries. It takes less than a decade."

"What do I do?" The wind was becoming even more erratic, and sand, dust, and detritus such as flower offerings, dead leaves, and cigarette butts were buffeting me from all sides. "I can't help him! I'm no fucking ghost whisperer."

Archibald cut through the howl of the wind with a noise that would've been called a melodramatic sigh had a human made it. Since it was coming from a cat, it reminded me more of the beginning stages of coughing up a hairball. "Take his hand."

A leaf smacked against my face, and as I dislodged it, I reviewed Archibald's words and weighed whether I'd actually gone round the bend after all.

"Archie. He is a ghost. I can't touch him." I left my *duh* unspoken but laid it heavy in my voice so he wouldn't miss it.

"Do not call me Archie. And just try."

Might as well, right? After all, yesterday I hadn't been able to talk to the ghost, and today we'd chatted like pals. Until he lost his shit and tried to send me to Oz.

I stepped forward with my hands in the air. "Hey. Hey! I don't know if I can help. I'm not a reaper, but I want to try."

The wind died almost immediately, and the vacuum of the sudden stillness and silence was shocking enough to nearly bowl me over.

"What's your name?" I asked as I got closer. "I'm Frankie."

"Adam." His voice was no longer threatening my eardrums, for which I was most appreciative.

"Hey, Adam. I'm going to reach out my hand to you." I stretched my arm toward him, and he reciprocated.

My hand met his with an icy shock. A chill spread over my body, and an involuntary cry burst from me. I yanked my hand back and tried not to hyperventilate.

Dust swirled around me for a minute until I got my breathing under control.

"Adam, I'm sorry. I'm not running away. I just need a minute to adjust." I took four more slow breaths. "Okay, let's try this again."

This time, the shock was less, but the chill was more intense. I closed my eyes but didn't let go.

When I opened my eyes again, he was staring at me with an intensity that shook me even more than the chill in his grip had.

Once I relaxed, though, and let the ice run over me instead of pulling it into my body, the material world faded the way it had in the fire. Adam's figure strengthened and solidified until he looked more real than the headstones and the mausoleum. His clothes lost their translucent quality. He was wearing a bright-pink T-shirt with a dinosaur skeleton on it and the words, *All my friends are dead.* His pants were dark-wash jeans. His skin was flawless, and his large eyes were the most beautiful velvety shade of brown I'd ever seen.

Once I adjusted to my new vision, I saw more than him. I saw his tether. He was tied to his body with the same sticky soul-stuff as Zach had been, which meant I knew how to separate them.

"What will happen when I sever his soul from his body?" I asked Archibald, who'd come up to rub against my ankle. He glowed the dusky purple of dusk, and nearly obscuring the orange of his fur. "He won't be stuck in the cemetery anymore, but I can't take him to the next place he's supposed to go."

"Ask him where he believes he'll go," Archibald instructed.

It seemed silly to ask him when Archibald had clearly just said it aloud, but I turned obediently to Adam and asked, "When you're no longer stuck here, where will you go?"

He smiled and lifted his shirt. Two ravens were tattooed across his chest, and some runes that I almost but not quite could read shimmered below them. "I didn't die in battle, but I at least deserve Fólkvangr, don't I? My mother taught me the old ways, and I want to join her there now."

I was familiar with Norse mythology, although my knowledge was more Valhalla and less Fólkvangr. Valhalla was the one that stories were told about, the Norse afterlife where brave warriors who fell in battle and were chosen by the Valkyries got to hang out, drink mead with Odin, and train while they waited for Ragnarök. Fólkvangr was the afterlife ruled by Freyja, and where those who fell in battle who weren't chosen for Valhalla went. My mother had always said that Freyja would welcome anyone, though, who believed that's where they belonged, whether they were a warrior or not, and it sounded like my mom wasn't the only one with that belief.

Even if I didn't believe in the gods of myth, it was as good an afterlife story as any.

"Freyja will welcome you to her halls with open arms, Adam." I yanked at the base of his soul. It didn't take as much force as Zach's, which probably spoke to the difference between removing a soul from a live body and one from a dead body.

Once he was free of his mortal coil, his spirit expanded, as if taking the first full breath he'd had in years. Then he stared at me expectantly.

Shit, there was more? I looked down for Archibald's guidance, but he wasn't there. Of all the times for him to decide to be a cat and wander off...

Still, I'd come this far. Maybe I could figure out how to send him to Fólkvangr, no matter how unlikely that seemed. After all, everything that'd happened in the past few days had been unlikely. What was one more thing?

I looked at him and thought about his ravens, trying to imagine Huiginn and Munin taking flight and showing me the way.

Nothing happened. And why would it? Odin wasn't in charge of Fólkvangr.

I took my free hand and placed it over the tattoo of a skeletal winged cat on my shoulder blade. As soon as I thought of Freyja, it shifted under my hands. Since my tattoos had never wiggled before, I took that as a sign something was happening. It was too early to decide if it was a positive sign or not.

In a second, the answer didn't matter. A path opened in my mind's eye, and although I couldn't see the end, I knew where it led.

"Adam, there's the road for you. Go to Fólkvangr and find your mother. Freyja's blessings are upon you." I crossed my fingers over my cat tattoo and hoped I wasn't about to get in trouble with the goddess I suddenly believed in a little more than I had a couple minutes ago.

"Thank you." He dropped my hand and sprinted for the shimmering path almost before the words were out of his mouth.

Once he and the shimmer disappeared, I fell to the ground, feeling like I'd been hit with a proverbial load of bricks.

"You did well," Archibald said, wending around the nearby headstones and settling at my side. He collapsed against me with a *whump*.

"I feel worse than I did this morning with my champagne hangover," I groused. "That was hard and stupid."

"It won't always be that difficult. Most souls leave their bodies easily with a little encouragement. It's only the long dead and the completely alive that are difficult. And the souls of the latter are much harder to choose, because you're not only taking their souls, you're choosing the living, something that should only happen on the battlefield, if then."

I wanted to ponder his words, but unless I was also willing to take on a hefty dose of guilt along with them, now wasn't the time. I'd have to deal with what I'd done to Zach at some point or another, but today was not that day. There was already too much happening for me to add one more piece to the full-on banana-crackers puzzle.

"I just want to grab my meds and head back to Ash's," I said. "You can give me another death lecture later."

"Back to Ash's?" Archibald asked. He didn't say anything else, but the weight of the judgment and disappointment in his voice threatened to crush me. God, cats really were the judgmental assholes we'd all suspected.

"For the night," I said. "Then it's time to leave town."

He purred, vibrating my leg. "Good choice."

"I just need to see if I can round up the funds to execute my plans. And find a landing place to settle."

"And what are you doing toward that end?"

I heaved a sigh and forced the words past the lump in my throat. "I'm going to call my mom."

"It's about damn time."

THIRTEEN

I settled back in my room at Ash's with three bottles of water— it really had been too hot for a run, especially in my less-than-ideal fitness condition—and stared at my phone on the nightstand.

Archibald lounged on the end of my bed, looking for all the world like he was fast asleep. His ribs rose and fell evenly, and every fourth breath a slight snore emanated from him. It was so fucking cute, but I wasn't sure he'd appreciate me cooing, "Who's the best, cutest boy in the world with the most adorable little snorsies?" at him.

"Are you going to call or not?" Archibald asked without moving.

"I said I would, didn't I?" I snapped. Ugh. I was an asshole. "Sorry. This is hard. I haven't talked to them since I left the state in the middle of the night ten years ago."

"Why'd you go?"

I looked down at where my hands were twisting in my lap. "I was immature, angry, and scared. They saved my life and did their best to protect me when I couldn't—or *wouldn't*—take care of myself. They loved me, and I didn't want it."

"That might be a good way to open," Archibald suggested. "An apology, an acknowledgement of what they did, and an explanation of why you did what you did. You may have been wrong, but you were sick and your frontal cortex was still far from being fully developed."

"Aren't they done by twenty-five?"

"On average. You are not average."

I decided to take it as a compliment, even though I couldn't figure out how to interpret it that way. "I need to just do it. Rip off the bandage."

"Yes, you do. Pick up your phone."

I picked up my phone, then dropped it again. "Or I could give you a recap of the last thirty years of my life."

"No, thank you. I am quite pleased with what I know thus far. I'm sure there will be plenty of time for you to fill me in later."

I blew out a breath and pulled up the contact. I'd changed my number a few times since I'd moved, but hopefully Mom hadn't.

I pressed *Call*, then immediately hit *End*. "No answer," I told Archibald.

If a cat could roll his eyes, Archibald would've. As it was, he made a valiant effort.

"Fucking fine," I muttered. I hit *Call* again and waited for the ring.

One ring. Two. Three. Four. A click. "You've reached Katrin Ström. I'm probably dressing up a corpse right now and can't come to the phone. Leave a message or call back later."

I hung up.

"Dressing up corpses?" Archibald asked.

"She's a funeral director. One of the things she does is prepare bodies for funerals. That's obviously her personal phone," I said. "I hope, anyway. That message is new."

Archibald stood and stretched. "You didn't leave a message."

"What difference would it make?"

"Well, a missed call from an unknown number is unlikely to elicit a call back. A message from the daughter she hasn't heard from in ten years probably would."

It made sense, but... "But what if it doesn't?" I hated the smallness of my voice. It was the smallness I'd felt when Gwen broke things off. The smallness I felt when I'd lost my job. The smallness I felt when I tried to look at the big picture, the long game, my future. Everyone I'd ever known had future plans—five-year, ten-year, fifty-year. I never saw anything when I looked ahead. I talked about my desires and dreams, but everything was fuzzy, and my goals felt like sandcastles at high tide. I'd always known my future would be shorter than other people's.

My time was brief, and I was small.

"Have faith, child. Have faith and call back. The worst that can happen is what you've already imagined will happen. Calling now will get your feared task out of the way, and you can move forward with knowing instead of dread.

I shook my head. "I can't. Not right now. But I can't stay here either."

"What will you do?"

I pulled up my banking app to check my balance, then looked at Greyhound prices. "If I don't eat, I can take the bus from here to Portland. It'll be a couple days, but I can probably stash a few granola bars in my bag or raid Ash's kitchen. It'll be fine."

Or... Or I could call Gwen. Ask for one last favor. She might be pleased enough that I was getting out of town, going back to the parents she'd urged me to contact for years, that she'd lend me the money to fly back to Portland—or at least have a couple meals on my bus ride.

The heap of possessions in the corner of the room caught my eye. Prominent among them was my sword. It was tucked away in its leather scabbard now, but the Viking-style weapon had a twenty-seven-inch blade etched with delicate Norse runes I couldn't read and was perfectly weighted and balanced for my height. My mother had given it to me on my twelfth birthday. Would I even be able to take that on a bus or plane? It was a good weapon. I hadn't had lessons or sparred with anyone more than a few times in the last couple years, but when I had, the sword's quality and craftsmanship always elicited awe and plenty of compliments. I thought about the word *craftsmanship*. Sexist. Craftspersonship sounded wrong, but who knew the maker's gender? Anyway, I bet I could sell it for more than enough to get a flight home. I even knew who to call first.

"Don't sell the sword," Archibald said. "You're going to need that. And besides, it's a family heirloom."

"How'd you know that?" I demanded. "You can't know what I'm thinking, and you don't know what it meant to my mother."

Archibald lay back down on the bed. "Your poker face is non-existent, and as for the rest... I'm a talking cat. Doesn't it make sense that I'd know a little more than the average humans you interact with regularly?"

"I'll ask Gwen," I decided. "If she gives me a couple hundred dollars, I can at least eat on the way to Oregon. And if my parents are okay with me staying for a while, they'll pay her back. I know they will."

"Why not ask Ash?" Archibald hopped off the bed and sharpened his claws on the rug.

I glared at him and hissed, "Stop that! It probably cost more than I'll ever see in my life."

"My point exactly. It's a rug in one of many spare rooms. If he can afford this, and he's truly your friend, couldn't he lend you the money to get home?"

He could. Of course he could. But all his gifts came with strings, and even when those strings seemed to be beneficial at first, they ended up fucking me over in the end. Ugh. What was wrong with me? He'd been nothing but generous. Treating me to food and drinks when I couldn't afford my own. He was giving me a place to stay—indefinitely, if that's what I decided. I didn't need to—*shouldn't*—ask for money. "He's done too much already. I can't ask for anything more." I narrowed my eyes at him. "Why don't you just teleport us the way you get yourself around?"

"I can't take passengers. At least not if I want to guarantee they arrive with all limbs intact."

I huffed. I hadn't expected that to be a solution, but I was more than a little disappointed. "Fine. I'll see how much a bus ticket is."

"I'm not riding on a bus. A plane, maybe, if you can keep me out of the cargo hold. We can fly first class. But not a bus. Never a bus." He turned his back on me and raised his tail in the air, giving me a better view than I wanted of his back end.

"I can't afford first class, but small pets can travel with their people as long as they're in a carrier."

Archibald shuddered. "No thank you. Why don't you ask for enough to rent a car? I am not a peasant cat, and I will not be treated as such."

"I don't think any cats are peasant cats. It's not in your nature," I answered absently as I tried to think of a way to get enough money to afford a rental car. Did they charge by time or distance? If it was time, I could make the drive in about twenty-four hours, and even grab a couple hours of sleep on the way. That quick of a trip could be fueled by nothing more than gas station coffee and a sandwich or two. It'd suck to drive straight through, but maybe it would be cheap enough to afford. I had to have one credit card that wasn't completely maxed out.

Archibald hissed softly and disappeared under the bed. A second later, Ash appeared in the doorway. "Ready for happy hour?"

"It's eleven-thirty in the morning," I said, already knowing how he'd counter my observation.

"It's afternoon on the east coast," he replied easily. "Besides, when has morning ever stopped us before? Let's get out of here."

I shook my head. "I can't. And I'm not staying in Santa Fe. I called my folks, and I'm going to head home as soon as I figure out how to get there." I steeled myself and pushed the request out, my words tripping over each other. "CanIborrowmoneytorentacar?"

"What?"

I took another deep breath and asked again. "Can I borrow money to rent a car? I'll pay you back as soon as I get to Oregon."

Ash laughed. "Of course I can lend you the money to get there! But I'll do you one better. Let's road trip it together. We can take Route 66 west, then head to Vegas for a couple days. Who knows? Maybe you'll hit the jackpot! Then we'll head to your parents' place. I haven't done a drive like that in a long time, and I've always wanted to take Route 66. Give me a few hours to get my schedule switched around, and we can take off. It's going to be so much fun!" He turned and exited the room before I could say anything.

Archibald crept back out from under the bed. "That is a bad idea."

"It'll be fine," I said uncertainly. I'd hitched the route when I came here, and it had been a cool experience. But a road trip with Ash? "I'll have someone to share the driving, and there's no way he'll want to sleep in a car, so there will be a hotel room every night—and food. It'll be better this way."

"It won't, and you know it," Archibald said. "But it's better than staying here." He sighed. "We might as well get ready to go."

FOURTEEN

I'd spent two days getting rid of everything I wouldn't need and repacking everything I would.

I texted an old high school boyfriend—aka Gary, the guy I'd made a "Let's-pretend-we're-both-straight" agreement with when we were juniors—who now lived in Vegas, and asked if we could crash with him when we passed through town. He worked at Caesar's Palace as a centurion and was the only person from high school I still kept in touch with.

I hadn't said goodbye to Gwen though. The idea of doing that was almost as scary as the thought of talking to my parents. The parents I was planning to drop in on with no warning or notice. I rationalized that decision by telling myself that it'd be harder for them to turn me away if I was already there. But what if they did anyway? What if, in front of Ash, they told me to leave? Then what?

I stuffed that possibility in the back of my mind. I'd cross that bridge when I got to it. For now, I decided not to think about what kind of reception I'd get at all. Everything would be fine.

"Everything will be fine," I whispered to the room I'd been sleeping in at Ash's.

"No, it won't," Archibald said from where he was curled up in a patch of sunlight. "Things are happening now, and nothing will be fine for a very long time. Maybe forever, if the people who choose what to do next make mistakes."

"That doesn't apply to me, though," I replied, ignoring the burst of panic that exacerbated the nausea already roiling in my gut. "I have nothing to do with choosing whether or not things will be okay. I'm just some weird... What am I?"

Archibald stood up and stretched luxuriously. "Why don't you figure that out on your own? I can't tell you everything. What are the facts?"

I mulled the question over for a minute. "I saved Gwen from death?" I offered.

"How did you do that?"

My shoulders crept up around my ears. "By taking the other guy."

"Taking?" Archibald was stern, and his unblinking gaze wouldn't let me look away.

"Yes. I detached his soul from his body so he could move on."

"Before his time."

"Fine," I snapped. "I killed him. It was the only way I could save Gwen. And I helped that second guy's spirit move on. I didn't kill him."

Archibald licked one paw, never breaking eye contact. "You did not. That was a job well and properly done once you committed to it. What happened once you helped that man move on?"

I visualized the scene, everything that had been said or done in the cemetery. "I sent his soul to Fólkvangr."

"To your knowledge, who can do something like that?" Archibald sounded impatient, and I didn't blame him. I was feeling particularly slow.

I'd chosen who would die. I'd sent a spirit to Freyja. A ray of sun flashed through the window and glinted off my sword. And I had a Norse sword with runes etched on my blade that had been my mother's.

"No," I whispered in denial.

"No what?"

Damn cat was going to make me say it out loud.

"I'm not a Valkyrie. There's no such thing." I said it with as much conviction as I could muster, which wasn't much.

Archibald resumed his bath and didn't offer any comment.

"I'm a Valkyrie." The knowledge of who I was, *what* I was, snapped into place. It was right. I was a mythical warrior, sworn in service to Freyja. I was a chooser of the slain. "Where's my pegasus? And my winged helmet?"

Archibald looked at me like I'd lost my mind. Which I frequently had, so it was fair. Shit. "I really have gone crazy. I'm probably in a psych ward right now, drugged to the gills and drooling on my straight jacket."

"You most certainly are not. As for the winged helmet and pegasus, they're both rather conspicuous, don't you think?" He settled back into the patch of sun that was slowly creeping across the floor.

"A pegasus would be a much cheaper way to travel than renting a car or getting a ride from Ash," I said.

"If you'd prefer, we can take the Ferrari," Ash said.

I jumped. He'd disappeared two days ago after making our road trip plans, and I hadn't heard him return. "Why the Ferrari?" I asked.

Ash grinned. "It might not be a pegasus, but it is a speedy horse —at least according to their logo!"

I laughed. "Definitely not the same. We can take whichever car you want, but the Ferrari might not have enough trunk space for all my shit." I gestured toward the neat stack in the corner. It turned out there were more possessions that I wanted to keep than I'd thought. Besides the sword, the pile contained three boxes of books, two suitcases of clothes, one backpack with my laptop, notebooks, meds, and five hundred—give or take—tubes of lip balm, lithium was super dehydrating, and a small box of mementos from my decade in Santa Fe and years with Gwen. I wouldn't have been able to take even half of this on the Greyhound.

Ash stared at my small mountain of stuff, caught sight of Archibald, then put his hands on his hips and glared at me. "You said you were going to ruthlessly purge. I was expecting one box and one suitcase. What is all this?"

"I'm going to need clothes," said, too defensively. "It's not like I'll magically have money to buy new ones when I get to Oregon. And I got rid of half my books, some old T-shirts I never wear, and most of my random crap. This isn't much for one thirty-five-year-old person to own." I gestured around the room, waving my hand dramatically. "You have more stuff in this room than I have in four boxes and two suitcases."

His expression softened for a moment, but Archibald took that moment to stand up and stretch luxuriously. "And that fucking cat? What's he doing here?"

"He's mine, and he's coming with me."

Archibald swung a contemptuous gaze between us. "I'm no one's pet."

Ash did a double-take, and his arms flopped to his side. He looked at the cat, then me. "He talks."

"Of course I talk. If you're really her friend—and I have my doubts about that—it might be time to listen to her and take what she says seriously. She's going to need a lot of support in the next few days, and it can't all come from someone as magnificent as me." He jumped onto the bed to where the sunbeam had moved, closed his eyes, and appeared to fall asleep.

I saw him open his eyes just a slit, so I knew he was faking, but I didn't tell Ash.

Ash turned and walked out of the room without another word, and I followed him. He stopped after a couple steps and swung around to face me. "Your cat talks."

His tone was flat, not astonished, and I narrowed my eyes at him. "You don't seem that surprised."

"Of course I'm surprised. I've never met a talking cat before. Is this because you're a Valkyrie?"

My jaw dropped. He knew. "You fucking knew and you let me believe I was crazy. *Told* me I was crazy. What kind of bullshit is that?"

His expression softened, and he took a step forward and slung his arm around my shoulder. "I didn't know, not for sure. But I overheard you a little bit ago, and then it all made sense."

Nothing was adding up, and I shook my head to try to clear my confusion. "What the hell is going on, Ash?" I paused for a beat, then another question occurred to me. "How are you taking all this in stride? Who are you?"

Ash grinned. "I've gotta maintain a little mystery, babe. Be ready at seven tomorrow morning. Bring all that shit if you need it. I think our trip is going to be quite the adventure."

FIFTEEN

I was in the driveway with all my things except for my cat at six-thirty. There was no way I was gonna be late and start the trip off with an irritated Ash.

I'd spent the night before packing and repacking my boxes and suitcases, trying to get everything into one fewer box and one fewer suitcase. I'd finally decided that I could lose a few more books, but Archibald had talked me out of it.

When I'd fallen asleep at one a.m., I was confident that I had everything I needed for the trip in my backpack. Three changes of clothes rolled tight, toiletries, two books, my laptop, and my meds. And obviously my five hundred lip balms. My meds dried me out, and I hated cracked lips.

My pack weighed a metric ton, but it wasn't like I was hitch-hiking this time.

At seven fifteen, the garage door opened, and I caught a glimpse inside. Five vehicles, including the Ferrari, occupied a half-dozen spots. But the sleek, shiny metallic grey sedan backing out looked almost staid compared to the sports cars being left behind. It looked expensive, and knowing Ash, it probably was.

The trunk popped open, and I heaved my boxes and suitcases in while Ash occasionally revved the engine impatiently. Once I'd stowed my stuff, I looked around once more for Archibald. He wasn't there. I hesitated for a minute before getting in the car. He'd been very clear that he was coming with me, and I didn't want to leave him behind. On the other hand, he was some kind of magical talking cat—although the possibility that I was in a mental institution still stood—and could probably catch up to us.

The passenger-side window rolled down. "Are you going to get in, or am I just driving all your crap to Oregon?"

I sighed and opened the door. "Just saying goodbye to Santa Fe." The impact of what I'd said hit a second later, and a sob caught in my throat. I was leaving Santa Fe, the city that'd been my home for over a decade. I loved it here—it was beautiful. Oregon was gorgeous too, of course, but its beauty was all green and lushness. Santa Fe was browns and reds and tans. There was so much life, but it wasn't as in-your-face as in the Pacific Northwest.

I'd miss the adobe houses, the blue doors, and the bluer skies.

"I'll be back," I whispered to the city. But when I said those words, I knew they were a lie. I was walking away from here forever.

I climbed into the car and nearly stepped on a large, orange, fluffy cat.

"Jesus Christ, Archibald," I muttered. "Just because you look like a cat doesn't mean you have to act like one and try to murder me."

"I don't *look* like a cat," he said, hopping into the back seat. "I *am* a cat. I'm just even more exceptional than my non-verbal kindred. And I wasn't trying to murder you. It's not my fault you stepped right where I was lying. He curled up into a ball on the seat behind me and closed his eyes.

"You'd better not have an accident back there," Ash said. "I am not cleaning hairballs off the leather."

Archibald opened one eye. "I do not get hairballs, and I am in complete control of my bodily functions. Should I have any needs, I will let you know. Now, shut up and drive. Drittsekk."

Ash revved the engine once more, then drove through the gates.

"What'd you call him?" I asked. I was pretty sure it had been Norwegian. I'd spoken a bit of the language when I was young—my mother had tried to teach all of us, but it didn't sound quite like what little I remembered.

"He called me an asshole," Ash muttered. "Your cat is rude."

"You speak Norwegian?" I asked.

"I speak a lot of languages," Ash replied in a tone that meant he wouldn't elaborate.

I turned and pinned Archibald with a look. "You shouldn't call him names. After all, he is driving us all the way to Estacada, and then he has to drive back in a—what kind of car is this?" All I knew was that it was sleek and grey and felt very expensive.

"Maserati Quattroporte." Ash said shortly without glancing at me.

I didn't know a lot about cars, but a Maserati was significantly more expensive than the fifteen-year-old Hyundai I'd driven until it'd fallen apart. "A Maserati is significantly better than a Greyhound, right? Or finding people who will pick up a hitchhiker and a cat."

Archibald flicked his tail but didn't answer.

If everyone was going to sulk in silence, this would be a very long road trip indeed.

CHAPTER

SIXTEEN

A couple hours after leaving Santa Fe in the rearview mirror, Ash pulled off the freeway at a town called Grants.

"I need a stretch and a drink," he announced.

He disappeared through the doors of the wood-sided building with peeling white paint, a bright-blue door, and blue trim.

A blinking sign over the door announced that it was *The Junkyard*.

Something about this spot... This situation felt familiar in a way that twanged in my chest and raised an unfathomable feeling of yearning.

Had I been here before?

I tried to shake off the longing. I probably had stopped in when I was hitching the Route. I followed Ash through the searing desert-in-August heat into the relative cool of the bar. It took a few seconds for my eyes to adjust. It was dimly lit, and light-blocking curtains covered the windows.

It didn't scream ten a.m. inside, but then anyone who was at a dive bar in a tiny town at ten a.m. probably didn't want a reminder. After a minute, I spied Ash. He was sitting at the bar, as far away

93

from the door and as close to the shadows as he could manage. Four shot glasses were lined up in front of him—two full and upright, and the other two already empty and upside down. The glasses were accompanied by a pint of what looked like lager.

I watched him pick up a shot, down it in a single gulp, and slam the glass on the table. Then he took a long drink of his beer.

I sat down next to him, looked at the shot glasses, and raised an eyebrow. "Little early in the road trip for the driver to get drunk, isn't it?"

He grunted and shoved the remaining shot at me. "Take it."

My hand was on the glass before my brain could tell me it was a bad idea, but my inner Jiminy Cricket popped up before it was too late. I inhaled deeply and dropped my hand back into my lap. "No thanks. It's a bit early for…" I leaned down and sniffed, then wrinkled my nose against the sickly sweet black-licorice odor. "Are you doing shots of Jäger in the middle of the morning?"

"Yes. And this one's yours."

I clenched my fists. I really, really wanted it. "No thank you," I said. My voice wasn't as sure and steady as I would've liked, but it'd have to do. I searched for a reason that Ash might accept. "One of us is going to have to drive, and it's probably better if I don't do shots before getting behind the wheel of your $100,000 Maserati."

"It was $150,000."

I couldn't quite muffle my gasp of shock. I'd meant to exaggerate the value of the car. Ash really, really liked luxury.

"I can drive," Ash continued. He didn't pick up the shot, leaving it in front of me. "You know I have an almost supernatural resistance to alcohol."

He'd described his near immunity to drunkenness that way before, but this time it hit differently. "Is it supernatural?"

He laughed. "Why would you even ask that?"

"Why wouldn't I? The last week made it eminently clear that there is a lot more going on in this world than I ever realized. I have no idea what else I'll encounter. Archibald didn't scoff at the idea of a pegasus. And also, he's a talking cat. And then there's me…" It was still hard to say the word Valkyrie out loud, so I skipped it. "What's next? Dragons? Freyja? Thor? Loki?"

Ash flinched, something I wouldn't have noticed if I hadn't been staring at him, looking for a clue as to who he was.

"Why'd you pull those names out?" he asked, his voice perfectly even. Too even.

"I watched Avengers last night," I said. "And Freyja is exceptionally fond of cats, so my talking cat seems right up her alley. As for the dragons…" I reached around and pulled the strap of my tank top down, displaying a dragon tattoo. It was flying across my back, and its wings were tattered at the edges and turning into a flock of ravens. It wasn't my only tattoo, but it was the newest. "I'm the girl with the dragon tattoo, and it might be interesting to see a dragon in real life."

Ash rolled his eyes. "You're being ridiculous. Of course there's more out there than you and the cat, but I wouldn't hold your breath for dragons." He finished the last shot, chugged his beer, and stood. "Ready to roll?"

I eyed him. Getting in a car with someone who'd had four shots and a beer in fewer than twenty minutes was a monumentally bad idea. "Can I drive? You might be nearly immune to the effects of alcohol, but I've had zero drinks."

"Fine." He tossed me the keys, which I barely snagged out of mid-air. "But if you break it, you buy it. And you can't afford to buy it."

Ash stalked out of the bar. I followed more slowly, and it was only when I was back on the road and heading west that I realized he'd skipped over denying we'd run into gods and just pooh-poohed the idea of dragons.

"What about the gods?" I asked, glancing over at him.

He was fast asleep, curled up in the corner of the passenger seat. A quick glimpse into the back seat showed Archibald in the same state. I sighed and turned on the radio, then tuned it to an all-classical station. Vivaldi's Spring filled the car, and the Route rolled out in front of me.

And for the first time in as long as I could remember, I felt part of something. Part of the world that I'd numbed myself to years ago. And I was curious.

SEVENTEEN

I opened my eyes and winced against the sunlight on my face. It took a moment to realize it was merely the brightness that was irritating and not a hangover. It was still weird to wake up without one, and I wondered if I'd ever get used to it.

After a quick shower and an even quicker repacking, I was out the door, Archibald at my heels, and ready to go.

Ash, however, was nowhere to be found. I shrugged on my too-heavy backpack, shot off a quick text to Ash, and walked to the coffeeshop at the end of the road.

I was on my third cup of drip and fifth crossword puzzle on my phone when Ash showed up. He looked as well-rested as I felt, but there was a rumpledness about his clothes—the same ones he'd been wearing yesterday—that implied he'd slept in them. Or picked them up from a heap on the floor and put them back on.

I raised an eyebrow. "Good night?"

He'd headed off to the hotel bar without me when I pled exhaustion to get out of it.

"You have no idea." He grinned and winked, apparently in a

much better mood than yesterday. Then he shuddered and glared at the floor.

I bit back a smile. Archibald was curled up under my chair. He'd had two cups of Earl Grey with a splash of milk, despite my protests that dairy and caffeine were bad for cats. And he'd just brushed the bare skin between Ash's trouser leg and sock with his cold, wet nose.

"You keep that cat under control, or I will," Ash hissed.

I bent down and scratched between Archibald's ears. "He's perfectly in control. Besides, there's nothing I can do. He's a cat, and even regular house cats don't listen. Now, do you want a coffee so you can tell me all about your latest conquest, or do you want to get on the road? Today is going to be a long day."

"Order me a quad shot Americano, and meet me at the car." Ash dropped three fifties on the table. "Get me a croissant, too. And whatever you want. Keep the change."

I wanted to protest, but I also wanted to keep myself in coffee while we traveled, so I pocketed the cash and smiled tightly. "You got it. See you in a few."

EIGHTEEN

The car ride was just as silent as it had been yesterday, and Ash ignored every request I made to pull over so I could take pictures of desert scenery, tourist trap towns, and oversized Route 66 signs. The only stop he made was when I insisted the four cups of coffee I'd drank had finally caught up with me.

It'd been almost two-and-a-half hours since we'd left Flagstaff, and twenty-ish since we'd left the freeway to stay on Route 66 for no reason I could discern, since it was taking us away from Vegas. But when I questioned Ash, he ignored me.

Ash was not one for following the speed limit—or even acknowledging that there was one—and when a vehicle appeared in front of us on the horizon, we caught up to it much faster than we would have if I'd been driving. Another one headed toward us. Nothing unusual, but something was off about the situation. The car we were catching up to crossed the center line, then jerked back onto the right side of the road.

I held my breath, willing the vehicle to stay in its lane until the one traveling toward us passed.

But that was not in my power. The sedan in front of us swerved into the path of the oncoming car again, and this time, there was no correction.

The crash of metal against metal churned my stomach, and the anguished scream that followed it tore at my soul.

I knew. I knew someone was dying.

Ash cursed and slammed on the brakes. I was out of the car and running to the scene almost before he'd come to a complete stop.

I got to the vehicles—or what was left of them—in time to see the drunk driver get out of his half of the mangled wreck and start screaming at the other driver.

She didn't answer. Her wracking sobs were the only thing I could concentrate on. My pace slowed the closer I got to her car. I already knew what I was going to see, what I was supposed to do, but I didn't want to. Not when it was children.

I looked through the jagged, shattered glass of the driver's side back seat. There were two children in there, and neither was moving.

I turned back to Ash, who was ambling along much slower than the situation warranted. "Get over here. You have to come help them. There are children in here."

Ash finally got to the car. "What do you expect me to do, Frankie?"

"You're an EMT. Do something!" I wasn't screaming, but I was close.

Out of the corner of my eye, I glimpsed another person who was being trailed by a translucent form that could only be a ghost. "Can you help? Can you do something?" I yelled at the stranger.

The woman, who looked vaguely familiar, regarded me with what looked like regret and a little anger. "I can't. You're the one who'll have to take their souls."

I shook my head, negating her words, even though they echoed what I already knew. "They're just children. It wasn't their fault."

"It's not about fault," she said. "It's about death."

"Please," the mother pleaded from the front seat. "Please help them. They're just babies."

I looked at the broken children, then at the drunk driver, who was still cursing under his breath, blaming everyone but himself.

"Only one person deserves to die today," I said.

"You can't do that," the stranger said softly. There was something about her—one moment she looked like a tall, voluptuous human, and the next she appeared otherworldly. She carried an enormous scythe that blinked in and out of existence and wore a hooded cloak that mostly hid her skull, which was flickering in and out of my perception in the same rhythm as her scythe. "You have to take the souls that are already untethering from their bodies."

"Maybe you can save one," Ash suggested. "If two need to be claimed, why not save one of them? You can take the drunk driver and one girl. That's better than nothing, right?"

I worried at my lower lip. I'd been wrong when I'd chosen someone to die in place of Gwen, but these were children.

"You cannot do that," the strange woman said again. "I did that once, and so many more people—so many more *children*—died because of it."

Archibald jumped out of the car and padded toward us. He rubbed against the woman's ankle bones, then looked up at me. I recognized that look. It was a warning.

I closed my eyes. I couldn't let anyone sway me right now. Tears formed at the corners of my eyes and spilled over to trail down my cheeks. "I can't. I can't kill them both."

"Of course you can't," Ash said. He reached out and patted my arm. "No one would ask that of you."

"You're not killing them," the other woman said. "You're only the conduit to their afterlife."

"I can choose," I whispered. "And I choose him." I spun around and placed my hand on the drunk driver, looking for the spark that animated him and tethered his soul to this body. When I found it, I wrenched it free. A wave of nausea overtook me, and I nearly collapsed with him.

"You need to take one more," Ash whispered. "Two must die here. Which child will it be?"

"I can't take a child, and I can't choose between them. They're so innocent. It's not fair."

"You have to," Ash said even more quietly than before. "It's the only way."

I choked on a sob, but he was right. Two souls were waiting, and if I didn't choose, they'd both die. I closed my eyes and thrust my hand through the jagged remains of the window. "I choose you," I said brokenly to the child nearest the door.

The little girl's soul blazed with light, and I felt the path open in front of her. Her soul turned and reached out toward her sister, but she faded quickly and disappeared. I had no idea why I'd been called for this family. My understanding of my role was weak and incomplete at best, but there was nothing in the myths and legends Mom had read to me about children. Choosing the slain was supposed to happen on battlefields. Not car accidents.

Warriors. Not kindergarteners.

But at least I could save one. I opened my eyes and reached across the now empty and broken body to the other child. This time, I gathered the soul that was nearly detached and cradled it for a moment. It brightened, but not with the flash of light her sister's had when she'd died. I thrust it back into its body and held it there until I was sure it would stay. It was easier than with Gwen, but whether that was because I knew more about what I was doing or because this girl was younger and more alive than Gwen had been, I didn't know.

The child coughed and gasped but lived.

"You did good," Ash said. "You saved a girl and meted justice to her murderer. This is what you need to do. This is how you can do good in the world."

"No." The strange woman stepped between me and Ash. "You did not do good. You disrupted the natural order. You haven't saved the girl, you've only delayed her death. You chose wrongly, and this will haunt you forever."

My shoulders slumped. She was right, and a glance down at the disapproval on Archibald's face confirmed she wasn't the only one who knew it. But what was I supposed to do now?

I looked back at the car. Another white woman, this one older than the vaguely familiar reaper, had wrenched open the driver's door. The driver got out and dropped to her knees to rock the body of her dead child in her arms.

"C'mon, Frankie," Ash said. "You don't have to listen to some random person hanging out in the middle of the desert. Let's find a drink and get out of here."

I hesitated and stared at the woman whose skull and scythe flashed so fast that it nauseated me. She was like me. I wanted to ask why she hadn't stepped in if I was doing everything so wrong, but before I could, Ash linked his arm through mine.

"Leave the crazy lady alone, Frankie. Let's go."

I tore my gaze from the woman and let Ash guide me back to the car. "Don't call her crazy," I said to Ash. "You know I hate that word."

"It's apt," Ash replied. "Get in the car. We need to get out of here."

I was settled in with my seatbelt on before it hit me. "We can't leave. The cops aren't even here yet. We need to give statements."

"There are two other people back there who saw even more than we did, even if one of them is even crazier than you. They'll take care of whatever needs to happen."

I twisted to look in the back seat. "Wait! Archibald isn't back yet."

"If that fucking cat won't stay in the car where he belongs, he can damn well get left behind," Ash snapped. He started the engine and stepped on the gas. He swerved around the wreckage, and I turned and watched the two women and one ghost until they disappeared behind us.

NINETEEN

This time, the now-familiar silence in the car was welcome. I replayed what had happened over and over. I'd been wrong. I'd chosen wrongly.

It'd been a test of sorts—that was the only thing that made sense. It'd been a test, and I'd failed.

My thoughts swirled through my head, but there was no resolution, no way to fix what I'd done. I couldn't go back and retrieve the drunk's soul and take the other girl's. Not now. He was gone, and no matter how wrong it'd been, taking the second child from her mother now would have been a level of cruelty I couldn't stoop to.

The reaper's—for that's what she had to be—words wouldn't stop repeating in my mind.

I did that once, and so many more people—so many more children— died because of it.

You disrupted the natural order. You haven't saved the girl, you've only delayed her death. You chose wrongly, and this will haunt you forever.

I hoped she was wrong. She had to be wrong. Even if my choices, my actions, hadn't been the right ones, it was over now. The only repercussions would be a mother who only had to mourn one child and not two, and a dead drunk driver who'd gotten what was coming to him.

You aren't a judge. The thought slithered through my brain, and I squashed it. If I was a chooser of the slain, that implied that I could choose. I had the right to choose. Maybe a car accident in Arizona wasn't a battlefield, but it was the field I was called to.

My stomach roiled, and the nausea I'd been feeling intensified. I rolled down the window, desperate for some fresh air.

"Ash, pull over," I gasped as the bile rose in my throat. "Now."

The car stopped so abruptly that if I hadn't been buckled in, I would've gone through the windshield. I undid my seatbelt and scrabbled at the door handle. The sudden clamminess of my skin made opening the door difficult, and I barely got it cracked before the contents of my stomach heaved up.

I vomited everything I'd consumed for what felt like the last three months. When I was done, I leaned back in my seat and tried to catch my breath.

"Did you get any on my car?" Ash asked.

I didn't have the strength to glare at him, but I managed to turn my head slightly so he could see my face. Sweat plastered the strands of hair that'd escaped from my braid to my forehead, and my tank top was damp with perspiration.

There was no sympathy in Ash's gaze. He got out of the car and walked around to my side. He made a disgusted noise when he got to my puddle of vomit but crouched to examine the car door. "You're paying to have it detailed," he said coldly.

"It'll wash right off," I replied. "Do we have any water?" My mouth tasted like acid and guilt, and I desperately needed to rinse it out.

"No. But we're only a couple miles from Oatman, so you can wash my car there." Ash slammed my door shut, stalked back to his side, got in, and took off.

Ash skidded to a stop, narrowly avoiding a burro wandering in the street.

"Fucking animals," he muttered, glaring at the burros that seemed to be everywhere. He spared a bit of ire for the cat who'd reappeared in the back seat somewhere between where I'd barfed my guts out and here.

Archibald didn't bother to acknowledge Ash's vitriol. Instead, he stood and stretched.

"This town is a fucking hellhole. I don't know why I'm here." Ash jerked the steering wheel and drove up to a ramshackle building with a neon sign half-heartedly advertising *old bee* and *f ee ice w te*.

"Um, we're here because you wanted to come this way rather than taking the interstate directly to Vegas," I reminded him. "This certainly wasn't my idea."

Ash opened the door to get out, but Archibald hopped out of the back seat and onto Ash's lap, then slowly and deliberately stood there for a moment, likely finding a way to ensure that Ash felt every bit of the mystical cat weight that could double and triple at will, before exiting the car.

"Fucking cat," Ash said loudly, earning several curious and contemptuous looks from nearby tourists. He followed Archibald out of the car, then turned and tossed the keys to me. "Clean up your mess."

I sighed. If only it was that easy to clean up my mess.

I took the keys and walked over to the General Store across the street. I bought a rag and two bottles of water to clean the car with, and got myself three bottles, one of which I drained before I even got to the register. The cashier was a short woman, barely older than a teenager, with long, dark hair and brown skin. She looked exhausted, although whether it was from lack of sleep, her job, or general malaise, I couldn't be sure.

"That'll be twenty-two fifty," she said dully.

I winced. That was a lot for five waters and a cleaning rag, but tourist towns, especially those in the middle of nowhere, didn't have a lot of competition.

I handed over two twenties. The girl counted out my change. Before she could hand it back to me, the bells on the front door jangled, announcing the entry of another person.

When the girl looked up, her face changed completely. Her brown eyes lit up and shone, and a wide grin spread across her face. "Hey Ms. Law! I didn't think you were due back till the end of the week."

"Hey Jess," the older woman said easily. I recognized her immediately. She'd been with the reaper out at the crash scene. "Had an anniversary to celebrate in town, so I headed back early."

"Is it that time already?" Jess asked. She was still holding my change and effectively keeping me there. "Is Dusana here, too? I haven't seen her."

"She rolled in earlier this afternoon. I'm sure she'll stop by."

The woman wasn't looking at the cashier anymore. Instead, she was eying me with an expression that was half contempt and half pity.

"Dusana..." I hadn't meant to say it out loud, but the way Jess looked at me made it clear I had. Now I knew why she'd looked familiar. She'd been one of my rides when I'd hitched to Santa Fe. There'd been a few minutes during the trip when I thought she'd hit on me, which happened a lot when I was on my own.

But there'd been more than a few moments later when I was disappointed she hadn't. She didn't look any different at the crash scene—well, except for the scythe and the visible skull—but the intervening years had been enough to erase the details of her face from my memory.

Both women were staring at me, and I grinned tightly at them. Now wasn't the time to reminisce. Now was the time to clean up Ash's car before he came out of the bar, then get the hell out of Dodge.

"Can I get my change?" I asked in as polite a tone as I could muster.

The girl flushed a little and handed it over. "Sorry about that, ma'am."

My eyebrows tried to rise off my face. Ma'am. I was barely thirty-five. Instead of telling Jess that, though, I said, "Thanks." I avoided Ms. Law's gaze and hurried out the door.

Unfortunately, I wasn't fast enough to miss hearing her last words.

"You're in a world of trouble, child. If you bring that trouble down on Dusana, you'll have me to deal with. And trust me, I'm a much more dangerous person than anyone you've met so far."

TWENTY

According to the Google Maps app on my phone, we were only about an hour out of Vegas. I was looking forward to stopping for the night. I hadn't seen Gary since he'd visited Santa Fe for some kind of backpacking adventure over five years ago. It'd be good to catch up.

The car halted so suddenly the seatbelt locked in place, and I lurched forward. "What the hell, Ash?"

"It stopped."

"Yeah, I figured that out for myself. Why?" I rubbed my sternum where I was positive I'd have a seatbelt shaped bruise later.

"Hell if I know." He pounded the steering wheel with the heel of his left palm.

It was probably my imagination, but it sounded like the steering wheel groaned under his assault.

I glanced at the map. "We're about a half-mile from a town called...Searchlight? They have a couple gas stations. There's probably someone who can tow us into town and fix whatever's wrong with your car."

"There is nothing wrong with my car," Ash gritted, despite all evidence to the contrary. "And there is no way anyone in that town will know how to begin looking for a problem with this car, even if there was."

I exhaled. I didn't want to antagonize him further, so I remained quiet. But his car wasn't running now, and each attempt he made to start the engine resulted in nothing but clicks.

"How about I walk into town and see if there's someone who can very gently bring the Maserati in, where perhaps it can be persuaded to start again?" I offered. I had to pee—the three bottles of water were catching up to me with a vengeance, and I didn't want to squat at the side of the road. "And if it starts before I get back, you can meet me there."

Ash grunted in response, which I assumed was a "Go for it."

"Coming, Archibald?" I asked.

"I'm not going for a walk," he replied. "I'll stay here with Ash. He probably needs the company."

The thundercloud marring Ash's near-perfect features belied Archibald's statement, but he didn't object.

I eyed my backpack but decided against grabbing it. I pulled my wallet out and tucked it and my phone into the back pockets of my shorts, then got out. "See you in a few," I said. I slammed the door, then winced at the noise. I took off down the road at a near jog before Ash could berate me for treating his car roughly.

I was in the middle of Searchlight in less than ten minutes and drenched in sweat from the summer afternoon heat. There were a couple gas stations, but I chose the one that had a service bay attached to it. I followed the sound of music into a large garage bay.

A wheeled, stretcher-looking thing was on the ground under a rusty, red Toyota something. A pair of worn, black work boots stuck out from under the car, but nothing else of the person they belonged to was visible.

I cleared my throat, but it was inaudible over the pulse of Ozzy Osbourne.

"Hey!" I shouted.

The music abruptly stopped, and the roller cart shot out from under the car so quickly, I shrieked and jumped back a foot.

The cart bore a tall white man wearing what looked like a long-sleeved grey onesie with blue pinstripes and "Hank" embroidered on the breast pocket and a camouflage trucker hat with *I Like it Dirty* written across the hood of a muddy car. He had so much grease on his hands, it almost looked like he was wearing gloves.

"What do you want?" he asked. He didn't sound unfriendly, not exactly. But he wasn't thrilled to see me. Although once he sat up and looked at me, his expression softened.

I braced myself for some kind of crude comment or suggestive leer, but neither of those were forthcoming.

"Sorry about that," he said, sitting up and climbing to his feet. "When I'm in the zone, I lose my manners."

Once I got an upright look at his face, I realized he wasn't as old as I'd first assumed. What I'd taken for deep lines were streaks of dirt. He wasn't any older than I was.

"No worries," I replied. "I'm Frankie."

"My name's Jordan."

"Um. Hank Jordan?" I pointed at the "Hank" embroidered on his onesie. It definitely, probably wasn't called a onesie, but I had no idea what it was called.

He laughed. "Nah, just Jordan. Hank used to own this place, but when he retired, he left me all his coveralls. It seemed silly to get new ones when these were perfectly fine."

I grinned. This was the nicest interaction I'd had with anyone in days. Weeks, maybe. I held out my hand.

He looked at my hand, then at his own. He wiped it on the leg of his coveralls—definitely a better name than onesie—but it didn't do much good. "Maybe we'll skip that nicety. What can I do for you?"

"I'm on a road trip with a friend, and his car stopped about a half mile south of town. I don't think it's out of gas—it didn't sputter at all. And besides, Ash isn't the kind of person to let the tank get low. It was almost like he turned off the car and slammed on the brakes at the same time. The engine just cut off, and we stopped. When he tries to turn it back on, it just clicks, like it's got a dead battery or something." I realized I was on the verge of babbling, so I clamped my mouth shut.

"You sound like you know a lot about all the ways a car might stop working," Jordan said with a laugh. "I can definitely come look at it."

I didn't tell him the reason I knew was because I'd often been too poor to maintain my vehicles, and I'd had more than my share of empty tanks and dead batteries. "Thanks. I really appreciate it."

"What kind of car is it?" he asked. He bent over and started gathering the few tools that were scattered on the floor.

"A Maserati..." I trailed off, trying to remember the model. "Quatro? Something like that."

Jordan stopped mid-crouch. "A Maserati Quattroporte?"

I snapped my fingers. "That's it!"

"Oh. Okay, then. Give me a few minutes to get cleaned up." He finished picking up his tools, then stripped out of the coveralls.

I was definitely not playing for his team, but watching him emerge from the too-large, shapeless garment was a pleasure to behold. Underneath, he wore denim jeans that weren't tight, per se —they'd need to allow for plenty of movement—but still showed off his powerful thigh muscles. He was also wearing a red tank top, which put his magnificent shoulders on display. I was a sucker for shoulders.

I sighed in appreciation. I'd much rather stay here admiring this dude's shoulders than rejoin Ash and his stupid car.

Jordan scrubbed his hands with some kind of soap, then turned to the simple utility sink along one wall of the garage, putting his perfect ass on display.

He turned around more quickly than I'd been prepared for and caught me looking. A grin spread across his face. "Is Maserati-owner a friend or a boyfriend?"

I grimaced. "Definitely not a boyfriend. At this point, even acquaintance is debatable."

Jordan looked at me, the question clear on his face.

I rolled my eyes at myself. TMI, Frankie. TMI. "He's a friend. He's just being a giant baby about his car." That was a true statement that didn't delve into any of the rest of our issues.

"So there's a chance I can talk you into dinner?" He winked, and I blushed.

"Um... Well..." I was at a rare loss for words.

"You can say no. It won't hurt my feelings. There just aren't a lot of beautiful people who wander through my garage, at least anyone I haven't known since we were kids. I always shoot my shot."

I finally found my words. "I am not going to pretend that you're not incredibly good-looking, but unfortunately for both of us, I don't date men. I just admire from afar."

"Probably safer that way," Jordan said. "Bummer for me, but I get it. I don't *date* men, either, no matter how pretty they are."

"Keep that in mind when you meet Ash," I said. "And definitely don't let him know you think he's pretty. If the urge overcomes you to fawn, direct it all to the car. Otherwise, he'll decide to seduce you."

Jordan laughed, dried his hands on a rag hanging on the edge of the sink, and snagged a set of keys from the key hook over the sink. "I think I'll be okay. It's been a long time since anyone's been able to seduce me."

TWENTY-ONE

Famous last words.

I sighed and watched Ash continue to wrap Jordan around his little finger. I grimaced at the unfortunate image that conjured.

I took another sip of my Sprite and picked at the burger that I'd order in a panic when the server had shown up.

It's not that I didn't like burgers, I just usually preferred something else. And tonight, that something else was anything that would take me away from the spectacle of Ash methodically and successfully seducing Jordan.

Jordan had lasted precisely fifteen minutes before his excitement over the car melted into awe at Ash's beauty.

And for his part, Ash was turning up the charm, probably because he'd been both gratified that Jordan truly appreciated the Maserati and delighted that the mechanic had the knowledge and skill to fix whatever weird thing was wrong with it.

I, however, was irritated. I didn't want to hang out with Ash, not really, and I hated being the third wheel.

"I'm gonna head back to my room," I announced after gulping down my Sprite. Neither man even looked at me.

Ash waved. "See you later. Have a great night."

I sighed and walked out of the restaurant, leaving the tab for Ash. He owed me for the hike into town, not to mention finding a competent mechanic and his date for the night. Besides, I didn't have the funds to pay for it, anyway.

I opened the door to my room and walked in. The motel was generic Americana—same bed, same tv bolted to the wall, same faded art on the wall as any room in any other roadside inn. The only thing my room had that most motels didn't was a giant cat in the middle of the bed.

"I sanitized the sheets, so no worries about sleeping on them," Archibald said.

"You did? How?"

Archibald made a noise that sounded suspiciously like a snort. "Of course I didn't. But they are clean. I wouldn't be on them if they weren't."

I didn't answer. Instead, I grabbed my backpack, pulled out my pajamas, and dug through it for my toiletry bag. "I'm gonna take a shower and order a pizza. There must be someplace that delivers here, right? And then we can veg out on the bed, watching true crime. If there's something you'd rather do, let me know."

Silence greeted my pronouncement, so I assumed either Archibald didn't have a problem with my plans, or, more likely, he didn't care.

I took my time in the shower. The motel might be inexpensive, but they hadn't skimped on water pressure. The hot water pounded out the tension in my shoulders. Unfortunately, my brain used this relative peace to bring to the forefront the reason for the tension.

The car trouble, the walk, Ash's flirtation with Jordan, and everything that'd followed had nearly driven the earlier part of the day out of my mind. The important part. The part where I'd fucked up so monumentally that a real-life fucking reaper had told me I'd face the repercussions forever. Or eventually. I couldn't remember. Either way, I deserved to suffer.

At the same time, it was so hard to regret preventing a woman from grieving over two children instead of one. And that fucking drunken douchebag didn't deserve to live after what he'd done. He hadn't even felt bad about it.

The heat of the water and the warring tension in my body fought for prominence, but the combination of guilt and—probable self-righteous—anger won.

With a growl, I turned off the water and reached for the towel from the cheap, faux-metal towel hanger. The towel rack ripped off the wall. The unexpected force tipped me backward, and I grabbed for something—anything—to maintain my balance.

Unfortunately, what I grabbed was the shower curtain. The tension rod collapsed into the shower, and the tenuous hold I had on my balance disappeared. I crashed into the tub, hitting my hip on the edge.

"Fuck!"

There wasn't a response from Archibald, not that I'd expected one. And really, what was a talking cat going to do for me, anyway?

I climbed out gingerly, briefly longing for my early twenties, when I could've sprung up without a second thought. I knew that mid-thirties wasn't old, but I'd started feeling things a little harder lately. Although... I stretched my arms overhead, turned side to side a couple times, then tentatively ran a hand over the curve of my hip, bracing for the pain.

I felt...fine. I'd probably be bruised tomorrow, but at least I didn't have to worry that I'd broken a hip or anything.

I put on a pair of rainbow-striped boxer briefs from my favorite gender-inclusive online underpants store and a long, worn Def Leppard T-shirt I'd found in a Target juniors' section more than fifty years after the band had topped the charts.

Clothing taken care of, I grabbed my phone to look for delivery.

Once my less-than-ideal chain pepperoni and black olive pizza plus bonus Sprite were en route, I finally took a breath. I would need to think through the repercussions of what I'd done and figure out what I should've done better. But I wasn't going to do it tonight.

I dried off my shampoo and conditioner bottles and stuck them back into my toiletry bag. Then I dug around in it for my prescription bottle. Might as well take the meds while I was thinking about it.

Nothing hit my hand that felt like a meds bottle. I pursed my lips and slowed down my rummage. Nothing.

"Dammit. I hate not finding shit," I said.

I left the bathroom and emptied my toiletry bag onto the bed. Deodorant, moisturizer, my shampoo and conditioner, and the couple mascaras and lip glosses I wore when I wanted to feel fancy. There was a nail clipper, an emery board I was pretty sure I'd never used, and three hair ties. No meds.

Shit.

I pulled out my laptop out of my backpack, then dumped everything else out next to my toiletries.

Clothes, a couple books, wallet, phone, eyedrops, and an orange pill bottle. Not the lithium, though. I might need a Xanax in a moment if the rising panic didn't subside, but that wasn't what I was looking for.

"Where the hell is my lithium?" I muttered.

Archibald finally stopped pretending to sleep and sat up, staring at me with an intensity that, in a cat, usually meant the bottom of their food bowl was faintly visible.

"Your meds are missing?" he asked.

"Probably not. Not really. But I can't find them. They have to be here, right?" The rising hysteria in my voice made me realize I was about to lose control. I took a deep breath. I was okay. This was okay. I'd taken them last night, and every night for the last week or so. They had to be here.

"They're here. Or maybe they fell out in Ash's car earlier. It's not a problem. I'll find them. It'll be okay."

"When was the last time you saw them?" Archibald asked.

"This morning in Flagstaff," I said. "I repacked them before I went for coffee."

"Interesting." Archibald stood and stretched. "Please let me out now."

I opened the door for him, even though it'd been made apparent that he didn't need such mundane assistance. I didn't expect him to be as frantic as I was, but I kinda hoped he would at least care.

I sorted through everything I had. Again.

Nothing. The lithium that'd saved my life more than once and that was keeping me from really believing I'd lost my fucking mind this time was gone.

I had nothing to keep the darkness at bay. Nothing to keep the mania in check.

I had nothing.

TWENTY-TWO

I wasn't sure how long I sat on the motel bed, but the light had died from the sky by the time I stirred.

I brought in the pizza box that'd been left on the ground outside my door when I hadn't answered the knocking earlier and ate three slices of now-cold pepperoni and black olive.

Once sated, or at least full, I pulled a loose, jersey-knit red skirt on over my boxer briefs, switched out my sleep shirt for a bra and tank top, and slipped my feet into a pair of black-and-white checked Rothys. Maybe the meds were in Ash's car.

I left the room and headed back toward the bar I'd left Ash and Jordan at earlier. I hoped they were still there, and that Ash would give me the car keys so I could look for my drugs. And that I could find some food I actually wanted to eat.

I was halfway to the bar when Archibald appeared in front of me so suddenly I nearly tripped over him.

"Dude. What. The. Fuck." I was fresh out of niceties, especially for creatures that were apparently actively trying to murder me.

Something dropped to the ground between me and the cat. It

was a cylindrical shape, dark orangish, and had a white cap and a white label. For all the world, it looked like a prescription bottle.

I bent over and picked it up, then read the label.

Frances Ström. Lithium Carbonate. 300 MG CAP. Take 3 capsules at bedtime.

"Where'd this come from?" I asked the cat.

He licked one paw. "Ash's room."

I nodded. That made sense. "He must've found it in the car and forgot to give it to me."

"That's one explanation," Archibald said. "There's another, of course."

I tilted my head, not following his train of thought. "What else could it be?"

He tilted his head and blinked slowly. "I'm sure if you think about it long enough, something will come to you."

I shook three pills out of the bottle and dry swallowed them, trying to figure out what Archibald was intimating. Well, I wasn't so much trying to figure out the what as I was trying to figure out the why. "There's no reason he'd take it on purpose." I meant to leave it there. Certain. But then the doubt crept in. "Is there?"

"Far be it from me to accuse a friend of yours of any nefarious motives, but it is suspicious—at least to me—that they went missing after you turned down his invitation to have drinks."

I pursed my lips and considered it. "I've turned him down more than once. Plus, he went out and got lucky last night, so clearly, he didn't miss me at all. Much like he won't tonight." I hated the doubt that colored my voice.

"There's no harm in asking, is there?"

I recognized the tone in Archibald's voice. He was stirring the pot.

"Why do you want me to pick a fight with Ash? He's driving me —driving *us*—all the way home." I did my best to infuse my voice with calm surety. "I have my meds now, so even if he took them for nefarious purposes, which I sincerely doubt, no harm, no foul."

"I'm sure you're right," Archibald said. "If you're content, then

I'm not going to argue anymore. If you want to avoid a repeat of tonight, though, I'd recommend keeping them on you." He didn't wait for a reply, just turned and walked off without a backward glance.

I looked at the pill bottle, then shoved it in my pocket and headed toward the bar.

TWENTY-THREE

When I wandered into the bar, it didn't take long to spot Ash. He was at a table in the back, surprisingly alone, and unsurprisingly with a row of empty glasses in front of him.

I slid into the chair across from him. "Where's Jordan?"

"Toilet." He swirled the tumbler of dark amber liquid slowly and stared into its depths as if mesmerized by the gentle whirlpool created by the alcohol.

Ash looked more than a little fucked up, which was weird, because I'd never seen him like that before. It might have been a good time to ask him a question that could, if I wasn't careful, sound accusatory.

Of course, it might be a shit time, too. I'd never seen him drunk, so I didn't know if he was an angry drunk or not.

"My meds weren't in my bag when I got to my room."

"Oh shit!" He looked up at me.

For a moment, I thought he was going to tell me he'd found them and it'd slipped his mind. A lot had happened today, after all.

"Are you going to be okay? Do you need to call your shrink and get a new prescription? I've never needed to take crazy pills, so I don't know how it works. I do know that if you want a Xanax or Adderall refill, you need to work with multiple docs and tell each of them you don't have insurance. That way, it's harder to track."

I'd done more than my share of drugs with Ash, but the one thing I never touched were prescription drugs. I couldn't articulate why, but it had something to do with not wanting my brand of crazy to impinge on someone else's medications.

"It's okay. I found them. Or rather, Archibald did."

The drunken persona dropped briefly when he met my eyes with a sharp look. A second later, the awareness disappeared back into a drunken haze. "Your magic cat found your meds? I'm willing to go a long way down the path of make believe to keep you feeling sane but agreeing that your 'magic talking cat'"—the air quotes felt superfluous—"found your missing meds makes it sound like you might need to take a few more drinks." He pushed a full beer over to me. "Local IPA. Pretty good, in my opinion."

I hesitated. I didn't want it, but whatever was going on with this conversation unbalanced me enough that I accepted the beer and took a drink. "You said you believed me. That you were on board with me being a Valkyrie. You were there when I chose who lived and who died today after the accident. You told me I had to choose two souls, encouraged me to take the drunk driver instead of both little girls. And you've talked to my cat."

"Oh, babe." The condescension dripped from his voice. "I think the heat is finally getting to you. I don't know what accident you're talking about. We barely saw another car all day. I'm just trying to keep you from falling apart. Why else would I offer to drive to the middle of nowhere in Oregon? I want you to make it to your family. They'll know how to take care of you."

My heart quickened, and my breath came in short, shallow gasps.

I'd thought Ash's confirmation of everything meant it was real. But if he'd just been pretending, then I could be mid-psychotic episode. I was bipolar and not schizophrenic, but it wasn't unheard of for my brand of crazy to have delusions of grandeur—and what was more indicative of that than the belief that I could choose the motherfucking slain?

I picked up the beer. What was the point of resisting if I was already on the fast track to Crazy Town? I downed half of it in one drink, took a breath, then finished it.

"Good girl," Ash said. He raised his hand, and a server appeared. "Another Catfish Point IPA for the lady, a double of Jameson for me, and a..." He looked up when Jordan reappeared. "...Long Island Iced Tea for my friend."

Long Islands were what Ash bought his dates when he knew it was already a sure thing.

Jordan laughed. "No way in hell am I drinking a Long Island. I don't care how hot you are, Ash. I'll have a glass of ice water and a Golden Shores lager. Give me that low ABV any night of the week. Especially nights before I have to fix a Maserati in the morning."

Ash laughed, but I saw the flash of irritation in his eyes. No one ever resisted him, and that must've stung. "I can't fault his reasoning since it's my car he's talking about. Thank you..." His eyes drifted down the server's chest until they caught her name tag. "Jessica."

She flushed, and Ash laughed.

"Right away," she whispered.

"You are a menace to society," Jordan said easily. "It's a good thing you're not staying more than one night. Otherwise, you'd leave a trail of broken hearts in your wake."

"Love that you think I won't anyway," Ash said. He reached out and stroked one thumb over Jordan's face from the top of his cheekbone to his jaw.

"You're pretty, and I fully intend to take what you're offering tonight, but my heart is safe from you." He glanced at me, and the look he gave me was full of too much sympathy to be comfortable. "Frankie is the only one here who could break my heart, and since she already turned me down, I'm safe."

I tried to answer Jordan's pity with a grin, but I came up short. "I'm not good company tonight," I said. "I'll head back to my room and leave you two alone."

"Don't be ridiculous," Ash said. "You're not a third wheel, and I just ordered you another beer. Stay a while longer."

"What he said," Jordan added with a devastatingly pleading smile it was hard to say no to.

I knew I was choosing wrongly—again—but I didn't argue. And when Jessica set the beer in front of me, I picked it up and drank it down.

TWENTY-FOUR

Even before I opened my eyes, I knew I was in trouble. My head was throbbing, and my mouth tasted like I'd licked the bottom of every ashtray I'd come across.

At the thought of that horrific action, my stomach joined in the hangover game. I bolted out of bed, which redoubled my headache, and barely made it to the bathroom in time to empty the contents of my stomach. I rarely throw up, and twice in two days was a not a trend I wanted to start.

When I'd purged everything I'd consumed since yesterday's vomiting episode, I rocked back on my heels and wiped my hand across my mouth. Once I was sure I was steady enough to stand without disturbing my head any more than I already had, I used the grab bar next to the toilet to hoist myself to my feet.

I gingerly brushed my teeth, careful to avoid triggering my gag reflex, until the taste of hangover was out of my mouth.

Then, I dug through my bag to find the ibuprofen I always carried, took four, and sat back on the bed with my head in my hands. I replayed the evening before, trying to figure out how many drinks I'd had, but I lost track after the shots started coming.

When the pounding in my head became manageable and the accompanying nausea dissipated as well, I donned my running clothes. Ash was never an early riser, and if he'd gone home with Jordan, it'd probably be noon before I saw him. There was plenty of time to caffeinate and run off my hangover.

"Mistakes were made," I said, looking in the mirror and adjusting my ponytail. I hadn't really looked at myself in a long time, and I didn't like what I saw today. My blonde hair that I kept dyed dark brown was showing several inches of roots, I had deep, dark circles under my bloodshot eyes, and there was an unsteadiness in my hands as I let go of my hair.

I couldn't be this person anymore.

I'd said it before, though, and I always had good intentions. Maybe I couldn't change. Maybe being a crazy drunk was my destiny. It wasn't a stretch to imagine myself alone, broke, and taking whatever money I could scrounge to buy my next drink.

"You don't have to walk down that path," Archibald said from where he'd appeared next to my ankles.

I snorted, then winced as the motion reverberated through my skull. "I stayed sober for what, three days?"

"And when was the last time you did that?" The cat tipped his head to one side and ran a paw over his face. It looked for all the world like he was admiring himself in the mirror as much as I was reviling my appearance.

I thought back. There'd been trips with Gwen without any booze —she was always insistent on that point—but it'd been a long time since we'd taken one of those.

"A couple years, maybe?" I hazarded.

"And you did that on your own, with no one reinforcing it. In fact, you did it in the face of the total opposite—nonstop encouragement. Next time you'll do better."

I laced up my sneakers. "I need you to follow me around, telling me what to do."

"I am not your Jiminy Cricket, and I will not sit on your shoulder dictating good decisions."

"No, you'll just be lurking about letting me know when I've done the wrong thing."

Archibald hopped onto the bed. "You don't need me for that. You already know. Now get going, or you'll be late."

I scowled at him, but without much heat. I didn't know the area, so wouldn't go far. It was unlikely I'd be late to meet Ash for the next part of our trip.

The last leg together. I planned to convince Gary to let me stay with him a few nights in Vegas until I could get ahold of my parents. They'd at least pay for a bus ticket to get me home, wouldn't they? I shoved the hotel key into the pocket of my spandex shorts, then opened the door. I was all the way to the edge of the dusty, gravel parking lot when paranoia hit me.

I headed back to my room and picked up my lithium. It wasn't comfortable carrying a prescription bottle in my pocket, but it was better than losing it again. Maybe Ash hadn't taken it, and Archibald had lied. Maybe I was trapped in psychosis. But regardless, if I was going to make this work, make new Frankie stick, I was going to need my meds. And if this was a delusion, perhaps adhering to my meds routine would help break me out of it.

This time, when I left my room, I kicked it into high gear immediately and headed out of town on the only road beside the highway that looked even remotely traveled.

Twenty dusty minutes later, I stopped. I'd pushed myself as fast as I could, and the pain in my glutes and ankles reminded me it'd been too long since I'd run on the unstable surface of a gravel road, needing to constantly adjust my gait to stay balanced. The burn in my lungs told me that going all-out without a warm-up and trying to match the pace I'd been able to hit when I was a regular runner had been stupid.

My breath was still coming in gasps when I remembered the words of one of my many therapists I'd visited for a while, then ghosted when I got tired of talking about myself. He'd said I was an all-or-nothing kind of person, and the sooner I learned to find my happy medium, the sooner I'd be able to find a place where I could be happy.

I wondered if it was part of living with the extremes of bipolar. I might be stuck with the bipolar forever—it was always there, even when in a meds-managed "remission"—I didn't have to let the all-or-nothing tendencies become an intrinsic part of my personality, right?

There was balance, even for someone like me.

"It's about fucking time."

TWENTY-FIVE

I whirled around. A tall white woman with long, honey-blonde hair twisted into braids that trailed to her waist stood behind me. She wore khaki capris, a rose-colored, silky tank top that matched the pink in her cheeks, and an unadorned gold circlet perched rather precariously on her head.

"Um…" As far as openers went, that wasn't impressive.

"I've been waiting for you to figure out that you could tread the middle ground. You won't always be successful, but at least you know it's possible."

"Who are you?"

She was standing between me and my way back to town, and although she didn't look threatening—not exactly—she was intimidating.

"You don't know?" She sounded genuinely surprised.

"We've never met before." That wasn't entirely true, though, was it? There was something vaguely familiar about her, just as there'd been about the reaper I'd seen yesterday. "Have we?"

"Not in person, but I did think you'd recognize me. Did your mother teach you nothing of who you are? Of what you are? Look at me, child."

A raven circled us for a minute, then settled on the ground near us.

"Shoo," she said, waving her hands at the bird. "This is none of his business."

The bird croaked once, then took off.

I followed its flight—it didn't leave, just did slow lazy circles nearly out of sight—and when my gaze returned to the woman, almost ethereal in her beauty, she was no longer alone.

A large chariot that looked like it'd been stolen from the set of *Ben-Hur* was behind her, but instead of horses, it was tethered to a team of four immense cats.

"Holy shit," I whispered. I stared at the cats, none of whom gave me a second glance. When I drew my attention back to the woman in front of me, she'd changed her appearance.

In place of the khakis and tank top, she now wore a knee-length, flowing gown with a shiny bronze breastplate and matching greaves and vambraces.

"Freyja." The name came out more flatly than I'd meant it to, considering the Norse goddess of love, beauty, war, and magic was standing in front of me. I'd grown up listening to stories about her, and now we were face-to-face.

She smiled, and it seemed like the world brightened for a moment. "Exactly! Now that we're friends, and we are friends, we can be frank with each other. I need your help. *We* need your help. And you need ours."

Freyja stared at me expectantly, but I was having trouble figuring out where to go with this.

"No," I said.

The goddess wrinkled her nose and tilted her head. "No? I don't understand."

"What's to understand?" My voice grew louder as the conviction that whatever she wanted was a path too far. "I am willing to believe that I have a talking cat. I can accept that he thinks I'm a Valkyrie—and the evidence I've seen so far supports it. But I am not doing favors for goddesses, no matter how many beautiful cats they have following them around. I just want to go home, apologize to my parents, and get my life back."

Freyja reached out and touched my cheek. "This is your life now. By all means, go to your parents. Your mother will be able to help you through this. But there's no turning around now that your powers have woken. You might not want to help me, but you won't be able to stop seeing the threads of death, and you'll be compelled to do something every time you do." She sighed, and the sadness in the sound nearly broke my heart. "And if you don't help us, the number of people you'll have to choose for Valhalla will increase exponentially."

"What do you mean?"

"Ragnarök is coming, and if you aren't there to stop it, this world will burn."

A laugh burst free from my mouth, and Freyja stared at me as if I'd either lost my mind or mortally offended her. Both might have been true.

"Listen, no offense, Freyja. But I am not some questing hero single-handedly in charge of saving the world. I am not walking into a training montage where you and a wise old woman teach me the ways of the Valkyries and give me the arcane secrets I need to trek to Norway, find the world tree, and stop Ragnarök. I'm Frankie. Broke. Mentally ill. Stuck with a shit friend, a worse hangover, and the self-control of a toddler being offered candy. If you need to find someone to stop the end times, look elsewhere. I am not your girl." I stepped off the road to walk around her and head back to town. The day was already heating up, and it was time for coffee, a shower, and Vegas.

Freyja's cats moved to block my path.

"Not single-handedly," Freyja said when I turned back to reiterate my refusal. "There's no way to do this single-handedly, nor would I ask anyone to. However, you are one of only a handful of Valkyries left in this world."

I pursed my lips so I could choose my next questions with care. I couldn't believe I was taking her seriously or considering agreeing to at least hear her out. I hadn't been kidding, nor was I trying to be self-deprecating. I really wasn't the hero type, and as much as my delusions of grandeur were extraordinarily grand, even they hadn't jumped into "save the world" territory.

"If not alone, then with who?" I asked. "And what would you need me to do?"

I might've imagined the relief that ghosted over Freyja's face, but I wasn't imagining it in her voice. "There are other Valkyries, and others similar enough that they can help you. You need to find out where the gods are hiding and plotting and lock them up so they can never escape. Because if Odin and Thor break out, they will have no compunction about starting Ragnarök as revenge for what we did to them."

I closed my eyes. None of this was making any sense. But the nonsensicalness of it all was what finally convinced me. I might be deeply imaginative, but there was no way my brain, crazy or not, would've come up with that explanation for becoming a questing hero.

"This is bananas. I don't understand anything you said. My brain is still hangover-fuzzy. I need a large cup of coffee and a shower."

"I can give you a ride back to the village where you're staying. Once you have showered, I will buy you a cup of coffee, and perhaps explain a little better. It may not all become clear, though, until you've spoken with your mother. After coffee, I will take you there. It will be faster than driving and will avoid any additional hazards on your route." Freyja stepped into her chariot and held a hand out to me.

I hesitated a moment before accepting it. I hadn't been looking forward to running back to town, and the sooner I got coffee and a shower, the better.

The offer of a ride to Estacada was even more welcome. I'd miss out on seeing Gary, but I'd be free of Ash that much sooner.

I settled in the chariot next to her, and she picked up the reins.

Freyja clicked her tongue twice, and the cats leapt into the air. Literally. The wheels of the chariot left the ground, and my delicate stomach lurched in response. I held onto the side tightly enough that my knuckles whitened. In a couple minutes, we landed just outside of town.

By the time Freyja was out of the chariot, she wore her earlier outfit of capris and a tank top once again, although her crown was now a circlet of flowers woven through the braids circling the top of her head instead of a golden band.

I hopped out of the chariot, and it and the cats melted out of view behind me. But before I could lead her into the coffee shop, she froze. I don't mean she stopped walking—she literally froze, something I wouldn't have thought possible in the Nevada desert summer. Her skin paled and took an icy blue tint, and frost formed in her eyebrows. She blinked once, so slowly I wasn't sure she'd open her eyes again, and a snowflake dislodged from her eyelashes, tumbled down her face, and froze to her cheek.

"Freyja?" I reached out and tentatively touched her arm. I snatched my fingers back immediately—Freyja was so cold, she'd burned them.

Her lips moved in slow motion, but no sound came out.

"I don't know what you're saying." I stared at her, hoping she'd try again and that somehow I'd be able to read her lips.

I'm sorry.

That time it was clear.

"For what? What's happening? What should I do?"

She shattered into countless pieces. The shards that had been a Norse goddess flared briefly into a cold, blue flame, and melted into the dusty road.

TWENTY-SIX

Coffee in hand, I pounded on Ash's door. After a full minute of steady knocking, it opened and Jordan, complete with bed head, peeked out.

When recognition dawned on his face, he opened the door all the way. He was wearing a pair of low-slung jeans and nothing else.

"Hey Frankie. Is that coffee for me?"

"Not even a tiny bit," I said. "Where's Ash? I need to be on the road immediately, if not sooner. Something's come up."

To his credit, Jordan didn't waste time asking questions. "Not sure where Ash is—he took off about thirty minutes ago. I was hoping he'd gone on a coffee run, but there's not a lot of town here, and only one option for coffee. And no way would it take Doris thirty minutes to make me a twenty-ounce quad shot caramel latte, no matter how busy the place is. I'll get dressed and get over to the garage. I think it's probably the alternator. I don't have the parts to fix it here, but I can lend you one of my cars and send for the part, then Ash can pick it up on his way back to Santa Fe."

I laughed a little despite the rush I was in and my complicated feelings about Ash. "Thus guaranteeing he'll be back."

"You saw through my subtle ruse," Jordan said. "Meet me at the garage in ten minutes. And if you have a coffee in hand for me, I'll lend you my classic Camaro instead of the VW."

"I don't care either way, but I know which will make Ash easier to deal with."

"Just tell Doris it's for me, and she'll fix you up." Jordan grabbed a shirt off the floor and disappeared into the bathroom.

I headed back to the coffee shop, appropriately named The Only Coffee Shop in Town, got a refill on my drip, and asked for a coffee for Jordan.

Doris, a tall, stout white woman with black hair sporting a single streak of white in the bangs and smooth skin that contrasted with the age evident in her gnarled, wrinkled hands, smiled and rolled her eyes. "Please tell me you're not his latest conquest. That boy couldn't keep his trousers up with suspenders *and* a belt."

I grinned back—Doris's cheer was infectious, and it broke through my worry and franticness. "Not me. I'm just trying to caffeinate him into finishing my car faster. I've got an appointment in Vegas this morning that I don't want to miss."

Doris shook her head and started on Jordan's latte. "A shop like that shouldn't stay in business in a town this size, especially since we're off the beaten track. But fortunately for Jordan, we get an unusually high number of breakdowns, and he stays busy. The few tourists who come through don't mind paying extra to get back on the road. If I didn't know better, I'd accuse him of using magic to stall the cars coming through—especially those with good-looking drivers."

I grimaced. A couple weeks ago, I would've laughed at her joke, but now I considered the possibility that it was the truth, and Jordan really did lure tourists here for money and sex.

Before I could travel too far down that rabbit hole, Doris handed over the latte. "Here you go sweetheart, and you tell Jordan he owes me a visit and an oil change."

"I'll do that. Thank you!"

She waved away my money. "This one's on Jordan. He can pay up later."

"Thank you again!" I headed out the door, thankful for not having to pay. I was down to less than a hundred dollars from the original cash Ash'd given me, and there was no fucking way I was asking for more. This would be all I had to get home on once I split with Ash in Vegas.

I stopped with my hand on the door. When had I started thinking of my parents' place as home again? I pushed the door open. It didn't matter how I thought of it. What mattered was getting there.

I walked the couple blocks to Jordan's garage and found him back in his onesie, hands already streaked in grease.

He took the coffee, pulled the lid off, and drank half of it down in one gulp. "You are a godsend."

I took a sip of my coffee to hide the sudden discomfiture his words triggered. I was a professional disassociator—is that a word? —but it'd only been a half hour since I'd watched a goddess die.

Coldness infused me. Maybe Jordan had done it. If he was powerful enough to break people's cars and seduce them—what other reason could there be for my fascination with his shoulders?— was he powerful enough to destroy other magical beings when they came into town?

"Are you okay, Frankie?" Jordan asked, concern writ large on his face.

I forced a smile. "Of course. Why wouldn't I be? Nothing wrong here." My voice was a couple octaves higher than usual, which did nothing to reinforce my assertion that I was a-okay.

"If you say so. I don't know you well enough to pry." He turned to a large board with a couple dozen hooks screwed into it, each with a set of car keys hanging from it. He grabbed a keychain with two keys on it and tossed it to me. "I didn't realize just how much stuff you had in the Maserati. No way does the Camaro have enough room for you. I thought y'all were just on a road trip, but this looks a lot more serious."

"I'm moving, and Ash is my U-Haul."

"He's a good guy," Jordan said. "Even if he took off this morning without a goodbye, leaving me to do the walk of shame alone."

"From what Doris said, you've had a lot of experience with it and never feel too much shame. She also said the coffees were on you, and you owe her a visit and an oil change." I held up my new keys. "If not a Camaro, what've I got?"

"Nothing that'll make Ash happy, I'm afraid. But it's not the VW." He led me around the garage to a small parking lot in the back.

Front and center was a blue BMW sedan.

I looked at Jordan in confusion. "Why won't he be happy with this? It looks nice enough."

Jordan shook his head. "It's the most basic model that exists, and it's a few years old. But if you have a few CDs with you, you could play those."

"This is nicer than anything I've ever driven. Thank you so much."

Jordan reached out toward my cheek. I tried to pull away but wasn't fast enough; his fingers touched my skin. His eyes widened, and he took several steps backward.

Something bumped against my ankles. I looked down, already knowing what I'd see. Archibald sat next to me, gaze fixed on Jordan.

The man visibly swallowed, and now his easy grin appeared forced. "It's been a pleasure, Frankie. Simply magical. Good luck with your move."

I watched him turn without a word. He knew something, and that solidified a lot of my suspicions.

He started back toward the garage. "Your boxes and suitcases are in it already. As soon as you find Ash, you're good to go. The tank is full, so no need to linger here. Goodbye."

He disappeared into the cavernous darkness of his workspace.

I looked at Archibald. "Is he a threat?"

The cat snorted. "Did you see the way he scurried away from you? He's not human, but he's nowhere near your level of power."

"So he isn't the one who killed Freyja this morning?" I wasn't sure if I was relieved to know he wasn't the culprit or worried because that meant I didn't know what'd happened.

Archibald jumped onto the hood of the BMW and stared at me. His body was rigid, his tail puffed up to at least three times its usual size, and he appeared even bigger than his usual chonky stature. "Explain."

I ran through the events of the morning, sounding as clinical as possible.

When I finished, Archibald again became the near boneless mass I expected from a cat. His fur lay flat, and he once more looked like his usual self.

"You scared me, Frances," he said, profound relief evident in his voice.

"Sorry, Archie." I didn't care what kind of emergency we were having. No one should be calling me Frances.

"Apologies. I hadn't felt Freyja's presence anywhere near me, and the way you dramatized events by saying she'd been killed set me on edge."

I opened the door and slid behind the wheel, waiting for Archibald to join me. When he got in, I drove out of the garage parking lot and headed down the street. "What do you mean, 'dramatized?' I told you everything as clearly as possible. Just the facts, ma'am, and all that."

"You think it's that easy to kill a goddess?"

I glanced at him out of the corner of my eye, then pulled into a parking spot in front of my room at the motel. "How am I supposed to know? I've never met one before. She froze, apologized, then shattered and burned. She looked pretty dead to me."

"You'll see her again. There's only one who could destroy Freyja, and Odin is not here to do it."

I gasped. "The raven!"

"What raven?" Archibald asked sharply.

"When we were talking, a raven landed nearby. Freyja shooed it away and said what we were talking about was none of his business. She meant Odin, right?" Fear clenched my stomach, and the nausea that'd been present too much in the last couple days threatened to rise again.

Archibald rolled his neck. "If he's already involved, it's even later than I thought. You must get home as quickly as possible."

"Ash will have to come with us," I said. I hopped out of the car, then grabbed my bag out of my room, tossing it in the back seat. "He'll need to drive the car back here and pick up his Maserati."

"I thought we were leaving him behind. That was your plan, wasn't it? If we start now, we can get there by tomorrow afternoon. He can wait here for his car. You need to see your mother, and Ash should not be there when you arrive."

"Why not? What aren't you telling me?"

"Yes, cat. What aren't you telling her?" Ash's voice was full of more malice than I could've imagined him capable of.

"Why don't you tell her who you really are?" Archibald challenged.

Ash laughed. "If you thought I was anyone else but Ash Messinger, you would've told her already. But you know nothing, cat." He turned to me. "Ready? I stopped by to see Jordan, and he told me the car plan."

I nodded, suddenly wishing I'd listened to Archibald and taken off before Ash had found us. "Yep. You drive. I need to call Gary and let him know we won't be staying with him. No more leisurely driving. We're making the rest of the trip in two days. Or less, if we can." I pulled the second key off the keychain, shoved it into my pocket, and tossed the keychain to Ash.

"Whatever you want, Frankie. Let's get out of here before that damn cat comes back."

I looked down, and sure enough, Archibald had disappeared again. I sighed. "Fine. Let's get going. I'm ready to be home."

TWENTY-SEVEN

I texted Gary as soon as we got on the road to offer my apologies and let him know that he should come home to hang out sometime.

Lol. There's nothing and no one—not even you—who could convince me to go to that hellhole. Can't believe you're going back after everything.

I grimaced. I'd sworn never to return, but here I was, on my way home. There was no way it could still be as bad as it was during high school, though, right? I texted him my reply.

I'll let you know where it falls on the hellscape scale when I get there. Thanks again for saying I could stay. Later. xoxo

Ash took the first exit for the Vegas Strip. "I'm hungry," he said in response to my questioning look.

Since I was, too—disassociating always had that effect—I didn't say anything. The more free meals I could get, the longer the few dollars in my pocket would last. I grimaced. I hated this. Hated relying on someone else for basic things.

Maybe that was how I ended up here. Refusing to ask for help when I was floundering and refusing to accept it when I desperately needed someone to have my back.

Ugh. Self-reflection and personal growth had no place on a road trip. There'd be plenty of time for that when I found a new therapist.

I focused my attention on the hotels rising from the strip. I'd passed through Vegas on my way to Santa Fe but hadn't stayed. It had an aura of sadness and desperation that made my skin crawl. Some people loved the noise, the energy, and the lack of windows inside the casinos that made the passage of time nearly impossible to clock. I bet vampires would love Vegas casinos if they existed.

"Oh shit," I whispered.

Ash spared a glance at me. "What?" He was curt—which was nothing new in my experience—but it was still upsetting.

"Are vampires real?"

He barked out a short laugh. "Why the fuck would you think that, Frances?"

I cringed. He usually called me "Babe," occasionally "Frankie," and only drug out "Frances" when he was too pissed off to bother humoring me. If he busted out the "Crazy AF"—short for "Crazy as Frankie"—then he'd need a timeout, and I'd need a drink.

Nope, not a drink. Some other tension reliever that wouldn't interrupt my trip with a hangover.

As mildly as I could, I said, "Well, if there are talking cats, reapers, Valkyries, and gods, why not vampires?"

There was a moment of silence, then Ash spoke in a voice absent of most of the curtness he'd demonstrated before. "I'd hoped you'd let that shit go by now. I can humor you if you want, but none of it is real. There are no vampires or werewolves, or anything of that ilk."

"So just gods and non-human monsters?" I prodded.

Ash didn't reply.

He pulled into the Caesar's Palace parking garage and killed the engine. "Normally I wouldn't be caught dead here, but Caesar's has an excellent all-you-can-eat buffet."

I gaped at him. Ash seldom ate—at least not that I ever saw. "You? A buffet? That's..."

"I'm hungry." When we got inside, he stalked toward the elevator bank, and I had to run to catch up.

There was no point in mentioning to him the disparity between his choice of eating establishment and his general germaphobia, especially when it came to food. Not when I had a buffet to look forward to. I could eat a lot here, and then eat lightly for the next couple days.

Once in the restaurant, Ash paid hurriedly and made a beeline for the buffet. By the time I'd secured a table, ordered a couple coffees, and found my way to the buffet, Ash had a plate piled so high with eggs, bacon, sausage, toast, and fruit that he was barely visible behind it.

I went to the omelet station and ordered a veggie omelet. While I waited, I made myself some toast and perused the rest of the offerings. It paid to be strategic in places like this. I didn't want to fill up on eggs only to find out that there were hashbrowns somewhere else. Potatoes were the best part of every meal.

Ash was nearly through his first plate by the time I returned to the table with my omelet, toast, and three kinds of potatoes.

He all but licked the plate clean, then pushed it to the edge of the table and went back for more.

Despite my intentions of stuffing myself, I only managed two plates of breakfast food and a trip to the sundae bar. In that time, Ash got more than his money's worth. I lost count of his trips after the fifth one.

Finally, he leaned back and groaned. "That hit the spot."

There were no words that I could think of that wouldn't sound rude. I didn't make it a habit to judge other people's food choices. I nodded and tried to look neutral.

"Ready to get going?" Ash asked. "I'd like to get as far as we can today, so I can drop you off early tomorrow and head back and ditch this ridiculous car."

"I just need to visit the restroom, and I'm ready to go." I stood and followed the signs to the ladies' room. I peed and washed my hands, then spent a moment staring at my hair in the mirror, willing it to stop growing so fast and revealing the unwanted blonde underneath the dark dye. When it didn't magically return to a shoulder-length, dark-brown mane, I gave up and turned to leave. I wasn't looking forward to pushing hard today—I hated long days of sitting—but I was getting excited to see my family again, even if I wasn't sure of my reception. And I was more than looking forward to a break from Ash for a little bit.

I couldn't discount his friendship as completely as Archibald wanted me to, but some time away from the snide comments about my mental health would be welcome.

As I exited the bathroom, I brushed against a person coming in.

Cold filled me, and I shivered. Something about this woman was wrong.

I spun around in time to catch her as she fell. She was dead before she hit the floor—or at least mostly dead. I could see her soul lingering and knew I could still bring her back.

"Mom!" a woman's voice called. "Wait up!"

A young woman, barely out of her teens, turned the corner and came into view.

She dropped to her knees. "What happened? Mom, are you okay?"

I relinquished the woman to her daughter, who lightly shook her mother, and crouched next to them.

By this time, a small crowd had gathered, and a couple people had rushed out of the bathroom to alert hotel staff to call 911.

The soul barely hung on now, and an indistinct shape was taking form, mirroring that of the woman from whom it'd separated.

"Mom. Mom." The young woman's voice cracked, and she sobbed. "Mommy."

My heart broke with hers. Here I was, running back to the family I'd abandoned, and a woman who was the age I'd been when I'd left was about to lose her mother for good. It wasn't fair.

I reached my hand toward the woman, intent on guiding the soul back into the body, then hesitated.

Nothing was fair, was it? I'd already fucked up once this week. Twice this month. It'd been made clear to me that not helping people move on when their deaths were imminent was screwing with the natural order of things just as much as taking those whose time hadn't yet come.

I extended my hand toward the unconscious woman, not sure what to do, just knowing I had to do something.

When I touched her arm, she grabbed my hand and held on tight. Her eyes opened wide when she saw me.

"Are you a Valkyrie?" She sounded both hopeful and afraid. "I thought you only came for those who died in battle."

I shrugged awkwardly—I'd thought so, too, until this week. "I'm here for you now." The words appeared in my mind, and I pulled her closer to me. "It's not Valhalla waiting for you, though, but Fólkvangr."

The woman—or her spirit, rather—smiled. "I wouldn't want to go to Valhalla, anyway. Drinking buckets of mead and training for Ragnarök is not the afterlife I desire. It's been a long time since I've felt any peace, and I'm ready for Fólkvangr."

A shimmering doorway opened behind me, and the woman stepped through with only one backward glance. Her gaze lingered on her daughter, who was now rocking back and forth, racked with silent sobs. "She'll be okay. I was the only thing holding her back. Now she can soar."

Her hand slipped from my grasp, but not before an almost ecstatic calm radiated from her to me.

The breath left my lungs in a soft *whoosh*, and I turned my attention back to the small crowd. I was ready for the stares my weird behavior would garner, but no one was even looking at me.

I'd done the right thing, and the gratitude and tranquility that'd passed from the woman to me was still echoing in my body. But seeing the grief of her daughter pulled back the guilt that'd almost disappeared.

I slipped out of the bathroom and returned to my table, then slung my backpack over my shoulder.

"What happened?" Ash asked.

"A woman died." I didn't want to elaborate—didn't want my actions reviewed, commented on, and found wanting.

"And?" He followed me out of the restaurant and down the hall toward the elevators for the parking garage.

"Can we talk about this later, when there aren't so many people around?" I crossed my fingers that he'd forget about it, and I wouldn't have to revisit any part of what happened.

"Sure. No problem, babe." He elbowed me in the ribs, much harder than a friendly nudge should've been, and unlocked the car. "Can't wait to hear how you made someone happy this morning."

TWENTY-EIGHT

"Tell me everything," Ash said as soon as we were back on the freeway. "Start at the beginning."

I told the whole story, only leaving out the woman's last words and downplaying the happiness I'd felt from her when she entered Fólkvangr.

"You let her daughter lose a mother? You watched her cry and didn't fix it? I didn't realize you could be so cold, so unsympathetic. You are cruel."

"It was her time," I protested, wrapping the rightness of what I'd done around myself as a shield against his accusations.

He turned his head and gave me a piercing glare. Doubt followed in its wake. Was I cruel?

No. I'd done the right thing. I had. The woman had even said she was ready for peace.

I shook my head. "It was the right thing to do. I know it was."

Ash turned his gaze back to the road, much to my relief.

The next eight hours passed in silence. Ash pulled over once to fill up the car with gas, affording me the opportunity to use the bathroom and grab a snack and a drink.

The sun was slipping toward the western horizon when Ash stopped again. He parked in front of a cheap-looking motel called the Donner Pass Motor Hotel and Laundromat, got out, slammed the door, and disappeared into the registration office.

A few minutes later, he reappeared. When he opened the door to grab his bag, he chucked a key at me. "Be out here at seven a.m. sharp, or I'll turn around and leave you here." He didn't look at me again before stalking off.

I sat dumbfounded for a moment. Had my taking the woman who'd died really been the wrong choice? So wrong that my friend was giving me the silent treatment over it?

My stomach growled, and that was enough to get me moving. I retrieved my backpack and sword and headed to room 115.

There was nothing remarkable about the room. Full-sized bed with a worn, faded pink-and-blue flower bedspread, a desk too small to use as anything but an end table, and a clunky-looking television that looked like it'd morphed from the CRT models to a flatscreen through force rather than design.

Further investigation showed that the bathroom, at least, was clean, even if the rest of the room was dingy. After a quick shower, I dressed in the same clothes I'd been wearing all day and left the room. I briefly considered making use of the laundromat, but one glance inside at the dingy, nearly abandoned building changed my mind.

Instead, I took what was left of my dwindling funds and went into the nearest fast-food restaurant for a burger, fries, and soda. It wasn't good, but it was hot, cheap, and filling. After eating, I wandered the town for a bit. We were on the eastern edge of a small range that might have been an offshoot of the Sierra Nevadas, and the mountains bathed in the pink and orange of the setting sun were spectacular.

I walked a little further, finally allowing myself to replay the events of the day.

It had been a lot. Enough that a few weeks ago, I would've been looking for the nearest dive bar to wash the day away instead of investigating it from all angles.

I would've liked to talk to Archibald about it, to process every-thing, but I hadn't seen him all day.

I headed back to the room, stripped the bedspread off, undressed, and crawled between the fitted and top sheets. When I turned on the tv, it was already on a true-crime channel. Nothing like watching murder shows when you were sleeping in what looked like the set of at least half of them.

At least I would never in a million years be described as "lighting up a room." I should be safe from serial killers.

I closed my eyes and tried to will myself to sleep with the soothing drone of the *Forensic Files* narrator, but sleep wouldn't come.

How did people shut their minds off without whiskey to knock them out? I turned off the lights and TV, then stared up at the ceiling and relived the deaths of Freyja and the woman I'd helped in Vegas.

Blue and pink flashes from the neon lights outside illuminated patterns on the walls, and I let them flood my brain and chase away everything else.

A SHRIEKING alarm pulled me upright and out of bed. The smell of smoke permeated the room, and I coughed.

It took a moment to clock that this was real, and not one of the many nightmares I'd had since pulling Gwen out of the burning building.

I grabbed my backpack, phone, and sword, wrapped a shirt around my face, and looked around. "Archibald?"

There was no answer, so I hurried out the door and joined the crowd in the parking lot. I hadn't seen Archibald since leaving Searchlight, and if he could pop himself around the country at will, always homing in on me, he could take care of himself in a fire.

I forced myself to turn and regard the building where I'd been staying.

The thirty-room Donner Pass Motor Hotel and Laundromat was completely engulfed in flames.

The fire department was already on site, breaking down doors on the first floor and hauling out anyone they found, relinquishing them into the custody of the EMTs.

I walked through the parking lot, looking for Ash, but didn't see him. His room had been in the south corner of the second floor, while I'd been about as far away from him as possible on the first floor.

I suspected that arrangement had been on purpose.

The more time passed without a sign of Ash, the more nervous I grew. He was the best firefighter with the Santa Fe Fire Department and had a nearly unerring instinct for what to do in a fire. He would not be surprised, and he would not be disoriented.

I glanced at my phone. It was three a.m. and the bars were probably closed. He hated bringing people into his space most of the time, but he'd brought Jordan to his room in Searchlight. Maybe it was only his home he wanted to keep sacrosanct.

I forced myself to take a deep breath. I was spiraling, and that wasn't helpful. I could fall apart later—with a glass of whiskey if I needed it—but right now, I had to make sure Ash was okay.

He might be an unmitigated douchecanoe, but he was my douchecanoe. Besides, I'd walked into a burning building before and come out unscathed. Surely, I could do it again, right?

Right?

TWENTY-NINE

"You know, instead of barging into the building, putting yourself and any firefighters tasked with stopping you in danger, you could just tell someone that Ash is in room 201."

I shrieked and jumped several inches in the air and to my right.

Archibald sat on the ground next to me, delicately cleaning one paw.

"You scared the shit out of me, Archie," I hissed, mindful of the odd glances I was getting from the few people who could be bothered to tear their glances away from the conflagration. I didn't waste any more time, though. I darted forward, looking for someone directing the show rather than actively trying to extinguish the fire.

It didn't take me long to settle on the tall, wiry Latino man dressed in protective gear, but without a helmet or any of the other tools of the trade. I knew his PPE would be close by, and he'd be ready to run forward and assist if necessary, but the fact that he didn't have any of that gear, accompanied by his low, tense conversation with another person in a police uniform made me sure he was the one in charge.

"Hi. Hi, I'm sorry," I said, pushing myself between them. "It's just, my friend is in room 201, and I haven't seen him tonight. He was gonna hit the bars before bed, and I'm worried he might be sleeping through the fire alarm." I crossed my fingers behind my back at the implication Ash might be too drunk to leave his room.

"Ma'am, we're doing the best we can. As soon as it's safe, someone will check all the rooms. In the meantime, please head back to the rest of the crowd and let us do our jobs."

A scream jolted me.

"There's someone there, burning!" an unknown voice yelled hoarsely.

My gaze followed their pointing arm, already dreading what I'd see. In the window of room 201, a figure I instantly recognized as Ash was pounding on the window, a soundless scream on his lips.

"That's him! That's my friend. Please…"

There was no one to yell to, though. Every firefighter, including the man I'd been talking to, was dashing up the stairs to help Ash.

"Do you care for that person?" a voice beside me asked. Their rich, harmonious voice echoed in my senses like reverberations in a cave.

I looked at them. They were tall, inhumanly beautiful, feminine looking, skeletally thin, and so pale they were almost transparent.

They wore a long cloak with the hood pulled up over their face. When they turned to look at me, their visage flashed between their human face and the skull underneath it so fast that I wondered if I was imagining it. The scythe that appeared in their hand convinced me that I wasn't, though.

"Are you here for him?" I asked. I held my breath, waiting for their response.

"No. But the motel had no vacancies, no working sprinkler system, and the alarm only worked in a handful of rooms." Their tone was vaguely regretful, but I couldn't tell if it was because the motel had violated so many safety regulations or that they weren't there to reap Ash.

"How many will die?" I asked.

"Five," they answered immediately. "But because you are here, I can give way to you if any of them are worthy of escorting to your afterlife."

"What? Fuck no. Definitely not." It was only after a few seconds of silence while the reaper regarded me with their otherworldly glowing eyes that looked like they might be laughing that I realized how rude I'd been. "Um, I mean, no thank you. You go right ahead and do what you've got to do. I'm full up on choosing today, and no one here is calling for me."

I wrinkled my nose. Why had I said that last bit? After a moment of concentration, I figured it out. Everyone I had helped—except Gwen—had pulled at something within me. They'd needed me. This reaper could've escorted the souls I'd helped, but I was made to take those slain who believed in the Norse afterlife.

The people here? No one here believed in my gods, not even peripherally.

Crashing lumber yanked my gaze back to the motel I'd been looking for any excuse to avoid.

The second-level walkway creaked as flames licked at it, destroying the structural integrity, forcing the firefighters away from Ash's room. His window shattered. Flames consumed his clothing and his hair. Our eyes met, and he winked.

Dozens of voices were screaming at him to jump.

He didn't.

His body collapsed, and he fell from his room into the street.

But his soul erupted through the roof, and it looked like nothing I'd ever seen before. An enormous winged snake made of smoke and shadow streamed into the sky, did a lazy turn around the motel, then flew off to the north.

"Huh," the reaper next to me said. "That's not something you see every day." They strode forward and disappeared into the motel.

I hit the ground. Seconds later, Archibald was in my lap. My hand automatically found its way to his head, and I scratched the spot he liked behind his left ear.

"What happened?" I asked. My breaths were too close together, and between the lump in my throat and the weight on my chest, I was having trouble catching my breath.

Archibald turned his head and gently closed his mouth over my left wrist, hard enough that I felt it, but not hard enough for his teeth to break skin. Once my breathing slowed and deepened, he let go.

"I don't know." The chagrin in his tone, as if he wasn't used to not knowing, shocked me.

Somewhere along the way, I'd come to think of Archibald as my all-knowing guide. Part of me had even started believing he might be a god—or an avatar of one. His cat nature suggested Freyja, but I'd entertained Odin as well.

The All-father wasn't much for cats, but the wisdom and foresight Archibald exhibited might be hallmarks of the god.

"I'll bite you for real if you don't stop that," Archibald chided, but there was no malice in his voice.

"Sorry, sorry, sorry," I chanted.

"You can be sorry later. Now, you need to figure out what to do next."

He was right. I could do this. I could deal with the death of my friend, and his smokey snake spirit, and the fire, the lack of money, whatever had happened to Freyja, and whatever was happening to me...

Archibald bit down again, and this time he wasn't gentle.

Blood welled up in perfect circles where his feline fangs had pierced my skin.

"Just tell me what to do," I said.

"No."

I took a deep breath, amazed that I could do so between the smoke and the grief, and closed my eyes. I was going to be okay. At least for a little while.

"Let's find an all-night diner. If I'm not getting sleep, I need coffee and pie. I have just enough money left for that." I glanced down at my stuff. I could bring my backpack into any diner, but the sword might prove problematic.

"Stash it in the car," Archibald suggested.

My glance swung to the line of cars parked in the cordoned-off parking lot in front of the burning wreck of the motel. Ash's car wasn't there.

"Across the street," the cat said.

I turned around, and sure enough, the BMW was sitting in a parking lot across the street. "Good thing he moved it." He'd probably gone out and decided to park in the dark parking lot of an abandoned dollar store rather than in the brightly lit motel lot. I recognized the dispassionate voice as the one I used when I was done experiencing my feelings. Usually it took a few glasses of booze to get me to disassociate this much, but watching my friend die in a fire so similar to the one that nearly took out my fiancée—ex-fiancée—was as good as a fifth of Jack, apparently.

"His foresight was almost perfect," Archibald said.

I glanced sharply at him. "What are you saying?"

"Nothing I want to say right now. Now, stow your weapon if you must, and then find yourself some coffee. You will have much to do tomorrow, and you need the fortitude. In addition, you might want to look in the envelope stowed under the driver's side floor mat." Archibald hopped off my lap, raised his tail in the air, and walked toward the twenty-four-hour diner that was quickly filling up with other displaced motel guests.

THIRTY

Steam curled up from my fifth cup of black—I hesitated to call the bitter, thick liquid coffee—caffeinated liquid.

Archibald's tip about the envelope had been a good one. It contained two thousand dollars in hundred-dollar bills—more than enough for a hot meal and whatever else I'd need to get home.

A plate heaped with huge, fluffy pancakes drenched in maple syrup dropped on the table in front of me, followed by a chocolate-peanut butter milkshake.

Irritation flooded me, and even though I knew the feeling was a distraction from having to process and react to everything else that'd happened in the last couple hours, I let it bubble free. "What's this town's obsession with Donner Pass? We're nowhere near the pass, and a diner named after it is in poor taste."

"We call it that just to piss off snotty tourists," snarked the server, whose name tag proclaimed her to be Chanterelle.

"Sorry," I mumbled, properly chastised.

Her eyes roved over me and for the first time she seemed to take in my ash-streaked face and hair and the acrid reek of smoke rising from my body. Her expression softened. "Were you in the motel?"

I nodded, unable to speak, and tears spilled down my cheeks.

"Sorry I was rude," she said. "Don't worry about paying. We're covering everyone who was staying in the motel tonight."

"I'm sorry too. I was rude first." I mustered a smile and fiercely told my tears to take a number and go to the back of the queue.

Chanterelle reached out and placed a hand on my shoulder, so briefly it barely registered, then disappeared back into the kitchen.

I took a long slurp of my milkshake, then followed it with a too-large bite of pancakes. I continued to eat slowly and mechanically, carefully chewing each bite and washing it all down with the shake.

As I was scraping the last bit of pancake across my plate, trying to soak up every last drop of syrup, someone dropped heavily into the booth across from me.

It was the fire chief I'd spoken to earlier.

"I'm sorry for the loss of your friend," he said with no preamble and no gentleness. "Since any identification he had is either missing or destroyed, I'm going to need you to identify the body and give some details to the police and coroner. Come down to the station after nine in the morning."

"Where am I supposed to—"

He cut me off. "Do I look like I run a hostel for displaced working girls? I have three injured firefighters, a still-smoldering building, and a lot of paperwork. Figure it out." He stood and walked out the door without a backward glance.

"Is this what it's always like?" I whispered.

"What do you mean?" Archibald said from where he was curled up next to me in the booth.

"Nothing but death. It seems like it's accelerating. Two yesterday —or the day before, actually. That little girl and the man who hit her car. Three today. Will this be the rest of my life now? Death finding me wherever I go?"

"Freyja didn't die," Archibald said. "She is a goddess and not much can kill her."

"Gods can die," I argued. He hadn't been there, hadn't seen what I'd seen. "I know the story of Ragnarök as well as anyone else."

Archibald gave a long-suffering sigh. "That's why I said not much can kill her. She is not dead."

I wanted to counter, but I knew what I was doing. I was pushing everything down. If I could fight about something, I would give me time to shove my confusion and grief at Ash's death into one of the many dark recesses of my mind where I hid all the things I didn't want to think about—not ever again.

"Are you done yet?" Chanterelle asked.

"What?"

"Just wondering if I can clear your plate. I don't want to kick you out, but..." She gestured at the door, where several soot-stained people were congregating.

"Oh. Yeah. Of course." I slurped up the last of my milkshake and pulled out my wallet.

"You're not paying," Chanterelle said firmly. "Tonight's policy stands."

I smiled sadly. "Your policy doesn't prevent me from tipping, though." I pulled a hundred-dollar bill from the small stash I'd shoved in my billfold. "Thank you."

Chanterelle took the money and tucked it into her pocket. "Thank you. And good luck."

I scooped Archibald into my arms, knowing he'd hate it but wouldn't protest in front of another person. Maybe it was impolite to carry him when I knew he didn't like being picked up, but I needed the comfort tonight. Maybe I could find another cheap motel that'd take cash and get a few hours of sleep before I had to...

I cut that thought off before it could gain purchase.

Motel. Sleep. That was all I could think about if I didn't want to break down.

I headed down the street toward a neon sign advertising the Quicksilver Motel. Before I walked into the registration office, I stole one last glimpse of the still-smoldering motel.

The structure was still visible through the flames, but there wasn't much left to look at.

Except for the tall, preternaturally beautiful grim reaper standing in front of it and looking at me. They raised their hand, but whether it was a greeting, farewell, or benediction, I did not know.

I grabbed the cold metal handle of the motel office door and stepped inside.

THIRTY-ONE

At nine o'clock sharp, I walked into the police station and approached the desk where a bored-looking young white woman sat.

I opened my mouth, but she held up her hand to silence me.

I waited while she finished whatever phone game she'd been in the middle of, letting my gaze rove around the dull station that radiated an aura of grey, even though colorful signs and posters covered the walls, and potted plants sat on almost every desk. Finally, I let my eyes settle on her. She had short, black hair, warm brown eyes, and a curvy figure. With her brow creased in concentration, she was absolutely adorable.

"What do you want?" she asked, slipping her phone into a desk drawer.

The brusqueness in her husky voice didn't match the soft persona I'd assigned to her while I was waiting. "I'm supposed to..." my voice faltered. The impatience on her face was the only thing that kept me going. "I'm supposed to identify a body."

"Of course. Why don't you have a seat over there"—she gestured at a bank of grey, plastic chairs that would've been at home in a middle-school classroom—"and I'll call Dr. MacKenzie to let him know I'm sending you down." Her voice wasn't as short as it had been before, but there still wasn't the sympathy I would've expected.

With a weak smile she didn't acknowledge, I followed her directions and sank into a supremely uncomfortable chair. It was only then that I realized I'd brought my sword into the police station. That was probably not a good thing. I'd been holding it tight with the tip of the blade just a few inches from the floor, so maybe the officer hadn't seen it, but now that I'd balanced it across my lap, there was no way it wouldn't be noticed.

I looked around, although what I was searching for, I didn't know. It's not like I could stash it in a handy umbrella holder and grab it on my way out, and if I ran out now, I'd have to start this ordeal all over.

My best bet was to make it super obvious and announce its presence before anyone had a chance to shoot me.

The door opened again, and the woman I'd spoken to earlier walked back into the room.

Before I could tell her I was carrying, and without a permit, no less—I didn't even know if one was required—she beckoned me forward.

I stood cautiously, gripping the sword in one hand again and letting it swing down to my side. Still, she didn't acknowledge it.

"Are you coming or what?" she asked.

Another voice floated into the room from beyond the door. "Stop being such a bitch, Jan. She's here to ID a corpse, not sell you raffle tickets."

Jan shot a glare through the open door but didn't respond. When she turned back to me, she'd pasted on a smile so exaggerated that made it look like she might be in pain. With a sugary-sweet voice, she said, "Please allow me to escort you to the morgue so you can do us a great service and tell us everything you know about the poor departed soul recovered from the fire last night. Should you need a tissue or a shoulder to cry on, let me know."

The saccharine sarcasm was worse than the bland unconcern, and the corners of my eyes stung. I would not cry in front of her. She did not get to see my weaknesses.

I tipped my chin up. "Let's get on with it. I have a long drive ahead of me."

Jan escorted me through the door and delivered me to who I assumed was Dr. MacKenzie. He gestured for me to follow him, and we walked down a long hallway.

"Sorry about Jan," he said easily, waving an ID card at the reader near the large doors at the end of the hall. "She's stuck at that stupid desk all day with nothing to do, and that makes her cranky."

I didn't point out that he was the one who'd crudely said I was there to ID a corpse.

A corpse.

Ash was a corpse now. A corpse with a flying-worm soul, but a corpse.

I was suddenly in the middle of a cyclone. The wind whipping around me echoed in my ears and snatched my breath away.

Something that felt cold on my neck pulled me out of the cyclone. Next thing I knew, I was sitting on the cold linoleum, head pushed down between my knees, and a wet paper towel on my neck.

"Take it easy, girlie," Dr. MacKenzie said. "It's not easy facing death for the first time. It gets easier, though. Every death hurts a little less and takes less time to get over. Soon, you'll be all but inured to its effects."

I looked up at him, and something sparked in his eyes.

"Are you..." Was asking him if he was like me, some kind of reaper, a rude question? Should I already know? Or was I reading too much into my post-panic-attack conversation?

"I'm the county coroner, and I see more than my share of death." He held out a hand to help me to my feet. The glow in his eyes was gone, if it'd even been there to begin with.

I stood without his help and followed him, sword in hand, to the room where they kept the bodies. I didn't know what it was supposed to be called. Was this the morgue? Or was there a fancy morgue word for it? I should know these things; my mother was a funeral director.

I'd half expected a room full of silver drawers like the world's creepiest, largest dresser, but there was a single table, and on it, a sheet-covered body.

Dr. MacKenzie went to the head of the table.

I braced myself for a fire-ruined body and a near-unrecognizable face.

He pulled the sheet down, exposing Ash's head and chest. I gasped, my hand going to my mouth. I looked at the doctor. "What?"

He shrugged. "I don't know. From all accounts, he went up in flames. I still expected him to have died from smoke inhalation rather than burning, but there was no smoke in his lungs, and I didn't find any other causes of death during the autopsy."

I gazed down at Ash's face. It was unmarred. Perfect. Beautiful.

"But..." I didn't know how to ask any of the questions swirling through my mind.

"How did he die?" Dr. MacKenzie asked for me.

I nodded mutely.

He shrugged. "I've no idea. I'll know more when I get the lab results back. It's possible he overdosed and died before breathing in any smoke."

"Or getting even superficial burns?" I asked, still staring at Ash.

"Like I said, I don't know. But now that you've seen him, at least we can get his ID taken care of. You recognize him, right?"

I nodded. "His name is Ash Messinger. Birthday is June 6, I don't know what year. He never wanted people to know how old he was, but he always had a birthday party. He probably is chock full of drugs and alcohol." I wasn't sure why I'd volunteered that last bit, but I desperately wanted to find something to explain his death.

Dr. MacKenzie nodded. "I'll grab the paperwork. Once it's all written down and you've given me your name and contact information, you can head out. Back in a minute." He disappeared through a door at the back of the room I hadn't noticed before, leaving me alone with Ash.

"You can't leave him here," Archibald said, hopping up onto the table and sitting on Ash's chest.

I bit back a scream and stumbled backward. "Jesus fucking Christ, cat. You can't sneak up on someone in a morgue. And you can't jump on dead bodies. It's rude."

"I'll apologize later. We have to go, and Ash cannot stay here. We certainly can't stay long enough for you to give your name and contact information to anyone. Pick him up and follow me."

I gaped at the cat, who'd jumped off Ash and was striding toward the door Dr. MacKenzie had disappeared through. "Are you kidding? You want me to steal a body? And *carry* it?"

"Of course I'm not kidding. I would never joke about bodysnatching. Now do it before that ridiculous man comes back. I messed up his office, but it won't be long before he finds what he needs and comes back."

I looked between the impatient cat and the dead body of the person I'd considered my closest friend.

"Fuck it," I muttered. Things were already almost too weird. Why not just ride the horror train as long as I could? I rolled the body over, slid my arms under Ash's shoulders, pulled him up, and hoisted him into the firefighter's carry that Gwen used to practice on me when she was feeling sassy and wanted to haul me off to bed.

I dismissed that memory—it was inappropriate considering the current circumstances—and adjusted the sword and backpack in my free hand, then followed Archibald out the door.

The street and parking lot were mercifully empty, and the short walk to the car had been—as far as I could tell—unobserved.

I popped open the trunk with the remote, dropped my stuff, and slid Ash off my shoulders, propping him against the car while I transferred my things to the back seat. Then I hoisted him up, rolled him in, and slammed the trunk closed.

What the fuck was I doing?

I looked around and caught sight of the multiple security cameras trained on the parking lot. Of course there were cameras. It was a cop shop.

"Get in and drive," Archibald commanded.

I buckled in and headed toward the freeway.

With a fucking body in the trunk.

THIRTY-TWO

Every time the speedometer edged above the posted limit, I slammed on the brakes, and the few times I caught sight of cop cars, I held my breath to keep from hyperventilating.

There was no way I could risk getting pulled over. For all I knew, there was already an APB out on me. My car hadn't been so far away from the police station that the cameras couldn't pick up the make and model of the car, even if they'd missed the license plate.

I was an hour past the Oregon border and on a four-lane highway before my grip on the steering wheel relaxed and the white in my knuckles slowly faded back to its usual tan.

Once I got rid of the immediate fear of getting arrested for body snatching or whatever this crime was, my mind started drifting back to the sheer horror of the last few days.

I glanced at Archibald out of the corner of my eye. He hadn't given a satisfactory answer at the diner when I'd asked if death would stalk me for the rest of my life—partially because the server didn't need to know I had a talking cat. He probably was also avoiding the subject altogether. He might be my spirit guide, or my familiar or something, but he was pretty tight-lipped about what was actually going on other than the small amount of guidance he gave with the young man in Santa Fe and the comments about everything I'd done wrong. And a few pointed jabs at Ash, when he wasn't encouraging me to body-snatch.

Ash.

The pressure in my chest returned, and I gasped. I slammed on my brakes and took the next turn, earning a honk from the car behind me. I drove a couple blocks off the highway, pulled into the first parking spot I saw on Main Street, and rested my forehead on the steering wheel. A few minutes of deep, slow breathing helped center me. I raised my head and looked around, trying to figure out where I was.

"Burns," Archibald said, speaking for the first time since we'd fled Winnemucca with a body in the trunk.

Burns wasn't a huge town, but it was big enough to have several restaurants to choose from. My stomach growled. It was time to eat —I'd had nothing since the diner, and my body was protesting.

Once again, I was delaying my return to my parents' house, but I couldn't have the deep discussions if I wasn't properly fueled, right?

I checked the gas gauge—I'd need to fill up before I left town. I wasn't sure if I'd have another chance before I got home—Eastern Oregon wasn't known for its plethora of amenities.

"I'm getting lunch," I announced. "Do you want me to grab you some Fancy Feast or something from the grocery store?"

Archibald looked at me with a level of contempt that was even more impressive than the usual contempt most cats mustered. "I'll get my own lunch, thank you."

He said nothing further, just got out of the car after me, then walked across the street and disappeared between two buildings.

I walked down the street a way and popped into a small, dark diner that had an average rating of 4.9 stars on Google Reviews, following the directions on a wall sign to seat myself.

The exchange with the server was short and to the point, much to my relief. The last thing I wanted was human interaction along with my open-face turkey sandwich, mashed potatoes, and strawberry milkshake.

The food was amazing and definitely lived up to the 4.9-star promise.

I left the diner but wasn't ready to get back in the car. Hearse, really, right? A hysterical giggle escaped my lips. So I walked down Main Street, taking in the storefronts. Some looked like they hadn't been updated since the town's founding in the 1800s, and not in a kitschy, touristy, ghost-town way like in Oatman. Several modern buildings were mixed in with older ones that appeared well-maintained, but looked nothing like the attractive adobe style I'd gotten used to in Santa Fe.

Once I could no longer pretend I was interested in the town's architecture, I headed back to the car. As much as I needed to ask Archibald the questions that were swirling in my mind, I didn't want to face the answers. Or, more probably, the reality that he didn't have any answers for me at all.

I couldn't deny that some of my hesitance was also due to the fear of what kind of reception I would receive at home. Ten years was a long time with no contact. Showing up and expecting to be welcomed with open arms was extremely optimistic.

My lunch churned in my stomach and sweat broke out on my forehead. Too many panic attacks in the last couple days. Too much everything.

I fisted my hands, then released them, repeating the action a few times until I felt at home—or at least present—in my body again. Next, I focused on my feet. I wasn't about to slip off my sandals to make direct contact with the ground, but I could still concentrate on the feeling of the earth beneath my feet.

It wasn't as centering as sinking my toes into the dirt, but it was enough to get me moving again.

Archibald was waiting for me at the car, and he jumped in the second I opened the door. Neither of us spoke until after I'd filled up the tank and was back on the highway.

"Ask your questions, and I'll answer what I can," Archibald directed.

"You'll tell me what you know or what you feel like answering?" I asked, wanting clarification before we dove into all the things that were bothering me. Some of the things that were bothering me.

"Everything I *can* answer."

That wasn't any clearer than his first answer, but it seemed like the only one I was likely to get.

I searched for the right words to use, but there weren't any. Just the words that started spilling forth. "Why am I suddenly seeing so much death? Why are there now so many choices to make?"

"The potential that was always in you is awake now, and you're seeing the world in a way you never were able to before. It's not just that, though. Death is part of who you are, and you'll always be aware of it now that the power's been woken." Archibald sounded almost sad, but I couldn't dwell on that now.

"And why am I being called to choose? I thought Valkyries chose on the battlefield and decided who was worthy of Valhalla. None of the people I've chosen have died in battle, and I haven't sent anyone to Valhalla. A couple went to Fólkvangr, but even that shouldn't be one of my responsibilities."

Archibald snorted. "And you know so much about the realities of what being a Valkyrie is like? Where'd you learn all that?"

"From the histories."

"From the myths, you mean. You can't tell me that you believe the stories have been handed down and recorded without a little bit of embellishment."

"But the stories mother told... Surely..."

"Your mother might be a Valkyrie, but there's a reason she stuck to the commonly believed myths and legends when recounting the histories. I'm sure you'll figure it out eventually." Archibald fell silent and delicately licked the fur on his left paw.

I'd think about it later. Right now, while he was in a sharing mood, I would plow forward to get more answers while I could.

"Okay. I'll accept that Valkyries do more than give dead soldiers a chance to remain soldiers for their entire afterlives in Valhalla. But that doesn't explain why I'm encountering so many dead. Maybe I'm more aware of death now than I was before, but I can honestly say that I've never experienced this much of it in such a short period of time."

"You're being tested. And so far, you're failing." There was no inflection in Archibald's tone, and he moved his attention from his left paw to his right.

"I didn't fuck up the woman in the Vegas bathroom, and I helped that guy in Santa Fe," I protested. It wasn't a great track record, but 50% had to be worth something, right?

"And you have forced death on two whose times were not up. That's different than ushering a soul already doomed into the afterlife."

My shoulders curled up around my ears, and I concentrated on the road for a while before continuing. "What happens if I refuse to choose altogether?"

"Without someone there to help them cross over, the dying soul will be trapped on earth between life and death. If they're lucky, they'll be strong enough to be a ghost."

"And if they're unlucky?" I whispered.

"Then you've doomed them to an eternity of being a wraith. A spirit less than a ghost. They can do nothing but feel the moment of their deaths until it drives them mad." Archibald curled up into a ball on the seat, scooting until he was in the sunniest spot, and closed his eyes.

"Won't another reaper show up to help them along? I've seen other reapers, and I didn't have to do anything for the others who died at the motel fire last night."

Archibald didn't answer, but he opened his eyes and blinked slowly at me.

I heaved a sigh. "Were the people in the car, the little girls, believers in the Norse gods?"

"Yes."

I heaved a sigh, decelerated, and merged onto Highway 26. I was back on roads I'd traveled before. It was still a long drive, but Estacada was creeping closer.

"What if I choose wrong? What's going to happen to that drunk driver?" I asked.

"You yanked his soul from his body, but you didn't do anything else. Maybe the other reaper helped him move on after we left, or maybe she didn't get a chance. The same thing will have happened to the man you chose instead of Gwen. You created ghosts—but not just regular ghosts. Ghosts whose lives weren't supposed to be over yet. That has a domino effect. Others will die because of what you did."

My sharp intake of breath caught in my throat. I hadn't wanted to know the other half of that equation, but Archibald was dropping everything on me now, and there was nowhere to go to avoid it.

"Aren't you going to ask about those whose lives you 'saved?'"

Cats couldn't make air quotes, but the intent was there in his tone. I shook my head, still trying to negate what he was about to tell me.

Mercilessly, he plowed on. "The dying soul, the one you forced back into the body it was leaving, will be trapped between life and death. They will be an embodied wraith. Reliving the moment of their deaths until they can do nothing else. It starts as nightmares, but it doesn't stay that way."

"What about Gwen? She's not a wraith. And she wasn't really dead yet when I saved her."

Archibald didn't answer right away, and when he did, the fear that had been creeping into me while he was talking took root. "What did you do to save Gwen and take her companion instead? Remember clearly."

I cast my mind back to the night I tried so hard not to think about. "I saw Zach's spirit and where it was attached to his body. Then, I held Gwen's down and..." My voice trailed off as I pulled up the sequence of events I hadn't really understood, and still didn't. "I grabbed Zach's soul—I needed to know *how* it was attached. It was sticky, and I had to yank to pull some away—I needed some of what held his soul to his body to reattach Gwen's."

"And in the process, Zach died," Archibald pointed out. "You used the soul of one who would've survived, and you shoved his into her along with her own."

I shook my head violently. "No, I only took the glue that held his soul to his body, and I didn't even take all of it."

"There is no such thing as 'soul-glue.' What you did was take what was his soul and entwine it with hers. Because his was still strong and not ready for death, it rooted in her body. Both souls are in one body. Because it is her body, she is at the forefront now, but if he proves to be stronger—a real possibility since it was not his time —he will gradually take over, condemning Gwen to slowly fade away without the chance to move on."

"But the girl I saved?" I could barely hear my words, but Archibald had no trouble doing so.

"She will be a true embodied wraith before too long. Reliving not only her death, but that of her twin. Your so-called mercy has destroyed more lives than taking those whose time was up would have."

"I have to go back. I have to find them. To fix this."

"It's too late. You made your choices. The dominoes are already falling."

"She's still alive. I can fix this." The desperation in my voice echoed in my body.

Archibald stared at me, an almost palpable gaze, until I glanced at him. Pity was written in his eyes. "How? Will you look at the mother who already lost one child and take her remaining daughter now? Can you do that?"

Tears fell down my cheeks. I couldn't. Maybe I should, but... "No."

"It is as I thought. You are not on an easy path. There is nothing fun about the role the gods have chosen for you, but there is purpose. You need to find that purpose now before you destroy more lives."

Steel slid down my spine, and I straightened. I'd wanted to be merciful, but I had failed. The true mercy was letting go when it was time.

"That's better," Archibald said in response to my unspoken thoughts. He laid his chin on his legs, and this time when he closed his eyes, he fell asleep.

The Cascade Mountains rose in front of me, and I drove on.

THIRTY-THREE

I stopped the car, put it in park, and stared straight ahead. It was mid-morning, and the sun was filtering through the trees. I'd stopped for the night in Madras. I'd been exhausted and not ready to show up on my parents' doorstep at dusk. It'd be easier for them to turn me away if they knew I had plenty of time to find somewhere else to go.

But I was here now. Not well-rested by any means, but at least highly caffeinated.

A gravel road parted the trees in front of me, disappearing around a bend. With the window down, I could hear the Clackamas River rushing northwest toward the Columbia River. I was a quarter mile away from the house where I'd grown up, and I wasn't sure I could make the rest of the trip.

"What if they hate me? What if they send me away?" I asked Archibald, who'd deigned to wake up for the final few miles of my road trip.

"What if they throw rotten vegetables at you and boo loudly?" my cat replied.

"That seems unlikely."

"No less so than them hating you and sending you away. They are family, and while many families are complicated in their relationships with each other, trust that yours is as you remember."

They'd never turned me away before. In fact, they'd done the opposite, trying so hard to help me, to keep me safe. I was the one who'd rejected them. Even if taking this step was difficult, and it would be, they wouldn't throw me out without talking to me.

Probably.

I took advantage of the tiny spark of hope in my chest and put the car back in drive. I didn't zoom up the road and around the curve that would bring their house into view, but I did get above twenty miles per hour until I was halfway around the bend and slammed on the brakes.

"What if they've moved?"

"I wish I could roll my eyes," Archibald said. "Perhaps they have, but you won't know if you sit here dithering about it. Drive forward and find out."

I took a deep breath and eased off the brake.

When the house came into view, it was like being pushed back in time. Everything looked the same. The sprawling ranch-style house was still red, the pines that grew around it were still bending protectively over the roof. The garage was open, revealing two blue Subarus.

It was only after a moment of staring that I picked out the differences. The cars were much newer models, and the house paint was fading in places. Instead of bicycles littering the front lawn, the grass had been torn out and wildflowers grew in its place.

I'd barely put the car in park when the front door opened and a tall, powerful-looking white woman walked onto the front step. She wore a bright pink apron and was stirring something in a huge, purple ceramic bowl she'd had since before I was born; the one she used to mix up the bread she made every weekend.

"It's about time you got here, Becky," she yelled. "You were supposed to be here two hours ago." The woman stilled and stared at the car. "Did you buy a new car? Again? I guess that explains why you're late."

I looked for the expected differences in the features of her face. There weren't any. Her skin was unlined, her hair long and blonde, and her body still bore the signs of the physical activity she did, both in the course of her job and from her love of running and sword practice.

My mother appeared to not have aged at all.

Slowly, I got out of the car, leaving the door open for Archibald. Not that he really needed it.

"Not Becky," I said awkwardly. "Sorry."

My mother stared at me for a moment, then the bowl dropped out of her arms and shattered on the steps. A poof of flour preceded a flow of dough creeping down the stairs like a bakery volcano. Her hands flew to her mouth.

"Frankie?" Her voice was barely above a whisper.

"Hey, Mom. Um, sorry to show up like this, but..."

I didn't even have time to finish my sentence before she was across the lawn. Her hands were on my shoulders, and she held me at arms-length while she stared at my face.

"Is that really you?" she choked out.

I nodded, not sure what to say. I didn't want to dive into why I was there, tell her I had nothing left in my life and needed help, and that was the only reason I'd come.

She pulled me into a hug that nearly crushed me.

"We thought you were dead," she whispered into my ear. "Ten years with no word, and after the way you left..."

"I finished school and went to Santa Fe," I said. I took a deep breath, preparing to disclose everything.

Mom pushed me back again to look into my eyes. "It must be going well, based on that car."

"It's not mine."

"Katrin, the cookies are burning. You and Rebecca need to get back in the kitchen where you belong," a man called out from the open doorway. He wasn't visible, but I'd know the voice anywhere.

"Dad," I breathed.

My mom rolled her eyes. "He still thinks he's hilarious. And he's still not." She half-turned and yelled back. "You know how to use the oven, and it's not Becky. Take the cookies out and get your ass out here."

"Your wish, my command," my dad called back.

A minute later, he appeared in the doorway. The sight of the still-oozing bread magma and the shards of ceramic gave him pause, but not for long. He strode across the lawn with long, deliberate steps.

"If it's not Rebecca, who is it?" he asked.

My mother stepped away from me, putting me in his full view.

"You're alive." There was no long stare from him. He threw his arms around me. His hug was not as crushing as my mother's, which wasn't surprising. She'd always been the stronger one.

My arms hung at my sides until I remembered what to do with them. I wrapped them around my father's torso.

After a few moments, he released me and stepped back. Unlike my mother, he had changed. His dark brown hair was sprinkled with more than a few greys, and laugh lines were etched into the surface of his dark brown skin. But he still didn't look like the sixty-seven I knew him to be.

"Where have you been?" he demanded.

"Santa Fe."

"She's a vet!" my mother said. "And look at her car."

I shook my head. "It's not my car, it's a friend's. Well, my friend borrowed it when his Maserati's alternator stopped working, and..." My voice trailed off when the knowledge of my friend's current location hit me again. I rallied but wasn't quite ready to confess to the body in the trunk. I took a deep breath. "And I'm not a vet. Not anymore. I am—"

I didn't get a chance to finish my sentence before Archibald hopped out of the car.

My mother blanched. I'd never seen her be anything but calm and in control. Even now, after her initial shock, she composed herself quickly. But Archibald was definitely throwing her for a loop.

"Um... That's my cat. Archibald Maelstrom." I wasn't sure how much further I should go with my explanation. My parents' last memory of me was of committing me to a mental hospital. Showing up after ten years and introducing them to my talking cat might make them wonder if they should give it another go.

"I know what he is," my mother said without taking her eyes off Archibald. "But if he's here, and he's with you..." She finally tore her eyes off my cat and swung them back to look at me. "Oh shit. Fuck. Shit. I'd hoped you were free and clear of all this."

"All this?" I knew what she was talking about, kind of. But it sounded like everything that had been happening was more than just an accident of nature. There was way more going on, and I didn't understand any of it.

A car tore around the corner and skidded to a stop behind mine in a spray of dust and gravel. A woman was out from behind the wheel almost before the vehicle had come to a complete stop.

"Sorry, sorry, sorry!" she chanted. "I know I'm late, but it's really not my fault this time. Jackie called and asked me to stop and get her. Apparently, she had a 'feeling' she should be here today." Becky rolled her eyes. "But unless she needed to be here to scope out the fancy car in the driveway, I can't imagine what—"

She caught sight of me, and her jaw dropped. "Jackie, I will never doubt you again."

"Yes, you will," Jackie answered, stepping out of the car.

My sisters were nearly identical, even though there was a year between them. They took after my dad's darker coloring. Light-brown skin, long black curly hair, and mahogany-colored eyes that always seemed to hide their true feelings.

"Holy shit," Jackie said. "I knew something interesting was going to happen, but I never would've guessed this."

Becky took three steps forward and threw her arms around me, my third familial hug in fewer than fifteen minutes. After ten years without hugs from anyone but Gwen, it was strange and wonderful.

"You're not fucking dead!" she exclaimed as she released me.

"I told you she wasn't dead," Jackie muttered, stepping forward and giving me a brief hug that was nowhere nearly as affectionate as the others I'd received. "But as usual, no one believes a godsdamned thing I tell you."

"I'm sorry." I didn't have any other words. Well, that wasn't true. I had a lot of things to say, but "sorry" seemed like a good start.

"You look like shit, Frankie. Are you using again?" Jackie asked bluntly. She was the youngest of us—seven years younger than me—and she'd been the one who'd found me after my last suicide attempt. She apparently hadn't forgiven me yet, which was fair. Eminently so.

I shook my head. "No, I'm clean and sober. I promise."

"How long?" She crossed her arms and stared at me.

I couldn't equivocate. Not with this. "Not long. Less than a week, with one slip on the road trip."

"That's not long," Jackie said.

Mom put her arm around me and pulled me close. "It's not, but it's something. Now, inside, all of you. We need to talk."

THIRTY-FOUR

om led us through the house and pointed at the expansive back deck that overlooked the Clackamas River. I followed my dad out and sat in one of the chairs scattered around.

Dad sat on my left, and Becky took the spot next to him. Jackie planted herself in the chair farthest away from me and stared at me.

Mom came out with a tray bearing a pitcher of lemonade, a stack of glasses, and a plate heaped with chocolate cookies fresh from the oven. My mouth watered. Chocolate chip was my favorite, and other than the meager breakfast offered at my hotel that morning, I'd had nothing but coffee. I had a lot of the cash that I'd found in Ash's car, but I didn't want to spend too much of it now in case I needed it to find a place to stay until I could find a job.

My dad poured the lemonade and handed out glasses while my mom shoved a handful of cookies at me, then passed the plate to my sisters.

"Are Jack and Devin going to show up any time soon?" Mom asked.

Becky & Jackie shook their heads.

"Devin's at work today and won't be done until late," Becky said.

Jackie added, "And someone had to stay home with the baby."

I stared between them. "Are Jack and Devin your...husbands?" It sounded weird to say that out loud. Last time I'd seen them, they'd been teenagers.

"Devin's my husband, and Jack is Jackie's life partner, or something like that. They're too cool to believe in marriage," Becky said.

"Your partner's name is Jack, and you have a baby." I nodded like those were in any way things that made sense in my head. "Please, please tell me your baby's name is Jacques."

Jackie glared at me, but I saw her lips quirk into a smile for a moment. "My partner's name is John, but our ridiculous family insists on calling him Jack. And the baby's name is Lenore."

I'd spent most of the time in the last few days either on the verge of tears or a panic attack. Tears were currently the frontrunner, and for once, they were happy ones. "That's my middle name."

"Duh," Jackie said. "I knew you weren't dead, but I didn't think you were ever coming back. I wanted to remember you the way you were...before. And this was my attempt."

It might have been my imagination, but it almost felt like she was softening toward me a little.

Mom clapped her hands. "Enough chitchat. There will be time to catch up on everything later. But now, there are things I need to tell you, Frankie. Things I should've told you a long time ago."

"If only someone had recommended that course of action!" Dad said brightly.

Mom shot a glare at him, but when he blinked innocently, she smiled. The love that flowed between them was so profound I felt like I was intruding on a private moment.

"Anyway, as I was saying before I was interrupted by Mr. 'I Told You So,' there are a few things about our family that I've never shared. Things I hoped would never be relevant, but that suddenly are." Mom looked at me, and I shrank back.

This was my fault.

"I'm sorry," I said. "I didn't mean to bring this here. I can go…"

"Don't be ridiculous," Dad said. "Just listen to your mother, and then we can figure out what to do next."

"If someone doesn't tell me what's going on, I'm going to scream," Becky said.

Archibald took that moment to walk up the stairs from the back-yard and stand in the middle of the deck like he owned the place. The moment he sat, a sunbeam broke through the trees, illuminating his ginger fur and making it look like he was on fire. He looked at Becky and flicked his tail back and forth a few times. "You're going to scream at some point," he said. "So you might as well get it over with."

Becky shrieked and jumped to her feet, scurrying until she hit the railing. "What the actual fuck is that?"

Archibald turned his back on her and raised his tail, likely giving her a stellar view of his backside. He stared at Jackie. "What about you, daughter of Katrin? Are you going to scream, too?"

"Stop terrorizing my children, Bygulson. Sit down, shut up, and let me explain. Then, if you want, you can continue with the theatrics." Mom turned toward me and grabbed my hands. "How much do you know already?"

I wanted to dissemble. Everything I knew would further my family's belief in my mental illness. But even though my sisters were shocked to hear Archibald talk, Mom hadn't seemed surprised at all. The only thing that'd shocked her was that he was here at all.

Still, saying it out loud was weird beyond belief. "I know I'm a Valkyrie. I can see the souls of the dead and help them cross over. I have a talking cat, and maybe met a goddess, who Archibald says isn't dead, no matter what it looked like. And—"

"Which goddess?" Mom asked sharply.

"Freyja," I answered. "We were talking, she offered me a ride, then she froze solid, shattered, burned, and melted.

Mom relaxed. "Definitely not dead, then. But no matter what Archibald says, her death is more of a possibility now than it ever was before. Now, you need to know my story." She exchanged a glance with my father.

"Like ripping off a band-aid," he prompted when her pause went on too long.

"I'm a Valkyrie," she said. "And I'm semi-retired."

"This whole family has lost their fucking minds," Becky muttered from where she was still pressed against the railing.

Mom ignored Becky and continued. "I'm not one of the originals, but my mother was. There's always the same number of Valkyries in existence, so when one wants to retire, she has a child. That daughter —and it's always a daughter—grows up to take her place."

"You said you were semi-retired," I said. "What does that mean?"

"When I got married, then pregnant, it was like I was relieved from active duty. I can still be called upon if there is need, but there seldom is."

"Seldom is still too much," Dad muttered.

Mom continued as if she hadn't been interrupted. "When I met your father, it was love at first sight. If it hadn't been for him, I don't know if I ever would've wanted to retire. I loved my job, but"—she reached her hand across my chair to hold his—"I love him more."

"Awwwww...gross," Jackie and Becky said in unison.

Becky seemed to have gotten over her initial shock, at least, and was inching back to her chair, although her eyes never left Archibald, who paid her zero attention. Instead, he was sitting up straight, all his attention focused on my mother.

"When you were born, the light of the Valkyries shone through you, and I knew my successor had been born."

"She means a literal light went through you," Dad interjected. "When you lit up like a beacon in the night, I realized why she was having a home birth with an 'old friend' named Lena as the only one in attendance besides me. When I finally could see again, there was a massive sword lying next to you. By that point, the light was fading, but I could still see it shining through the runes etched across your body."

Mom took up the thread of the story again. "With my successor born, I was able to step back so I could raise you to take my place."

"Kinda harsh, isn't it Mom?" Jackie asked. "Raising your kid to grow up and be some kind of battle maiden?"

Mom shrugged. "It's a living."

A laugh escaped me before I could clap my hand over my mouth and hold it in. "Does it pay well?"

It was Mom's turn to laugh. "Spoils of war aren't as easy to cash in as they once were, but they still exist, and most of the gods are generous."

"Okay, but if Frankie's a Valkyrie, why are you only semi-retired?" Becky asked. "None of this makes any sense."

"I don't know," Mom said. "There have been a lot of theories floated around. For a time, the leading idea was that something went wrong with my bloodline. I was the first in the second generation of Valkyries to give birth and retire. And then I had two more daughters—something that had never happened to anyone else. Valkyries give birth to one daughter and no others, no matter how hard they try."

"What's the current theory?" Jackie asked.

"That the Valkyrie blood is too diluted. No one in my generation has a daughter to take her place. A few others, like me, had daughters, but other than the sword and runes at birth, no other signs that Frankie or any of the others are Valkyries have arisen. Until now." She picked up my hands again. "Tell me what happened."

I chewed at my lip. I wanted to tell her everything, but the mistakes I'd made along the way were humiliating, and I doubted she'd grant me as much grace as Archibald had. After all, she'd done this job far longer than I had. "Hold on a minute. You said your mother was an original Valkyrie. That must have been a long time ago. How old are you?"

My mother grinned. "I'm a bit older than your father."

"You're a damn cradle robber is what you are," he countered. "I'm sixty-seven, and I met your mother when I was twenty-nine."

"I'm not ancient," Mom protested. "I'm practically a baby compared to some of the other active Valkyries."

"Don't hide behind 'it's rude to ask a lady her age.' Just tell us," Becky said. She was quickly regaining her composure, although she still wouldn't look at Archibald.

Mom sighed. "I'm not sure. I was born sometime before the Vikings settled Iceland, but after the fall of the Roman Empire. I like to believe it was 1300 years before the birth date I claim now. So, I'm still sixty-five."

"One thousand three hundred sixty-five is not the same as sixty-five," Becky muttered, but after a stern look from dad, she shut up.

"Close enough that I'm going with it. I was born in 665-ish. We can talk about my skin care routine later. Now it's Frankie's turn to talk." She turned to me and sighed. "But before you get started, I want to apologize. I honestly believed that not enough of my power had passed down to you to produce anything but a great sword and a fun light show. I wish I'd been there for you when your powers woke. What was the catalyst?"

THIRTY-FIVE

It was well past lunch time when I finally finished talking. I'd considered asking my mother if we could talk privately, but in the end, decided it was much better to own up to what I'd done in front of everyone.

I hadn't lingered on the parts where I'd hitchhiked to Santa Fe for a job, gotten fired multiple times—first from my vet job, then from every other job because of my inability to stay on my meds and stay sober—but I hadn't left them out either.

"So..." I spread my hands and looked down at my fingers. I hadn't made eye contact with anyone since I'd gotten to the part where Gwen had kicked me out. "Now I'm here. I know I shouldn't even ask, but I—"

"Of course you're staying here until you find a place of your own," Mom interrupted. "You can even have your old room back if you give me some time to get it ready for you."

"Ask for the guest room," Dad said in a stage whisper. "It has a bed and zero swords."

Mom grinned. "Your old room is the biggest in the house—it makes the perfect indoor gym."

My room had been in the basement. In fact, it *was* the basement. When I'd gotten particularly snotty as a teenager about having to share with Becky, my parents had first moved her in with Jackie. But that resulted in a different type of whining, and my parents told me that if I could make the basement habitable for humans, they'd put in a bathroom and I could have it.

I spent the summer between middle and high school working on that room. I ripped out the old, musty carpet, revealing concrete underneath. I'd stained the floor light grey, but the walls had unfortunately been painted during my "lavender is my favorite color" phase.

I added a few rugs I'd found at thrift shops in Portland, sewn some curtains out of old sheets, and moved all my stuff down the day before I started ninth grade.

True to their word, my parents had installed a small bathroom, complete with a tiny stand-up shower. It'd been a little ramshackle, but it was all mine. Well, mine and Princess Paprika's, my mottled calico cat.

"The guest room is fine," I said. "I don't want to cause any trouble. And I can stay in town if you'd rather. I have plenty of cash." Shit. I'd told them the whole story, including the weird town in Nevada with magical mechanics and visiting goddesses, but I'd stopped my tale in Vegas.

I don't know why I hadn't kept going, why I hadn't even realized I'd stopped too soon and let it sound like everything after was nothing more than a standard road trip.

Archibald sat up from where he'd been napping in a sunbeam and looked at me. "It doesn't matter why you didn't. You need to finish telling it now."

It was the second time he'd spoken since he'd arrived, and Becky shrieked again, although this time, her reaction was more muted.

I looked down at my hands again, then met my mother's eyes. "There's one more thing. Ash and I left Vegas two days ago, and we stopped in a town called Winnemucca for the night."

Jackie gasped softly, and I glanced at her. She nodded once, and I knew she was aware of what'd happened there.

"We stayed at the Donner Pass Motel and Laundromat, and in the middle of the night, the fire alarm went off. I got out just fine, and even got my sword and bag, but Ash..." I took a deep breath. "Ash didn't make it out."

"Wait, your friend *died*, and that's not what you led with?" Becky said, aghast.

I squirmed a little. It was weird that I'd put this off. I could argue that the wound was too raw, that the trauma of watching my friend die was overwhelming, but the truth was, it didn't feel real.

I continued, and my voice took on the flat, monotone quality it always got when I was overwhelmed. "It's been a weird few weeks, capped with some absolutely unbelievable days. I watched him die, and I saw his soul leave his body. And the next day, I had to go to the morgue to identify his body." I cringed a little at what I was going to have to say. "The coroner was baffled. There wasn't a mark on him, even though many people had watched him burn. No smoke in his lungs, either. When the coroner left the room to get the forms I needed to sign, Archibald told me we couldn't leave Ash there, so... I grabbed Ash's body and ran."

"You what now?" Jackie asked, scooting to the edge of her seat and regarding me with wide eyes.

"I took Ash. He's in the trunk right now, actually."

Mom stood up, shaking her head. "I guess we'd better go get him."

"I hate it when this happens," Dad muttered. "I'm too old to be digging graves."

"You did it one time, and it was thirty years ago," Mom shot back. "And I can dig the grave, you big whiner." She looked at me. "C'mon, Frankie. Let's go get your body."

I followed my parents to my car and held my breath as I hit the button to pop the trunk. Mom leaned forward and lifted the deck lid up. I closed my eyes and waited for something to hit me. It would likely be the stench of death that I probably should have anticipated from a corpse that'd spent twenty-four hours in a trunk driving across the high desert in the middle of August.

"Huh. That's interesting," Mom said, sounding completely nonplussed.

I stepped forward and peered in tentatively.

It was empty.

THIRTY-SIX

"He was there, I swear!" I said.

We'd retreated to the kitchen after discovering the absence of Ash's body.

"I'm sure he was," Mom said. "I don't doubt you at all. However, he's definitely not there now, and that leads to a lot of questions."

"When did you say your last drink was?" Jackie asked. "And are you sure you're taking your meds? I was with you until you got to the part about the body—and your strange lack of emotion around it, considering it sounds like Ash was your only friend—but now I'm not so sure that any of your story has been real."

"Jackie, I think it's time for you to head home. I'm sure John and Lenore would love to see you," Dad said firmly. "Becky, why don't you take off and give your sister a ride home. You and your families should join us tomorrow afternoon. We'll grill and catch up."

Jackie opened her mouth, but when Dad held up a finger, she snapped her mouth closed and spun on her heels and walked out of the house.

Becky came over and gave me a hug. "I don't *not* believe you. But you have to admit it's all a bit weird. I'm glad you're home, though. I missed you."

I gave her an extra squeeze. "I missed you, too, Bex. I can't wait to meet Devin and see what kind of man was lucky enough to catch my sister."

"Bye Frankie." Becky followed her sister out the door.

"Jackie will come around soon," Mom said easily. "Your absence has been harder on her than any of the rest of us. And even though she has gifts of her own, it's difficult for her to believe in anything beyond her vague sense of knowing, which is wrong almost as often as it's right."

"She'd be right more often if she believed all the way or talked to Sasha about it." Dad didn't quite roll his eyes, but it looked like it had been hard to resist.

"What's Aunt Sasha got to do with it?" I was going to seize on anything that wasn't Ash's missing body while I tried to figure out where I might've lost him.

"She has the sight too and is never wrong. After one conversation about it, though, Jackie has refused to speak to her aunt again, and neither of them will tell me what they talked about." He shrugged, then added, "Like your mom said, Jackie will come around eventually. Until then, that's nowhere near being our biggest issue. You are."

A sharp pain pierced my sternum. They'd been glad to see me, but it'd been unrealistic to believe that I wouldn't still be a problem. Ten years' absence followed by a sudden reappearance and a missing body—not to mention everything else—wouldn't erase every problem I'd caused in the ten years prior to my disappearance.

"I understand," I said. "Thanks for the place to stay tonight. I'll take off tomorrow and see what I can find in Portland. I won't run again, though," I added when he looked about to protest.

"Nonsense," my mother said, finishing her inspection of my sword, which I'd grabbed out of the car along with my backpack when we'd finally closed the trunk and given up on figuring out how

Ash's body had dematerialized. "You've kept her in good shape. I suppose it's too much to expect that you've kept yourself in as good of shape as the sword?"

I winced. "I've been running a few times in the last couple weeks. I've got nowhere near the endurance and speed that I should have, but I didn't lose it all. As for the sword, I haven't practiced regularly. I took some classes in college, then found a place to practice in Santa Fe, but it was expensive, so I had to quit after I lost my job."

She handed it back to me, and I cradled it to my body. It wasn't exactly a security blanket, but it was comforting when I had nothing else. "I thought about selling it," I confessed.

Mom waved away my confession. "There's no way she'd let you do that."

"She?" I wrinkled my nose quizzically. "She who?"

"Your sword, of course." Mom leaned forward and regarded me, resting her chin on her hands. "You do not have to leave tomorrow and find a place in Portland. That is not what your father meant. *You* are not the issue. At least not in the way you're thinking. But everything that's happened to you—the deaths, the tests, and Freyja's visit, not to mention the missing body—those are what we need to think about."

"I don't know what to do, but Freyja and Archibald both said I needed to come home, that you'd know what to do."

Archibald strolled into the room. "I didn't say your mother would know what to do. I said she'd have answers for you." He huffed out a long breath. "No sign of Ash anywhere. I didn't notice any difference in the way the car felt between when you put him in there and today."

"I never opened the trunk after putting him in," I said. "Maybe I should've checked."

"Don't beat yourself up," Mom said. "You shouldn't have opened it. You never know who's watching. Besides, why would you check on a body? They're not notorious for running off."

"Speaking of someone watching, we should probably get rid of the car," Dad said. "Want me to take care of it?"

I bit my lip. "Technically, it belongs to Jordan in Searchlight. I should probably figure out how to get it back to him."

"I have a burner phone you can use to text the incubus and let him know the Maserati's his as long as he doesn't report this one stolen," Mom said. "You don't want to give any indication of where you are—or even who. Someday we'll figure out how to get the Maserati's title signed over to him."

I looked back and forth between my parents, not knowing which question to ask first.

"We'll try to answer all your questions later. Right now, I need to figure out who—or what—Ash was and call in some help. I don't know if I'll be able to bring you up to speed fast enough on my own, and it sounds like you need to be ready sooner rather than later." Mom stood and paced the length of the kitchen.

"You should warn your cousins," Dad said. "If the power has woken in Frankie, maybe it's waking in others of her generation too. No one deserves to be surprised the way Frankie was. They might not handle it as well as she did."

I stared at my dad for a moment. "How could someone handle it worse than me? I made my fiancée into a two-souled monster and turned a little girl into a wraith." A new thought hit me. "Do you think... Do you think that I somehow raised Ash from the dead, like how I saved Gwen?"

Mom was shaking her head before I finished my question. "Absolutely not. That's not something you could do unconsciously, and since you were sober, you know you didn't black out and shove someone else's soul into the trunk. Besides, once someone's been dead for a few hours, it's nearly impossible to get a soul to take up residence in a body."

I filed away the "nearly impossible" for future questions when I had enough reserves to deal with it.

"I've got to go. Marty, come with me. We have things to take care of, and I'm sure Frankie needs some alone time. Archibald, with us please." My cat followed my parents out of the house, and I was alone in the home I hadn't been in for more than ten years.

I GRABBED a soda out of the fridge and walked back out onto the deck. I loved it out here. It's where I'd always done my homework when the weather was nice. It's where I'd had my first kiss with a girl, something she later claimed didn't happen. I'd spent hours out here reading, and when Mom wasn't home, practicing sword work on the outdoor furniture.

The longer I sat and stared into the trees, the river providing some background music, the more anger welled up in me.

Nothing I'd said had been a surprise to them. Maybe my parents hadn't anticipated everything I'd done, but they'd known I was a Valkyrie, or at least a potential one. They'd had years to tell me, years to prepare me, and had just...hadn't.

They'd left me in the dark—a place I was intimately familiar with since it never quite left the corners of my mind. To have them confirm what I'd had to find out on my own felt like a betrayal.

I walked down the stairs and around the outside of the house, regarding the car. Dad said he'd "take care of it," whatever that meant, but it was still here, and I still had the keys. They might've claimed I wasn't the problem, but there must be something wrong with me that they'd kept my identity a secret from me for so long.

The truth hit me and nearly knocked me back.

They hadn't told me because I wasn't worthy. They were surprised, not because they thought the Valkyrie powers would never wake, but because they hadn't believed it would happen to their screwed up crazy daughter.

And not only had it woken in me instead of in one of my more deserving sisters, I'd fucked up every step of the way. No wonder they needed a time out from me.

There was no point in staying here any longer. I didn't have a body in my trunk, and there was no evidence I ever had. I had enough cash to live in Portland for a month, as long as I got a room at one of the extended-stay places in Felony Flats and ate Ramen and PB&J.

I headed back toward the house but stopped when I heard voices.

"After all this time, why now?" my mother asked. "You'd think Freyja would have more sense than to start kindling latent Valkyrie powers now."

"I don't question the goddess," Archibald replied. "That's a Valkyrie's role. I was just told to show up and do my best to get her here."

There was a long moment of silence, then my mother spoke again. "It isn't fair to her. She isn't ready, and I'm not sure how much I can do."

I didn't wait to hear Archibald's reply. I turned on my heel and headed to the river. There was a path down there that would take me upstream, farther into the rolling hills, and away from what might never be home again.

CHAPTER

THIRTY-SEVEN

Once I was firmly ensconced in the tree that I'd claimed as my own when I was six, I finally took a breath and thought over what I'd heard. It was clear my mother didn't think I should be a Valkyrie, and she wasn't impressed with whatever Freyja was doing.

I closed my eyes and leaned back, letting the branches of the huge conifer support me. I'd spent hours here as a child, hidden within the boughs and nearly invisible from the ground unless one knew exactly where to look. My hair, once more completely blonde like my mother's, rippled in the late summer breeze that was cooled by the river and the thick, dark forest.

Listening to the wind and the rushing river below, clarity crept in, and with it, rationality.

I knew better than to eavesdrop, much less on a partial conversation without context, and take what I'd heard as the entire story.

Mom might have said she didn't know how much she could help me, but she hadn't said anything untrue. I wasn't prepared, and it sounded like most women started training for their role when they were young. Other than knowing the old stories and learning how to use a sword passably well, I'd had no other training.

Not because I was crazy, though. The effects of my mental illness hadn't been apparent until I was a junior in high school. No, it was because they thought it was unnecessary. Mom had believed I wasn't a Valkyrie. Maybe she still should've told me—it was a shitty secret to keep, regardless of whether or not I was Buffy material—but she didn't keep it out of malice or because she believed me unworthy.

Heat crept up my neck as shame suffused me.

I was an idiot. An idiot who once more ran away from my problems rather than face them.

At least I hadn't run very far this time.

I stayed in the tree for another half hour. I finally felt my connection to this place returning. I'd lived here for the first eighteen years of my life, and although it'd been ten years since I'd even set foot on this land, I knew every nook, every branch of every tree, every secret path used by the deer that were passing through. This place reminded me that I wasn't unmoored. I had this place to keep me grounded. I had family to lift me up. And sure, maybe Jackie wouldn't forgive me and welcome me with open arms right away, but she hadn't completely written me off yet.

I took a deep breath, inhaling the earthy, rich scent of the forest, and exhaled some of the tension that had been riding my shoulders for the last few weeks. Maybe I still didn't have all the answers, but at least now I felt like there might be some.

I hadn't realized how much I'd missed having someone else take care of me, to hold my problems for me. It was a relief to know that someone else could help me handle this ridiculousness.

THE DESCENT from the tree was harder than the ascent had been and was much more difficult than I'd remembered it being. Once I was down, I slipped my shoes back on and headed back to the house. I crept around the side, hoping to be back on the deck before anyone noticed I'd been gone.

Instead, both of my parents and Archibald were on the deck, drinks in hand—not Archibald, obviously—and serious expressions on their faces.

"Hey," I said weakly. "I went for a walk. Visited the tree. Inhaled the piney air. Like you do."

"After eavesdropping on a conversation you hadn't been invited to?" Archibald asked.

I started to protest, but there was nothing to push back on. "I didn't mean to. I was..." I'd been running away. Again.

My mother arched an eyebrow, which always meant trouble. "You were what?"

I didn't want to answer. They already thought poorly of me. Was there any reason to make it worse?

When was I going to grow up and stop being such a disappointment? All I wanted, all I'd ever wanted, was to make my parents proud. Becky was an all-state volleyball player and had been a freshman in college on a swimming scholarship when I'd cut off all contact. Jackie was one of the smartest people I knew. She'd been in the process of deciding which of the many universities that had been courting her she wanted to attend. Plus, she could play just about any instrument you put in front of her. And it seemed like she was some kind of psychic, too.

And me? I couldn't even keep my part-time job at a cat shelter.

"I was going to head into town," I hedged. "There are a few things I need."

"Were you planning on coming back?" my dad asked.

I hesitated, and that pause answered my father's question. The look of disappointment on my father's face and the resignation on my mother's were so much worse than anger would've been.

"I'm sorry," I said. "I know I'm a huge disappointment. I don't know what's going on, but I'll do whatever you tell me to. I just want you to be proud of me. I don't know if that's possible anymore, but I am going to try."

"Oh, Frances," Mom said, shaking her head. "You don't have to do anything to make us proud. I've always been proud to have such a wonderful daughter. You have been through so much, and you always make it to the other side. You are one of the strongest people I know, so don't discount yourself."

My dad nodded. "Your mother's right. You have to work so much harder than either of your sisters to fight the dragons in your mind. You are amazing, and I am so happy you're home. Asking for help is difficult, but you did it."

I blinked several times, searching for something to say. In a million years, I wouldn't have expected this reaction. Not only were they not angry, they were...proud?

"But," my mother said.

I hunched my shoulders, waiting for the statement that would negate all the good feelings my parents' compliments had engendered.

"We're not going to tell you what to do. I'll help you, offer advice, but whatever happens from now on has to be your decision. You have to do more than choose the dead. You have to choose your life."

The tranquility I'd found in the forest redoubled. I could choose what happened to me. I wasn't just a game piece with no control. I was a whole person with agency.

"You're right. I've spent too many years hiding from myself and expecting other people to fix my shit. Maybe it's time I grow up and stop screwing up."

"No." Dad glared at me.

I knitted my brows in confusion. "What? Mom just said—"

"Your mother said you have to make your own choices, but she didn't tell you to berate yourself for previous ones. Whatever did or didn't happen before is over. We can learn from our mistakes, but if we spend too much time holding them close, we get stuck with them and can never truly move on. Maybe you did things the wrong way before, but that was then. You are not your past. Only when you can let go—without forgetting the lessons learned—can you live your best life."

"I don't know if I can do that," I confessed. I wanted to, lord knew I would love to make all the mistakes I'd made look a little smaller in my rearview mirror, but I'd fucked up so many times that I didn't know if that was even possible anymore.

"You can," my father said confidently. "All you have to do is listen to me and believe in yourself."

I grinned through the lump in my throat his words created. "I thought you weren't going to tell me what to do?"

Mom huffed out a long sigh. "There is still so much more you need to learn, and if you're already getting divine visits, we can't afford to go slow. I've called a few of my cousins to let them know about you and asked if any of them know what's going on. I don't have answers yet, but I do have two Valkyries and Adele descending on us this Monday."

Dad closed his eyes and pinched the bridge of his nose. "Please don't tell me Lena's one of them."

"Of course she is. She's Frankie's godmother. She has to be here."

"Aunt Lena's a Valkyrie?" I hadn't seen my honorary aunt since I was sixteen, and I couldn't imagine the tiny woman hoisting a sword and riding into battle. "She's so short!"

Mom cocked her head at me. "Valkyries aren't flight attendants, you know. There's no height requirement to reach the overhead bins." She turned back toward Dad. "Lena, Kara, and Adele are all going to be here. I'm going to need help getting ready for them."

"Where's everyone going to sleep?" That might not have been the biggest issue facing the impending arrival of three Valkyries who were going to evaluate me, but it was the only one I could give voice to.

"Valkyries don't need to sleep, and neither does Adele," my mother said. "At least not much. They'll be fine."

I exhaled slowly. "I need to."

"How many hours a night do you get on a regular basis?" Mom asked.

I pursed my lips and counted. "Three or four, usually."

"It'll become less and less as time goes on. I only sleep every few weeks unless I really want to."

"Huh." I had nothing else. I'd run out of words—something no one I knew would've thought possible. "I need..." I didn't know how to tell them I needed a break. I hadn't seen them in a decade, and I'd already taken a walk.

"You need some time to settle in without us around," Mom said. "I understand. Let's get the rest of your stuff out of your car and into the guest room. You can use the shower, put on some fresh clothes, and catch up on your laundry. When you're ready, come back out and we'll have dinner. Do you want to eat here or head into town?"

The thought of potentially running into someone I knew made me cringe. "Here, please."

"No problem. I'll put together a lasagna, and your father will make a salad. In the meantime, I need to restart that bread that I didn't get to finish this morning."

"Thank you."

"You're welcome. Now let's get your stuff," Dad said.

In five minutes, I was alone in the guest room. My few boxes were piled in the corner, and fresh towels had been placed in the adjoining bathroom.

I turned on the water, grabbed a book out of one of the boxes, and got into the bathtub. For the first time in a long time, I felt safe.

THIRTY-EIGHT

I picked my way through the forest, heading down to the river to watch the sunrise. My spandex shorts and tank top were not enough to insulate me against the early-morning chill, although I knew that once I started running, I'd warm up quickly.

This had been my ritual in high school—at least on the mornings I wasn't waking up with a hangover. There was one spot on the river where I could see Mt. Hood, and I loved watching it gradually take shape as the eastern horizon lit up.

I'd tried to talk Archibald into coming with me, but he said he'd much rather stay inside where it was warm than get his feet wet in the morning dew. I didn't mind. I was quite fond of my cat, although I was becoming more aware that he wasn't *my* anything. Even so, twenty-four hours wasn't enough time for me to get used to parental presence, and every bit of solo time I could manage helped keep my whelm from going over.

"I thought I'd find you here," a familiar voice said.

I spun around. Jackie was picking her way through the undergrowth of the forest. Unlike me, she'd dressed for warmth—jeans, long-sleeved shirt, and a puffy vest along with hiking boots.

"Hey Jackie. I didn't think I'd see you until later."

"You won't see me later," she said.

There was something wrong with her tone. Even yesterday, when she'd been angry and accusatory, she hadn't been this snide.

"In fact, this is the last time you'll see me."

I tilted my head and looked at her. I could hear what she was saying, but none of it made any sense. "What do you mean? I thought you and John and Lenore were coming for dinner today?"

"I agreed to that just to make Mom and Dad happy, but there's no way I'd let you anywhere near my child. If you really care about our parents, you'll make this your farewell meal. Leave your phone number so they can make sure you're not dead from time to time and get the fuck out of here." Jackie's face twisted into a sneer.

Nausea roiled in my stomach. "I don't want to make things worse."

"You already have. Do you know how many times Mom cried about you? We had a fucking memorial service for you. You've never been anything but a burden. A parasite. It was a relief when you left and no longer needed to be watched and cared for, and given everything you ever asked for, only to give nothing in return. I almost wish I hadn't called 911 when I found you. That would've made everything easier."

My jaw dropped, and I stared at her, unable to speak.

"You're nothing but a crazy addict. You might claim to be clean now, but we both know it's only a matter of time before you fuck up. Again. Why don't you crawl back into the hole you've been hiding in the last ten years—and this time, stay there."

Jackie turned around and walked out of the forest, but not back toward the house.

I almost let her go, but I couldn't leave it like that. I ran after her. "Jackie, wait!"

She didn't turn around. I picked up my pace, and although she didn't seem to move any faster than me, in a few seconds, she disappeared into the early-morning mist, and by the time I got to the road, she was nowhere in sight.

I leaned against one of the trees lining the gravel road and slowly sank down until I was sitting, my knees drawn up to my chest. I wrapped my arms around my legs and dropped my head and let the tears flow.

THIRTY-NINE

The sun was well over the horizon by the time I got up from where I'd been sitting. I debated skipping my run, but I needed it now more than ever. I thought best when I was running and could clear the cobwebs from my brain, and if I didn't go for a run, I'd probably go for a drink.

And I wasn't doing that, no matter how much my little sister thought it inevitable.

We'd fought in the past, but nothing like this. I was seven years older than her, though, so it was usually over minor stuff, like when she briefly wore the same size shoes as me and kept "borrowing" mine. I couldn't imagine how awful it must have been for her to find me unconscious and unresponsive, to be the one to keep me alive until the paramedics arrived. There was no way to go back in time to change the situation, and I didn't know how to make it up to her now. But I'd have to try.

Just maybe...not yet.

I jogged in place for a couple minutes to warm up my muscles that were stiff from sitting on the cold, hard ground for so long. Then I picked a direction—east toward the mountains—and took off at a slow run. Once my gait became easy and my breathing was hard but steady, I picked up speed.

It was easier here than it had been in Santa Fe. Even after living there for ten years, the elevation still affected me, apparently.

With the speed came clarity. My sister was angry—she had every right to be—and I couldn't do anything to change that now except apologize and be there if she ever wanted to talk. But doing what she'd told me to do, to run off again, wouldn't be the right thing, either, no matter how much she might think so.

It was long past time that I took responsibility for myself and my actions. I still didn't know what was coming and what I'd need to do to stop it, but I wouldn't hide from it. Not again.

By the time I got home, it was almost noon, and I was red-faced, dripping sweat, and determined.

I slipped past the kitchen where I could hear Mom and Dad arguing about the best way to prepare potatoes. Dad was vociferous in his belief that there was nothing superior to a baked potato, while Mom was waffling between vodka, lefse, and scalloped.

"Mashed!" I called back on my way to my room. A burst of laughter followed me down the hall, and I smiled. Belonging was kinda nice. It'd been like this when Gwen and I had first moved in together—friendly banter in the kitchen, inside jokes that drove our friends bananas when we used them in public, and casual affection that was even more important than the serious affection we had for each other. This right here was family.

I'd thought I'd need more alone time after I got cleaned up to process my life, the last week, and this morning, but after I put on clean clothes, I was ready to face my parents, Becky, and her husband, and find out what explanation Jackie would give for not coming. Would she tell everyone what she'd said to me, or beg off with a more polite excuse?

By the time I'd towel-dried my hair and French braided it, I could hear Becky's voice and a deeper one that must be Devin.

I metaphorically girded my loins—seeing family after a decade of absence was hard. Meeting someone new who'd probably heard all sorts of stories about me was another level of stress. It only took a moment for me to prepare, though, and I was out the door.

The great potato debate was over, and everyone had moved out to the deck. I walked through the sliding door. I hadn't even gotten both feet onto the deck before Becky was up and at my side. She grabbed my hand and pulled me forward, halting me in front of the only person I didn't recognize.

"Dev, this is my sister, Frankie. I know you've heard all about her, so I don't need to tell you anything else. Frankie, this is Devin Wulfe. My husband."

Devin was a tall Black man with laughing light-brown eyes, close-shorn dark hair, and a grin so wide and friendly it could light up the whole state. He stood, and I held out my hand to shake.

"Don't be ridiculous," he said in a deep, husky voice dripping with honey. He pulled me into a hug. "You're family, and family hugs. That's what Bex told me, anyway."

"It's nice to meet you, Devin." I pulled away from him. It's true we were a hugging family, but a person had to work back up to this level of casual affection. "How'd you two meet?"

Devin sat again and snagged Becky around the waist, pulling her down onto his lap.

"We met the first day of grad school, in the bookstore," Becky said. "It was a total meet-cute."

"She dropped a textbook on my head," Devin said, shaking the referenced body part.

Becky snorted. "It wasn't that dramatic. I dropped a paperback of *The Yellow Wallpaper* on his head, but I only did it so he'd look at me."

"It worked. I looked, and I've never been able to look away since." The look he directed at her was panty-meltingly hot, and the love and adoration on her face confirmed that she'd found a good one, and that he was one lucky man.

"Don't ask them any more questions about their relationship," Mom advised. "They've known each other for almost five years, been married for three, and they're still disgustingly affectionate like this."

Dad leaned over and planted an enthusiastic kiss on Mom. "Maybe they'll get over it as soon as I get tired of looking at you."

Mom rolled her eyes but blushed. The earlier feeling of belonging, of family, faded a little as a wave of jealousy lapped over me. I'd had that, too, with Gwen. And I'd fucked it up. Just like I'd fucked up my family relationships before that.

Maybe it was just a matter of time before I screwed up again.

A head butt on the ankle jolted me out of the self-pity I was about to wallow in.

"Thanks, Archibald," I whispered.

Becky tore her gaze away from her husband and narrowed her eyes at my cat, then she looked at Devin. "Um, there might be a couple minor details I left out when I was telling you about Frankie's appearance yesterday. Nothing huge, you know. I covered most of the basics."

Devin's easy smile never left his face, but his eyes narrowed slightly. "What kind of details?"

"I assume part of what she's referring to is me," Archibald said, hopping onto the chair next to me. "But for the other item, she'll have to tell you herself."

To his credit, Devin's reaction was nothing like Becky's had been yesterday. His eyes widened, and his jaw dropped a little before he recovered. "Huh." He closed his eyes for a moment, then trained his stare on Archibald. "What's your name?"

My face scrunched in confusion. There was taking it well, and there was asking a talking cat what his name was.

"Archibald Maelstrom." The cat dipped his head a bit. "Pleased to meet you."

"I'm Devin, and I have to say, it's been a very long time since I've chatted with an avatar."

"I'm not an avatar, just a messenger," Archibald said. "And I didn't expect such politeness from someone like you."

No one in the room was giving the talking cat another look. All eyes, including Becky's, were trained on Devin.

"I think you've left a few details out of...everything, too," Becky said to her husband, a dangerous lilt in her voice. She started to stand. "Someone like you?"

Devin grabbed her around the waist and held her in place. "C'mon, Bex. Tell me what you would've said if I told you when we started dating that I sometimes talked to animals, and they talked back?"

Becky seemed to concede that point, but she wasn't done. "Fine. That's an off-putting first date conversation. But we've known each other for five years. Surely you could've mentioned it at some point. If I'd known that was a thing, maybe I wouldn't have freaked out when a cat talked to me yesterday!"

"What's the other thing you didn't tell me last night?" Devin asked.

While Becky composed her answer, I stole a glance at my parents. They'd recovered from Devin's bombshell much more quickly than I had, and were now leaning back in their chairs, watching Becky and Devin like they were in a mildly interesting sitcom.

"My mom's a few thousand years old, she's a Valkyrie, now my sister is a Valkyrie too, and Jackie really can predict the future. Oh, and Frankie had a dead body in her trunk, but it disappeared, so that part's alright." Becky spoke so quickly her words ran into each other and tumbled around until her quick confession was nearly incomprehensible.

"Huh," Devin said. "That explains a lot, doesn't it?" He glanced over at my mom. "Not the age thing, Katrin. You don't look a day over thirty."

"Anyone need a refill on anything?" I asked. I'd thought I'd brought the weird home, but choosing the slain and having a talking cat were barely enough to make waves in this household, apparently.

"I've got it," Dad said. "I have to check on the potatoes, anyway. Jackie and Jack should be here soon, then we can dig into the feast."

"I don't think she's coming," I said. "Didn't she tell you?"

Mom looked at me. "No. I talked to her while you were in the shower, and she said they'd be here around one."

"Oh." My head felt like it was trapped in a pinball machine. Maybe she expected that I'd packed up and left already and was coming to celebrate my departure?

"I should skip this meal, then. I can hide out in my room with a potato and a book," I offered. "I don't want to make her uncomfortable."

"Is this about what happened yesterday?" Becky asked. "It's fine. She was pissed, but she was practically over it by the time I dropped her off. She didn't know you were coming back, and she hates being surprised."

A car door slamming drove home the truth that Jackie was coming.

"Don't hide," Mom said. "You want to meet the baby, right?"

I let out a deep breath. I did, in fact, want to meet the baby. I could always hide later if things got weird. I pasted on a smile. "I would love to meet little Lenore."

FORTY

Lenore was the most beautiful baby in the world. She had the same light brown skin and black hair as her mom, and beautiful hazel eyes. Right now, she was sleeping in my arms and had a firm hold of my finger.

I looked up and saw Jackie watching me hold her daughter. She didn't look angry, just contemplative. It was such a change from earlier that I didn't know what to think. She hadn't balked a bit at Mom's suggestion that I hold the baby. Sure, she'd sniffed my breath before handing Lenore over, but once satisfied, relinquished her daughter.

I'd barely had a chance to say anything to John—a short, roundish white man with sandy hair and hazel eyes that perfectly matched Lenore's—before Mom hustled him off to the kitchen with everyone else, leaving me, Jackie, and Lenore alone on the deck.

Awkward.

"So," I said, not sure how to broach the topic, but knowing I needed to.

Jackie raised one eyebrow in an almost perfect imitation of my mother. "So?" she prompted.

"About earlier today. I've thought about what you said, but I don't think I can go right now. And not just because I don't have anywhere to go. I'm just tired of running away."

Jackie wrinkled her nose. "What the hell are you talking about, Frankie? What did I say? When? We haven't talked today."

I stood and handed Lenore back to her mother. Either Jackie was messing with me, which was unlikely—Ash was the only one who'd ever done things like that—or none of it had happened.

"Shit. I must have been hallucinating. I'm so sorry."

Jackie stared at me for a moment, then handed Lenore back to me. "Sit down. Let's talk a moment before you decide you just bought a one-way ticket on the crazy train."

I cradled Lenore to my chest and took my seat. "I shouldn't hold her if I'm this unstable."

"I trust you not to hurt my daughter," Jackie said. "Before we go too much further, I want to apologize for how I acted yesterday. I'm not ready to completely forgive and forget, but I was out of line. A disappearing dead body is hardly any weirder than a talking cat, a thirteen-hundred-year-old mother, and a magic sword."

"It's fine. I deserve the suspicion and mistrust. I hope to earn your trust back someday, but I don't expect that to happen overnight. And for what it's worth, I am so sorry you had to be the one to find me. I can't imagine how horrible that was. I can't take it back, but I can promise you'll never have to go through that again."

Jackie squeezed her eyes shut for a moment and took a deep breath. "I can't talk about that now. Maybe not ever. But apology heard." She opened her eyes. "Now, let's talk about your halluci-nations."

Lenore opened her eyes for a second, then reached up and touched my face before falling back asleep.

"You found me in the forest where I watch the sunrise and were... mean. Truthful, but not kind."

"I showed up at sunrise and walked through the woods? On purpose?" Jackie shuddered. "I do not rise with the dawn. You, Mom, and Bex are the morning people in this family. Dad and I are the sensible ones.”

“A hallucination doesn’t make sense, Jackie. That’s why it’s a hallucination.”

She held up a hand. “How many times did you mock me for sleeping in when we were younger?”

“Every weekend I came home from college for several years,” I admitted.

“That detail might not be something you could pull up without prompting, but you know I’m a late sleeper. Your brain has that detail in it.” She tapped her finger against her mouth. “I can’t believe I’m going to say this, but after yesterday, I’m willing to believe almost anything. Do you think it could have been some kind of magical thing trying to make you feel bad and run away? It’s a little insulting that it used me as its mean shape, but also completely understandable. I was a total bitch yesterday.”

I brushed a thumb over Lenore’s cheek to avoid looking at Jackie. “You didn’t say anything that wasn’t true.”

“Maybe not, but there were so many kinder ways I could’ve approached it. And calling into question your disappearing corpse was way out of line. Now, let me think. I know what’s going on, but I just can’t put a finger on it.”

I stayed silent for a good thirty seconds before asking the question that’d been at the forefront of my mind since the second Jackie dismissed my hallucination theory. “How come you’re taking this so well? I mean, Becky looks fine, if a bit freaked out by Archibald”—I gestured toward the cat lightly snoring in the sun—“but I can tell she’s overwhelmed. Not doubting necessarily, but maybe three revelations away from needing a family-free vacation for a week. But you... You’re taking this all in stride.”

Jackie turned her focus from the woods to me. “When you’ve spent most of your life having visions of things that haven’t happened yet and later come true, it’s easy to believe there’s a lot more going on than meets the eye. I talked to John about it last night, still pissed off and ranting a bit about you, and he totally called me out. I've been having this recurring vision for the last three weeks of you and a pegasus standing on a pile of skulls. You're holding your sword aloft, and are dressed in chain mail, like some Valkyrie-themed episode of *He-Man*."

"A pile of skulls? I kinda hope that's more of a daymare than a prediction."

Jackie waved my concern away. "It's almost never literal. Besides, standing on a pile of skulls would be difficult. They don't make for a stable surface. But there was also a huge fire behind you, lighting striking your sword, a black, shadowy dragon circling in the sky, and your ginger cat rode a flying horse, and all that seemed more relevant than the skulls. Do you think Archibald is a Pegasus in disguise and the vision was just showing me both of his forms at once?"

She stared at Archibald as if she could make him grow wings through sheer force of will.

"I am not a pegasus," he said without opening his eyes. "But I would like to hear more about your vision. About all of them related to Frankie."

Jackie shrugged. "For a while, I would see her alive and... Maybe not well, but alive. I could never tell where she was, although it was typically in a poorly lit bar."

I winced. Great. She only saw the dark bits. "No wonder you didn't think I was clean and sober," I muttered. "Nothing good ever happened in dark bars."

"They weren't great visions," Jackie admitted, "but they were confirmation that you were alive. Then, a few weeks ago, the fire dreams started. The setting changed a little. At first, there were zero skulls and no pegasus. Just you, the sword, and your cat. Gradually, the other details showed up. Like I said, they aren't literal, but there is something about fire that is tied to you. Now, whenever I get visions of you, which is almost every day now, I see the same six things. Flames, your sword, Archibald, that weird-ass flying horse, a dragon, and death."

I puffed my lips, then blew out a long breath. "Everything but the pegasus and dragon make some kind of sense. My powers 'woke,' I guess you'd say, in the fire I ran into to save Gwen. Archibald was there, and I do have a sword. And Ash died in a fire a couple days ago. At least I thought he was dead."

"Being autopsied usually leads to a pretty definitive diagnosis of dead," Archibald said. "I don't think it's weird that you believed your eyes."

"It was weird that you stole his body from a morgue, though," Jackie said. "Why'd you tell her to do that, Archibald? Can I call you Archie?"

The cat opened both eyes and stared at Jackie with so much contempt it was palpable. "My name is Archibald. If you'd rather call me something else, you may call me Mr. Maelstrom. As for the body snatching... I had my reasons."

"You don't know, do you?" Jackie asked. "You made my sister a body-snatcher because you had a hunch."

"He would've left the morgue eventually anyway," Archibald said. "So really, we were just helping."

"Except instead of a body walking away, you had my sister carry a body and dump it in the trunk. That is not helping."

"Hey guys, maybe instead of arguing about something that's done, we talk about my pile of skulls?" I was desperate to keep things civil on the deck, especially since Jackie and I were doing so well. "Or about the mean Jackie who was in the woods today?"

"You're right," Jackie said. "Body snatching motivations are not the important thing here. Once Mom and Dad stop playing peacemaker, we can talk about the fire visions. But until then, let me think. I'm almost got it. In fact, go inside, both of you. Come back in twenty minutes."

I stood and held out the baby. "Do you want Lenore?"

Jackie shook her head. "Take her inside and hand her off to whoever looks most enthusiastic about it. There will be no shortage of volunteers."

I did as she said, handing Lenore to her very demanding grandmother. Before I could pour myself a glass of iced tea, the Buffy theme song announced a text message, which was weird, because I'd silenced my phone before my run that morning and hadn't turned it back on.

I read the message. "I'm calling you in five. We need to talk about what happened."

I blanched. Shit. Did she know about Ash? Was it her or the spirit of Zach residing within her calling?

"I have to take this," I said. "It's Gwen, and she wants to talk."

FORTY-ONE

I paced in front of the house, staring at the phone, willing it to ring. It'd been seven minutes since the cryptic text. Gwen was always punctual—she was the kind of person who thought being five minutes early was late.

The phone rang, and I answered it immediately.

"Gwen? Is that really you? Are you okay?" My words poured out of me as soon as the call connected.

"It's me. I'm okay. Well, not okay. Things have been weird since... Well, since, you know."

I hunched my shoulders. "I'm sorry. I couldn't let you die."

Her voice softened. "I know, Frankie. And I'm so happy you pulled me out of that fire. But something changed in me, and I don't understand. Can we meet in person? I need to see your face and make sure you're okay."

Something brushed against my ankles. Archibald was winding through them in a move that had the potential to trip me up more than comfort me.

"I can't meet," I said.

"Oh." She sounded dejected, and my heart ached. There were few things I hated more than hurting Gwen, although that had been almost the complete basis of our relationship for the past few months.

"Not because I don't want to," I hastened to say. "But I'm in Oregon with my family."

"I know," she said. "I called Ash a few days ago to find out why he was skipping work, and he told me he was driving you to your parents' house. I figured you were there already. I'm in Portland. Please."

"Okay." I nodded, even knowing she couldn't see me. "Where do you want to meet?"

"I don't know Portland very well, but I'm staying at a bed-and-breakfast in some weird industrial area, a fact that was not on their website." She paused, and all I could hear were rustling papers. "I'm somewhere called Swan Island? That sounded really pretty, but there are no swans that I can see. My room does have a view of the Willamette River, but it's just past some kind of car factory." She pronounced the river as *Willa-MET*, which made me smile.

"I didn't even know they had houses on Swan Island to make into Airbnbs," I said. "That sounds awful. And the river is pronounced *Will-AM-it*. Rhymes with dammit."

"Whatever," Gwen said. "Can you meet me here? I don't have a car, and I have no idea where you live."

"Sure." I looked at my wrist, like it'd magically tell me the time. "Um, I'm not sure how long it'll take me to get there. My whole family is here, and we're supposed to be having a big Sunday family meal."

"I have a flight home late this afternoon, but I'm hoping to have a reason to reschedule. Please come now," she pleaded.

I could never resist Gwen when she really wanted something. "Okay, let me tell my folks I'm leaving. I can't just take off, not after the way I left last time."

"Fine. But don't take too long. I don't know how much more of this place I can stand."

"Text me the address, and as soon as I have an ETA, I'll let you know." I hung up. I tripped over Archibald on my way back to the house, nearly hitting the ground. As it was, my phone went flying.

"Dude, what the fuck?"

"Please, never call me dude again," he said. "It is undignified."

"And tripping me isn't?" I scrabbled for my phone, scratching my arms on one of the ubiquitous blackberry bushes that were always encroaching on my parents' property. No one ever did too much to get rid of them. They might be thorny pests, but they made the most delicious berries.

"You need to think about what you're doing before you go rushing off. Don't mindlessly react. Is there anything about this situation that seems off?"

I grabbed my phone and checked my messages. Gwen had sent me the address, and when I mapped it, I squinted in confusion.

"There is nothing here but factories, barges, and the UPS Customer Center. Where the hell could she be staying?"

"Sounds like a red flag to me," Archibald pointed out.

I shook my head. "People do all sorts of weird things. Maybe some enterprising worker opened an Airbnb in the backroom of his building to scam unwary tourists."

"You don't think it's weird that Gwen would show up here without calling to make sure you made it home first?"

It wasn't a bad point, but still... "Ash told her where I was going, and probably told her when we expected to arrive. She doesn't know exactly where I am, but she knew my parents lived outside Estacada. Archibald, I owe her this much. She called me from her actual cell phone."

He huffed, a sound that reminded me of the beginnings of a hairball ejection. "Fine. I see I'm not going to talk you out of it. But please, please don't go alone."

"I'm so glad you want to join me on my road trip!" I said brightly.

Archibald muttered something that sounded suspiciously like "motherfucker," and I grinned.

"Back in a minute!"

CHAPTER

FORTY-TWO

While Archibald waited for me outside, I glossed over the parts of the situation that he'd found more problematic when I announced I was going to have to miss our first family meal to go meet Gwen in Portland. I told them she was at an Airbnb in North Portland.

No one was thrilled that I was taking off, but when I agreed to take my sword and drive my parents' Subaru instead of the BMW that I'd transported the not-dead-yet body in, they acquiesced. They probably thought I wouldn't disappear if I had to return their car.

It was only about an hour drive from the lush forests of Estacada to the industrial not-quite-an-island of Swan Island. Archibald didn't respond to any of my attempts at conversation. Instead, he alternated between muttering under his breath and glaring at me.

I slowed as I turned onto Going Street, the road that would take me onto the island. Since it was a Sunday afternoon, there was barely any traffic, and I was suddenly nervous. Whether it was at the thought of seeing my ex-fiancée, the weird almost-abandoned-looking industrial area, or Archibald's mutterings, I wasn't sure.

But I was here now. No backing down. No running away. Not this time.

I followed the GPS's directions to the back of a machine shop.

"Oh my god," I said when I saw the sign over the door. It was a large yellow piece of pasteboard with two cutouts of swans inexpertly pasted on it and *Swan Island B&B* written in messy block letters that were just a little off-center. "This should be illegal."

"It probably is," Archibald said. "But we're here now, so we might as well get this over with."

I turned off the engine and opened the door.

"Take your sword," Archibald said.

I glanced back over my shoulder at him. "I hardly think I'm going to need my sword to talk to Gwen. I haven't needed my sword for anything so far."

"Please."

I shrugged and grabbed my sword out of the back seat. I didn't have a scabbard, and it was awkward carrying it unsheathed toward a body shop, even with the creepy sign, but if it would make Archibald feel better, I could give him that much.

I knocked on the door under the sign and fidgeted, shifting my weight from foot to foot, until it opened.

Gwen ushered me into the room.

The inside of the room fulfilled the promise of the sign. Concrete floors covered with three worn rugs in varying sizes, patterns, and shapes gave way to a twin bed with an industrial-looking metal bed frame, sheets that reminded me of the '70s, a flat pillow, and decorative pillow with *Live, Laugh, Love* messily embroidered on it.

When she saw my expression of horror, she grimaced. "This definitely doesn't look like the pictures online."

"It looks like the set of a horror movie," I said. "Wanna go somewhere else to talk?"

"No," she said quickly. "This is okay."

Okay. She obviously didn't want to get in a car with me. Fine. I could work with this. I looked around her to see more of the room. There was a single metal folding chair under a bare lightbulb.

"That's the reading nook," Gwen said, correctly interpreting the question I hadn't yet asked.

"Maybe we can sit outside," I said. "There must be a bench somewhere. There's a bus line on this street."

Gwen stepped out of the room and pulled the door shut behind her. "I'd much rather breathe in the diesel fumes this island runs on than spend another second in that hellhole."

It didn't take long to find a bus-stop bench. We perched on opposite sides as far away from each other as possible, and I set my sword on the ground next to me.

The silence drew on awkwardly until I couldn't help myself. Someone had to say something.

"I'm sorry."

She waved away my apology. "Like I said on the phone, you don't need to be sorry. You saved my life. But I need to know what happened. Why am I having thoughts that don't feel like they're my own? And most importantly, why do I miss you so goddamned much?"

I opened my mouth to explain what'd happened when I'd saved her and why she was no longer alone in her mind, but her last question caught me completely off guard. "You...miss me?"

Gwen reached across the space between us and took my hand. "Frankie, I know things weren't perfect between us, but I was wrong to push you away like that."

"I broke every rule you asked me to follow. I stopped taking my meds and drank and drugged myself into near oblivion. I shopped like it was my job, and that was about the only job I had left. You know I got fired from the cat shelter, right? How could you miss that?"

She put her hand on my cheek, then looked me in the eye. I blinked once. Hers were blue, which is not the color I remembered them being. Another blink, and they were back to their usual soft brown. I must have imagined the change.

"Sure, there were a lot of bad things, but they didn't negate the good. I know you have it in you to take care of yourself better. Just come home with me, and we'll figure it out together." She scooted along the bench until she was pressed against me. The hand on my cheek slid down to cup the back of my neck, and she licked her lips.

I followed the path of her tongue with a longing so acute I almost vibrated with it. "Don't mess with me, Gwen. I couldn't stand it if you pulled the rug out from beneath me."

She brushed her lips against mine.

I leaned into her kiss, and for a second, everything seemed perfect.

Then she pulled back and laughed. "You are so gullible, Frankie. One of the dumbest people I've ever met." She laughed again, and stood up while I stared, dumbfounded and broken-hearted.

"What are you doing, Gwen? You didn't have to come all the way here to call me stupid." My voice didn't waver, something I was more than pleased with.

"Ahh, but then I wouldn't have gotten to see the look on your face, and I so dearly wanted to experience that one last time."

As she spoke, her voice changed from its usual huskiness into something softer, more melodic. Her long, brown braid shrank and disappeared, turning into a pale-blonde pixie cut, and her features morphed into a face I knew almost as well as Gwen's.

"Ash? What the actual fuck?"

FORTY-THREE

I stood and moved into a defensive position, sword held in front of me. Maybe I was gullible, but no matter what Gwen/Ash said, I was not stupid.

"You show up alone without reinforcements. And now you think that sword is going to save you?" Ash laughed again.

"I'm not alone," I said with a bravado I didn't quite feel. Fake it till you make it was a tried-and-true method to get a person through anything, even a confrontation with a shapeshifting asshole who'd pretended to be my girlfriend.

"The cat hardly counts," Ash said. "What kind of help do you think he'd be able to give you? Will he shed on me? Cough up a hairball?"

Fear threatened to creep into my body, raising the hairs on the back of my neck, but I squared my shoulders and refused to let it take over. I could be scared later. Now, I just needed to figure out what was going on and how to get rid of Ash.

"Why all this?" I gestured at our surroundings, taking in the quiet, abandoned industrial setting. "What is the point?"

Ash shrugged. "Fun, mostly. I love fucking with people, and you are oh so easy to fuck with. So innocent. So trusting. But now, unfortunately, I have to kill you."

"Why now?" I slowly backed up, desperate to put as much space between us as possible. "You could've killed me at any time between Santa Fe and here, and no one would've known. Gwen knew I was going home, but she never wanted to hear from me again. My parents didn't know I was coming. Why go through this?"

Ash rolled his eyes and pulled a long, wicked-looking knife from the backpack I hadn't noticed him wearing. He shrugged off the pack and tightened his grip on the blade. "Fun. I already told you that. Watching your homecoming, seeing your parents embrace you back into the fold, letting you have that day of security only to yank it all away was worth it. Not to mention the pleasure it gives me to let your sisters believe that you just took off again."

I shifted my balance and held the sword a little higher. Thunder rumbled in the distance. I stole a glance at the sky. Dark clouds were piling up over the west hills, and the scent of rain and petrichor washed over us with a gust of wind.

Frowning, I adjusted my stance so my back was to the wind while still keeping my eyes on Ash. "I don't understand what's wrong with you, but I'm not just going to stand here and let you kill me."

He cackled, and lightning flashed, thunder only a few seconds behind. "You can wave your stupid little sword around if you want to, but it won't help. Even if you somehow manage to escape—which you won't—I still win. I destroyed your job, your relationship, your life. Not that it was hard. You were so desperate for a friend, so desperate for a drink, that it was easy to become your 'bff.' All it took was a little coke, a few drinks, and some late nights, and you were mine." Ash sneered at me.

The tip of my sword dropped a little as the impact of his words hit me. "Why?"

He shrugged. "Why not? It was more fun than outright killing you, and as long as it had the same end result, taking you off the game board, who cares how it happened? You were never anything but a weight I didn't want to carry. A parasite."

His words echoed what Jackie had said to me that morning, and I gasped.

"You? It was you this morning?"

His smile was smug and self-congratulatory. "Figured that out, did you?"

"Who are you?" I whispered.

In answer, he burst into flames, laughing maniacally as he did so. "I'm the one who killed the last Valkyrie."

He rushed me, and I lifted my sword. This was nothing like the sparring matches I'd had in the past, but my muscle memory still worked. I deflected him, but the fire radiating off his body singed the hair on my arms.

I spun around, keeping him in view. Lightning arced across the sky, nearly blinding me. Fortunately, Ash was easy to spot, even through the bright flashes that were the after-effects of the bolt, and I blocked his knife again.

"You're more fun than I thought you'd be, considering how pathetic you are at everything else," he taunted me.

I rotated my wrist a bit to get a better feel for the sword I'd barely used in the last year and ignored him. I wasn't going to let a little trash talk get through my defenses. I was out of practice, but it didn't look like Ash had any experience wielding a blade.

I could have ended the fight quickly if he hadn't been on fire; the heat and smoke kept me at a distance. I couldn't go on the offensive without getting a lungful of smoke.

"Ash." Everything came together. "The fires?"

He cackled again. "I wanted to see what would happen. I thought you might die rushing in to save your stupid girlfriend, but what happened was even more interesting. Not everyone agreed that it was the best way to get rid of you, of course, but you created enough havoc to make up for surviving. Nothing like a little chaos, a few wraiths, and a pissed-off reaper to add a little spice to this adventure." He danced forward again, slashing with his knife.

I stepped back. I couldn't tell if he wasn't trying, or he really wasn't as good as me.

The sky opened up and a deluge hit us. Ash dropped his knife to his side, but his flames didn't dim.

"I probably shouldn't have let you get to your parents' house, but it seemed like a good idea at the time," he admitted. "I do not recommend riding in a trunk, though. I was so motion sick by the time I got out."

"Do you ever shut up?" Archibald asked. He padded to my side through the downpour. His ginger fur was dripping and matted to his body.

"Not if I can help it. Glad you're here, cat. Now I get to kill two annoyances with one knife."

Lightning struck the ground between us, and the force threw me back. Something knocked the wind out of me, and I had to fight to stay conscious. When I finally blinked the grey away, Ash was standing over me, knife held to my throat.

"Not even your tricks are enough to save you, Frankie. You're an inexperienced Valkyrie and crazy AF. And I'm a god. Thanks for the laughs."

The knife plunged toward my throat, but not before another bolt of lightning tore through the sky, striking Ash and creating a smoking hole in his torso.

FORTY-FOUR

It took a few nudges from Archibald to get me to move. Ash hadn't stirred, which really shouldn't be weird, but he had survived his own autopsy after all.

"Take a breath, Frankie. We need to get out of here."

I followed his instructions, and when the ringing in my ears had faded and the smell of burnt flesh dissipated in the rain, I straightened and took in the scene.

The electricity in the air built again, and it seemed likely that this time, lightning would hit me. I wasn't sure why I believed it was after me, but it might have been too many *Mighty Thor* comic books as a youth combined with a visit from Freyja.

I took a step away from Ash, just in case he was the target, but the static electricity running over my body didn't dissipate.

I raised my sword, the only defense I had, and cringed.

A bolt of lightning struck my sword and rattled my teeth. The light spread through me, rooting me to the ground.

When I could open my eyes again, Ash was no longer at my feet. Instead, he was standing, knife at the ready.

He laughed, although it sounded more unsure and slightly less deranged than before. "Trying to reenact some kind of Castle Grayskull fantasy? The lightning sword *was* pretty impressive, but I'm tired of playing games now."

My jaw dropped as his reference hit me.

He-Man. Fire everywhere. Sure, there wasn't a pile of skulls or a pegasus, but Archibald was here. I wish I'd asked Jackie more questions, like what happens next?

I didn't have time to dwell on Jackie's precognition or my lack of flying horse. Ash attacked, and the speed with which he wielded his blade made clear that he'd been taking it easy earlier.

It was all I could do to block his blows. There was no way I could return his attacks.

He pushed me back, step after relentless step. I didn't dare take my eyes off him to survey the ground.

I stumbled, and my sword dropped, just far enough that Ash got a strike in. His knife slashed across my chest, and burning pain followed. I resisted the urge to clap my hands over my boobs and instead took advantage of his momentary expression of victory to move forward and get my sword in under his guard.

I didn't make contact, but I pushed him back a few steps. I was going to count that as a win until I got a real victory.

Movement out of the corner of my right eye momentarily pulled my attention away from the fight. A curvy woman with brown hair, a black cloak, and a huge scythe stood ninety degrees from where we were fighting.

I recognized her immediately.

I turned my attention back to Ash but spoke to her. "Dusana?"

"One and the same," she replied.

Dread washed over me, and it was only muscle memory and training, no matter how long in the past it had been, that kept my sword arm from wavering.

Ash's grin was victorious when I faltered, but I took another step forward, forcing him to fall back to protect his abdomen.

"Are you here for me?" I gasped. I might have been working on my endurance the last couple of weeks, but I was not in fighting form. I should save my breath, or at least keep Ash from knowing how winded I was, but I had to talk to her.

"Yep," she said, much more casually than I'd expected a reaper to sound, especially when she was declaring her foreknowledge of my death. "I mean, no. Not in the way you mean. Watch out!"

Her warning pushed my full attention back to Ash. He'd raised his knife and was bearing down on me.

Panic fluttered in my throat, but then a calm clarity washed over me. I was going to win.

I raised my sword to block his. Then, with two quick movements that my last instructor had despaired I'd never pick up, I pushed him back and skewered him.

He looked down at the sword in his torso, then glared at me. "Seriously?"

I peered at him. I could see where his soul anchored to this body and knew what I had to do.

I raised my sword, held my breath, and slashed.

FORTY-FIVE

I stared at Ash's corpse. Between the hole that'd been created by the lightning and the stab wound by yours truly, it was in terrible shape.

The connection between his soul and body, however, was intact.

The storm moved on and the sky lightened, blue patches appearing between the clouds.

"You should behead him," Dusana said. She'd walked forward to stand next to me when Ash had finally fallen. "I don't know what the fuck he is, but beheading takes care of most things."

"Why is his soul still attached?" I grabbed at the hem of my T-shirt and ran my sword along it. It wasn't enough to clean it, but at least it got some of the blood off. Of course, that meant the blood was now on my T-shirt. I grimaced.

"I don't know," Dusana admitted. "But he's not human, and he's somehow associated with Hel."

"Like a demon? I just got used to being a Valkyrie. I am not ready for Satan to be a thing."

Dusana laughed, but she never took her eyes off Ash. "He's not Satan. I meant Hel. H-E-L. The Norse goddess of the underworld."

Dammit. Of course.

Smoke rose from Ash's body, and I took a step back, raising my sword.

The smoke formed the pattern I'd seen at the Winnemucca motel, taking the shape of a giant fucking snake with wings. This time, though, instead of dissipating into the sky, it solidified, took a few slow turns around us, and laughed.

"Your stupid weapons can't kill me, and the reaper can't take me."

Archibald walked forward from wherever he'd been hiding. "Get out of here, Ash. You can't hang out and gloat because you lost. So leave."

To my surprise, smoke-snake Ash listened. He hissed, his forked tongue flickering toward us, and left.

"Huh," Archibald said. "I didn't think he'd listen."

Dusana took a few steps closer to me. She smelled like lavender and sea spray. I bit my lip as my attention was drawn to her cleavage. It wasn't blatant, but her body wasn't hidden by the corset top she was wearing, either.

I shook my head. "If you didn't come for me, or for him, why did you?"

She wrinkled her nose and pursed her lips. "I'm here for you, but not *here* for you, if you know what I mean."

"I can honestly say I one hundred percent do not know what you mean," I answered.

She huffed out a breath. "You know I was the reaper at the accident outside of Oatman, right?"

I nodded.

"You looked like you needed some help. The soul I was tethered to was doomed to haunt Route 66, but he elected to move on after that. So I decided to follow you. It took me awhile to catch up with you, even with your weird cat's help, but you need me."

"Um…" There weren't a lot of ways to respond to that declaration, and I couldn't find any of them.

Her expression turned uncertain. "I mean, I'm sure you're more than capable of figuring things out, but you *looked* like you might need someone more experienced."

I raised my eyebrows. I knew what she meant, but I couldn't help myself. Everything was so ridiculous, and I needed to say something, anything, to break the tension growing in my body.

To my surprise, Dusana blushed. "Dammit. I'm not saying anything right. Ugh. I am a reaper. I have millennia of experience. I've made so many mistakes, and I've learned from them. I want to help you make fewer than I did."

"Plus, she finds you attractive," Archibald added.

Dusana's flush deepened, and I grinned. I was never the one on solid ground in flirting situations, but for once, I had the secure footing.

"Would you like to come back to my parents' place with me? My mom's a Valkyrie, and my youngest sister's a psychic or something. A couple Valkyries and another friend of my mother's are arriving tomorrow, an event my father believes will be pure pandemonium, and there is a lot of family-related chaos, but—"

"Yes," Dusana said before I could finish my caveats.

This time, the heat that rose in my chest had nothing to do with embarrassment.

"Cool. Cool, cool, cool." I was babbling. Time to move on and pretend I was not an awkward teenager.

"Cool," I said, then winced. "I mean, yeah. Let's get going. Do you have a car?"

Dusana laughed. "I have a car, and I can follow you there, as long as you give me the address in case we get separated."

"If you give me your number, I can text it to you." I held my breath—that was a level of boldness I seldom attempted.

Dusana recited her number, I texted her my parents' address, and heard the *ping* that announced receipt.

"Okay. Well, I guess I'll see you soon, then?" I shifted from foot to foot.

Dusana straightened, and her cloak and scythe disappeared. "For sure. But not in a reaping sense. Just a hanging out sense." She muttered something I couldn't quite hear. It sounded like she was cursing under her breath.

I grinned. It was nice not to be the only person discombobulated by our conversation.

"Cool," I said.

She grinned at me. "Cool." She strode off and climbed into an older Lincoln.

I headed to my car, Archibald at my side. "I suppose you're going to tell me about all the mistakes I've just made, including inviting a reaper to my parents' house."

"Actually," he said, "you've done remarkably well. The lightning trick was unexpected but effective, and you vanquished your enemy. At least for now."

"Who is he?" I asked.

There was no answer for a while, and I looked down to make sure my cat was still there.

"I don't want to make baseless conjectures," he hedged. "I need to consult a few other people."

"Just tell me what you think, then. I promise not to hold it against you if you're wrong."

Before he could answer, I noticed a woman in jeans and a tank top with a gold circlet twined through her long, thick, blonde braids striding toward us on a path I could've sworn was empty seconds earlier.

"Freyja! You're okay!"

She grimaced. "Okay is relative. I am alive, although not at full strength. But we are not here to talk about my injuries. There are spies who could take news of my well-being to the gods. You have done well. You have defeated your enemy—temporary though it may be—on the field of battle. You have chosen right when the choice was presented. And you have offered truth and accepted aid. I am pleased."

"Um, thank you?" I hadn't meant to make it a question, but that's how it came out.

Her smile was brighter than the sun that was peeking through the clouds. "You are welcome. We will talk again soon. In the meantime, please pass on my greetings to your mother, Kara, and Lena. You may also let Adele know that I am aware of her."

I nodded. "Okay." I didn't have a chance to ask why Adele didn't get a greeting, because she disappeared in a burst of light, although at least this one wasn't as blinding as the lightning had been.

"Okay. This has been...an adventure. Ready to go home, Archibald?"

He didn't answer, but his head butt pushed me toward the car.

FORTY-SIX

An hour-and-a-half later, I pulled into my parents' driveway. According to my phone, I'd been gone fewer than four hours. Not nearly long enough for everything that had happened.

My mom appeared on the front porch seconds after I turned off the engine, and Dusana pulled up moments later.

Mom looked between me and Dusana with obvious confusion, then walked toward us. "Is this...Gwen? I didn't know Gwen was a —" She looked between us again.

"Mom, this is Dusana. She's the reaper I saw in Oatman. The one who told me how much I was screwing up."

Mom's smile widened, and she held out her hand. "It's a pleasure to meet you, Dusana. It's been a long time since I've talked to a reaper. Most of you don't show up at the conventions."

My eyes widened, and I was gratified to see Dusana was equally surprised. "There are conventions, Mom?"

My mother laughed. "No. But your faces made my little white lie worth it. There used to be occasional informal get-togethers, but in recent years, there have been so few of us." Her face drooped for a moment, and I saw the sadness behind her mask. Then, the perpetually sunshiny face returned. "But you're both here, and I'm here, and three more amazing women are showing up tomorrow. Maybe it's not PompCon, but we can still have drinks and gossip, right?"

Dusana grinned at my mom, but I couldn't quite manage to. I couldn't have drinks and gossip. Not now, and maybe not ever.

"So many iced teas," Mom said without losing a beat. "And—if everyone is good—homemade lemonade."

"You can drink, Mom," I said. I wasn't sure if I meant it, but I wasn't going to make my issues anyone else's.

"Don't be ridiculous," she said. "None of us lose anything by having non-alcoholic beverages, and if it makes your life easier, why wouldn't we?"

She slid her arm through mine and tugged me forward. "Come in. We ate sandwiches for lunch. We didn't want you to miss out on the potato judging."

"Is judging potatoes a Valkyrie thing or a family activity?" Dusana asked. Her earlier awkwardness appeared to have disappeared, and she was settling into the rhythm of my mother's banter.

"It is a human thing," my mother answered. "The three of us might not be entirely human, but everyone has a favorite way to prepare a potato. What's yours?"

"Home fries," Dusana said without hesitation.

My mom stopped walking. "Oh shit. That is a good one, and not something that made today's tournament." She tipped her head back and pinched the bridge of her nose. "This invalidates today's results completely, unless Marty can find enough potatoes to make a batch. I'll have to rework the brackets, but that can be done…"

She dropped my arm and strode into the house, muttering about potatoes and cursing her own forgetfulness.

Dusana slid her arm through the one my mother had released. "So. Here we are."

"Indeed." I was a brilliant conversationalist today.

"I followed you all the way here. I was only a day behind you in

Vegas, but your cat"—she glared at Archibald, who was trotting sedately behind me—"steered me wrong after that, and I lost your trail."

"I didn't steer you wrong," he said.

"You told me to head to Tahoe, then to Portland," Dusana protested. "That is the very definition of steering me wrong."

"You found her, didn't you? And only a day or two later than you would've, anyway."

I looked back and forth between them, then to Dusana. "You can track me?"

Dusana wobbled her hand back and forth. "Not in the way you're probably thinking, but when I chose to stay here on earth instead of returning to the After, it was for you. And because of that choice, I'll always know where you are. Vaguely, at least."

That was more than a little creepy, but I tried not to let it show on my face. I failed, though, as was evidenced by Dusana's reaction.

She dropped my arm and rubbed the spot between her eyebrows. "Ugh. Sorry. I've been human for ten years, and I'm still awkward as fuck sometimes."

I laughed, and the tension dissipated for a moment. "I've been human for thirty-five years, and same. I think awkward is the human condition."

"Neither of you are human," Archibald muttered. "Barely even mortal at this point." He stuck his tail up in the air and stalked off around the house and into the woods.

I stopped walking and looked at Dusana. "I have a lot of questions. About your choice to stay here, about the tracking, about the why of it all. And that doesn't even start to get into the other things. Ash the flying snake pyro, goddesses, Valkyries, talking cats, a magic sword. And where's my pegasus, anyway?"

Dusana held up her hand as if to ward me off, but her laugh sounded amused and sympathetic. "My life is a story, and one that has intersected with yours a couple times. I don't know if you remember—"

"Of course I do! You were the hot chick who picked me up when I was hitching to Santa Fe."

Dusana grinned. "And you're the hot chick I picked up when I was cruising the route with my ghost-friend Percy." She sobered for a moment and shook her head. "He decided to move on after everything that happened in Oatman. We were together for ten years, and as much as he was a pain in my ass, he was my first friend here, and I miss him."

I didn't really understand what she was talking about, but I could feel sadness radiating off her. I placed my hand on her arm. It wasn't enough, but I didn't know if anything would be. "I'm sorry for your loss."

Dusana shrugged. "It's harder than I expected, but it was time for him to go. It was supposed to be my time to go back too. Who would've thought after ten years trapped Earthside, banished from the After for fucking up a reaping, I would've chosen to stay here. Here. Where I am forced to menstruate!"

"But yet..."

She smiled at me. "But yet. I thought when I decided not to leave, it was because you needed me. Needed someone to guide you to make better choices. But I think what you really need isn't a teacher or a guide. It's a friend."

"Pretty sure I need a teacher, too," I said wryly.

She leaned toward me, and my hand slid off her arm and hooked through her elbow. "I'm happy to answer any questions you might have and offer any advice. But as a friend and not a mentor. I think your mom is more than capable of teaching you everything you need to know."

"I can't remember the last time I had a friend," I said. I'd meant for it to sound light-hearted, but the truth of my statement rang through my words, and my smile faltered. Ash and I hadn't been friends. Even before today, I'd known that. And Gwen had been my girlfriend. It's not that we weren't friends, but we'd started off as a couple, and that was different.

My last friend, the last person I could remember exchanging confidences with, was Gary, and we hadn't been close since high school.

I dismissed the pain to be dealt with later. With all the things I was shoving in the overhead luggage compartments, I was going to need to find a few therapists to help me unpack some other time.

"I'd very much like a friend," I said. And maybe, someday, it'd be more than that. But for now…

Dusana held up her middle finger and pointed it at me.

I looked at her finger, then at her face. "I do not understand."

"We'll middle finger swear to our friendship," she said. "I know most people pinky-promise, but I met this kid at a diner once, and she told me, in the most solemn voice, that middle-finger swearing was ever so much more binding than a pinky promise."

"Well, if a kid told you that, it must be true." I laughed and held out my finger, linked it with hers, and we shook on it.

"Of course, she also told me that swearing on the River Styx was an unbreakable oath, and that flipping the bird was called 'middle fingering.' I laughed so hard at that, but when she asked why, I told her to ask her parents."

I burst out laughing. "I'm not opposed to middle fingering, but I'm not sure that one all by itself is enough to be effective."

"Dirty," Dusana said.

I exhaled in a rush. "Friends," I said firmly.

"Swear on the River Styx," she replied. "Just friends."

FORTY-SEVEN

I snuck away while the great potato debate was going strong, Dusana joining in with no hesitation. Mom hadn't been able to find enough potatoes to make home fries and declared the entire contest invalid. That didn't stop people from sampling, judging, and vociferously defending their choices.

Jackie's gaze caught mine as I was leaving, and I nodded at her, hoping it was enough to assuage any fears she might have had that I was running off. I held up my phone as if that was somehow more evidence, but she'd already turned her attention back to her baby.

When I was alone on the deck and the glass slider was closed, I dialed Gwen's number.

She didn't answer. I hadn't really expected her to.

Once her voicemail picked up, I gave my carefully prepared speech. "Gwennie, hey. I know you don't want to talk to me ever again, and that's okay. I'm back in Oregon at my parents' house, so I'm not gonna show up on your doorstep. No worries about that. I won't reach out again after tonight, but I need to know you're okay." I took a deep breath. "Ash called me today pretending to be you, and I'm worried. Please, just call me."

I sat in my Adirondack chair and leaned back, watching the setting sun change the sky from blue to lavender.

My phone rang. I fumbled it in my haste to answer and it dropped onto the deck. For one horrific moment, I thought it was going to slide between the slats, but it didn't, and I picked it up before it could get up to any more shenanigans.

"Frankie, make it quick. I have plans."

My guts twisted and I could feel beads of cold sweat on my brow. Plans meant a date. If it'd been work, she would've said she needed to get to the station. If it'd been friends, she would've said she was headed out with Daphne and Craig. But plans.

"Frankie?" Her voice was sharp, but it also sounded just like Gwen. Not that I'd been able to tell the difference before, when it'd been Ash.

"Hey. I just wanted to make sure you were okay, like I said. Ash's joke was not funny at all—I almost got hurt—so I needed to make sure he hadn't hurt you."

"I haven't seen that bastard in a week," Gwen said. "And good riddance. He might have been a great firefighter, but he was weird."

"If you investigate any of the fires without a clear cause, I think you'll find that Ash is the thread that ties them together. He as much as admitted that to me today before he took off." I crossed my fingers she wouldn't ask for more details.

Gwen sighed heavily. "I'd suspected. He was under investigation, but everything kept coming up clean."

I wanted to draw this moment out. The subject was grim, but for a moment, it felt like we were partners again.

But it wouldn't last, and I owed it to her to get through what I needed to say.

"Gwen, I'm sorry. For everything. I'm clean now. It's only been a week, but it's just the beginning. I'm back on my meds, and my psychiatrist in Santa Fe is finding someone here to refer me to. I'm staying with Mom and Dad until I get back on my feet. I just wanted to let you know."

Her voice softened. "I am so happy to hear that. It doesn't change anything between me and you, but I want you to be okay, and there were so many times I didn't think you ever would be."

I bit my lips. There was something else she didn't know, something that might be important. But I just couldn't.

"Anyway," I said. "Thanks for calling me back. I'm glad you're okay. I'll let you get back to your date. Be safe."

"Goodbye, Frankie," Gwen said before ending the call.

I put my phone on the table next to me and dropped my face into my hands.

"Decided not to tell her about the second soul?" Archibald asked.

I wrapped my arms around my body. "I don't know how. She wouldn't believe me, and even if she did, there's nothing I can do about it. It'd just freak her out more."

He nodded, then hopped onto my lap. "I don't know how your skills will develop, but it's possible that you can fix it someday. It won't bring her back to you, though."

"It doesn't matter. I screwed up too many times to ever expect that door to open again. But maybe eventually we can be Facebook friends."

Archibald laughed, and his claws dug into my legs. "High aspirations indeed."

My fingers found the sweet spot between his ears, and I scratched until I made him purr. "The highest. Thanks, Archie."

He didn't protest the nickname. "For what?"

"For being there for me, even when I was majorly fucking up everything."

He didn't move, but his form exuded a shrug all the same. "My pleasure. At least some of the time."

I smiled and redoubled the scritches. I tipped my head back and watched the stars pop out, one by one. There was so much left to learn, to understand. In the soft glow of the emerging Milky Way with my cat in my lap, everything felt almost achievable now that I was home.

I closed my eyes and let a smile spread across my face. Home. I kinda liked the sound of that.

EPILOGUE

I woke to what sounded like an explosion followed by the crash of a car accident. The window rattled in the frame, and my bed shook beneath me.

I was out of bed, in my robe, and in the kitchen in a flash.

Instead of a smoking crater or some other natural disaster in the middle of the room, I found four women ranging in age—or at least appearance of age—from forty and five million. My mother was snort-laughing, and a familiar-looking gorgeous white woman with long, silver braids was rolling her eyes. Early morning light was streaming through the windows, and the clock on the stove read 5:13.

One of the other cacklers was a white woman with cropped, fiery red hair. She was short, barely topping five feet, and if she weighed more than a hundred pounds soaking wet, I'd have been shocked. She had one of those faces people called "ageless." Light creases to denote age and experience, eyes that looked like they'd seen some shit over the years, and a youthful countenance that was in stark contrast to her laugh lines.

"Aunt Lena!" I said. "I haven't seen you in a million years!"

She opened her arms for a hug, and I walked into them, then

grunted when her surprisingly strong grip threatened to crack my ribs.

"Frankie! We thought you'd be up when we arrived." This was from a tall, fierce Black woman with a stern expression and no traces of laugh lines—all the deep grooves in her face were severe. She looked much older than my mother, but I had no doubt she could kick the ass of anyone who got in her way. "I didn't come all this way to be kept waiting by some layabout too lazy to get up and greet the women who will help get her shit in order."

"Um…" I looked at my mom, who just smiled encouragingly. "It's a pleasure to meet you…?" I held out my hand.

The woman stared at it as if I'd offered her a dead fish instead of a greeting, but when I didn't waver, she gripped it and grinned. Her wrinkles rearranged themselves into softer lines around her eyes and mouth. "I'm Kara. I trained your mother, and if I can't get you into shape, no other Valkyrie can."

"So no pressure, then?" I asked.

"None whatsoever," Kara confirmed. "At least not on you. Imagine if I fail after a one-hundred-percent success rate? I'll be cast down in shame, my name erased from the rolls of Valhalla. Freyja herself will appear to take my sword and slit my throat."

"She means we'd make fun of her the next time we got together," Aunt Lena said. "Everyone knows Freyja outsources all her throat-slittings."

Unfamiliar footsteps behind me announced Dusana's arrival. I turned to greet her with a smile, but her expression was dumb-founded.

"Adele? What are you doing here?"

The pieces clicked. Adele looked familiar because I'd seen her in Oatman.

Adele shrugged and grinned mischievously at Dusana. "I love me a bit of chaos, and your girl has plenty of that following her around. Besides, I'm old friends with Katrin, and she needed help."

"You're not a Valkyrie," I said.

"Nope." She didn't elaborate.

I glanced back at Dusana again. Her eyes were narrowed in suspicion. "You've known this whole time," she accused Adele.

Adele smiled and addressed Dusana. "'Known' is such an amorphous term. But we met Hel, and now you're in the company of Valkyries. And based on the CliffsNotes I've gotten on Frankie's friend Ash, who was your odd desert encounter, someone of my talents will be useful."

"What do you mean?" I asked, stepping into the conversation between Adele and Dusana. "What about Ash? What are your talents?"

Kara looked at me, pity evident in her eyes. She glanced at my mother. "Do we tell her?"

"I've kept too much from her for too long. I won't hide anything now," my mother said.

"Child," the Black woman said. "Your Ash is Loki. He is chaos, a shape changer, a trickster, and a god. And he wants you dead."

KEEP READING for a sneak peek at Calling the Blood, Book 2 in the Ghosts of Valhalla series, then pre-order now for a March 19, 2024 release date!

WANT MORE AMY CISSELL?

And why wouldn't you?

Love it, hate it, somewhere in between? Please leave a review for **Choosing the Slain** at Goodreads, Bookbub, or your favorite online retailer.

Links to all retails sites are at:
https://books2read.com/choosingtheslain

Reviews are always appreciated & allow me to keep writing what you love!

Sign up for Cissell's Epistles at https://amycissell.com for new release updates, exclusive content, and a bevy of book recommendations! (You'll also get to choose a free book as a thank you for hanging out!)

Come hang out in my Facebook Reader Group - the Amyzonians can always use another shenaniganator. (It's a word. Promise.)

https://www.facebook.com/groups/amycissellauthor/

Join my patreon for early access to books, free copies of my digital books, free paperbacks, and access to my entire back catalog!
https://www.patreon.com/ACissellWrites

CALLING THE BLOOD

GHOSTS OF VALHALLA BOOK TWO, CHAPTER ONE

Sweat dripped down my face and my stomach churned as I collapsed to the floor. My pulse pounded in my throat, and my vision wavered.

I swallowed hard, trying to stay conscious and keep the contents of my stomach where they belonged. Through the dripping strands of hair that'd escaped my ponytail and stuck to my face, I saw my mother.

I hadn't known she was here. I squinted, bringing her into focus. Her expression was completely shuttered.

Fuck. I'd disappointed her. Again.

I pushed myself into a seated position and scrubbed at the tears and sweat, wincing at the sting in my eyes.

"Sorry!" I gasped.

Mom sighed. "You don't have to be sorry."

"Yes she does," Kara snapped. "That was pathetic."

My chip dipped to my chest, and a flush of shame burned my cheeks.

"Get up." Kara stalked away and paced in the middle of the floor, never taking her eyes off me.

I used the wall to push myself to my feet, then bent down to pick up my sword. My hand cramped, and I almost dropped it. Only fear of Kara kept it in my hands.

"What are you waiting for?" Kara snapped.

My mother offered me a half-smile. I would've preferred an intervention, but I'd take what I could get.

I straightened my spine, shifted my grip to ease the cramps, and shook the tension from my shoulders. I raised my sword and bounced on my toes. She would definitely disarm me in less than a minute, but I was not a quitter.

Kara attacked without warning. I'd taken sword-fighting classes on and off since I was thirteen, and the one thing I'd learned about all my opponents is that watching the eyes was more important than watching the body if you wanted to know what was coming next. It didn't work with Kara. She telegraphed nothing. One second she was still, the next, she was inside my guard and my sword was on the ground. Again. At least this time, it was only my sword and not my body. I was covered in bruises from the six weeks of training, and no closer to proficiency than I had been before.

Kara strode to the far wall of my mother's basement training room and picked up [sword cleaning materials]. She whipped a towel at me. "Dry yourself, clean your sword, and hit the showers. Be back at eight tomorrow morning, and we'll go again." She finished cleaning her sword without another word and left, her steps light and almost silent on the creaky wooden stairs that led to the main floor of my parents' house.

I took the towel and mopped at my face, then walked over to the bench that held my stuff, gulped some water, and started cleaning my sword.

My mother sat down beside me. She was fair-skinned and flaxen-haired, or at least that's how she was described in the sagas. In reality, her white skin was tanned from hours outside and her hair was a dark blond, rather than the golden color attributed to the Valkyries by the old stories. She was, however, built powerfully. She would never be described as slim—nor would I—but she had a muscular solidity about her that was inspiring and intimidating.

"You're doing great," she said.

"Yeah, real great," I replied. "I'm black and blue all over, I spent more time on my ass today than on my feet, and I have never managed to get a strike on Kara, a woman who is a million years older than me."

Mom laughed. "Not quite a million. And she's your teacher because she's the best swordswoman we have."

"She's also the biggest bitch you have," I muttered under my breath.

My mom gently smacked the back of my head. "She's not a bitch. She's a hard-ass. And no one likes her during training. She'd probably be offended if you did. Her goal is not to be your friend, but to train you to stay alive."

I sighed. Everything she said was true, but it still sucked. "I hurt all over and may never walk again."

"So dramatic," my mother said mockingly. "With those skills, you could skip saving the world from Ragnarok and become a Broadway star. I smell Tony!"

Teenage Frankie wanted to roll her eyes, but adult(ish) Frankie leaned into my mom and rested my head on her shoulders. "You're ridiculous, Mom."

She slipped her arm around my shoulders and pulled me in close. "That's my job." After one more squeeze, she let go and stood up. "Take your time, but don't sit too long or you'll stiffen up. I'm going help your dad finish getting lunch set up. Once you're showered and clean, come eat. You need the calories." She ran her gaze up and down my body and frowned. "And not just because of the amount of energy you're expending with Kara. You are running on empty, Frankie."

I brushed off her concern with the same light tone I'd perfected over years of ups and downs with bipolar, substance abuse, and the resulting health and body changes that went with it. "I'm fine." I met her gaze and pushed sincerity into my eyes. "Seriously. I feel better than I've felt in ages. I'm just crap at sword fighting at the moment." I set down my sword, stretched, and took another drink of water. "Go help dad. I'll finish cleaning up in here, then take a shower and meet you in the kitchen."

The narrow-eyed look she shot me wasn't convinced, but she let it go. At least for now.

When she disappeared from the room, I slumped onto the bench. She was right. I was running on empty. I might be clean and sober for almost two months, but things were not getting easier.

"You okay?"

A smile crept across my face. I turned around to face Dusana and tried to keep my jaw from dropping. She always looked good—she was a tall, dark-haired white woman whose lush curves needed a warning sign and whose brown eyes were deep enough to capture my soul—but in her tight blue jeans, scarlet corset, and knee-high leather boots, she was stunning.

No! I chastised myself. *Reapers are friends, not fuck buddies.*

"Hey Dusana," I said, going for casual and not quite hitting the mark. Fortunately my new friend and secret crush was not the greatest at reading body language—it took more than a decade as a human to pick up all the skills—and my awkwardness went by without comment. After a moment, I remembered that she'd asked me a question. "Um. Fine. Everything's perfectly all right now. I'm fine. Thank you. How are you?"

A smile flitted across her face. "Love a Star Wars nerd almost as I love the planning and preparation that goes into the Great Potato Showdown Redux, as your mother calls it. Once you're showered, can we go for a walk?"

My head spun with the pinball of her subject changes, but I caught up quickly. "Of course! Showering is good. Food, better. Potatoes best. I'm gonna grab some lunch once I'm clean, and then we can head out. Anywhere in particular you want to go?"

She looked past me, and I knew Archibald had appeared back

there. "Why don't we figure it out as we go." She reached forward and lightly ran a thumb down my jawline.

Friends. I told myself, clamping down on my libido. I was too fucked up now for anything else.

She grinned at me, then walked out of the room. I turned around to face the large, fluffy orange cat in the corner. "How long have you been here?"

He delicately licked his front, right paw. "Not long. I missed seeing Kara knock you around. Any better today?"

I finished cleaning my sword, then sheathed it and hung it on the wall. "No. I'm never going to get it. I'm useless as a fighter. There must be a better role for me."

Archibald walked over to me and headbutted my ankle, then twined around my feet. "You're not just a fighter, Frankie. There is so much more waiting for you. But fighting is going to be a part of it all, and if you can't keep yourself safe, then you can't keep anyone else safe. Don't look at this as PE class punishment. You're not running laps. You're learning how to channel the most elemental, powerful parts of your soul and become a weapon."

"I don't wanna be a weapon," I sulked.

Archibald snorted. "You are a Valkyrie. You can not only escort souls to the afterlife, you can pull them from a person before they're ready. You're already a weapon. The least you owe the world is control."

He wasn't wrong. But still... "I'm not learning how to stop inadvertently stealing souls. I'm learning how to kill people with a pointy stick."

Archibald strode towards the door, tail straight in the air, giving me a view I could've done without. "Tell me later how anything you're learning isn't teaching me control." He disappeared before he reached the stairs, and I glared at the space where he'd vanished. Why couldn't I be learning how to teleport instead of stab people?

With a final huff of disgust and self-pity, I walked up the stairs, skirted the kitchen and living room, and ducked into my room. I shed my clothes on the way to the shower, stuck my tongue out at my reflection, then turned the water on to just below boiling. I let the scalding water beat out the tension of the fight, my nerves, my crush, and my crazy.

Preorder Calling the Blood today!

THE CARDINAL GATE

AN ELEANOR MORGAN FANTASY
ADVENTURE #1

I am faced with an impossible choice: destroy the world of my birth or the world I call home?

I was minding my own business, giving Hedge Antilles—my laurel hedge big enough to warrant its own name—a much-needed trim when bam! Vampire! At least that's what he called himself, and he did have pointy fang, try to bite my neck, and died with a stake to the heart. He also called me a fairy before he bit it—literally and figuratively.

Now I'm in a race I don't quite understand to open gates I'm not entirely sure should be opened to save the Fae Realm, the home I don't remember. Finn—up until now, my best friend—is guiding me on this quest, but we both need some personal growth if we're gonna make things work. He needs to get over the hope that I'll ever be in love with him, and I need to get over the fact that he deliberately infiltrated my life by order of my absent Fae father.

Not everything on this whirlwind quest is bad, though—Isaac, Mr. Tall, Dark, and Handsome werewolf, is along for the ride (that's what she said...). There are too many secrets to sort out, and I feel like I'm the only one playing this thing straight.

Everyone seems to think I'm going to shatter this world, but only some believe I'll save it. Am I trusting the right people, or will my faith in my friends be the straw that destroys it all?

Meet Eleanor Morgan as she begins her quest to open the gates between Earth & the Fae Plane. Come for the magic, stay for the puns.

The Eleanor Morgan Fantasy Adventure series is a contemporary/urban fantasy series with adult themes (read: explicit naked times and a fair amount of violence). It is a complete series at seven full-length novels.

https://books2read.com/cardinalgate

ACKNOWLEDGMENTS

This book wouldn't have been possible without the many, many people who took part in my mental illness survey. For everyone who shared their experiences with living with or parenting a child with bipolar, thank you so much. Your willingness to share so much personal and often deeply painful information is more than appreciated. I hope I captured, at least in part, your experiences.

Thank you to Kim Snyder - Overall Beauty Minerals, The Great and Powerful Oz, Debb, Ian, Jennifer H, and especially Treasa Lynn's mother, as well as everyone else.

So many thanks to my great beta readers and all my advance readers! Y'all are beyond fantastic.

I'm grateful to my editor Andrea at Two Birds Author Services and my proofreader Christopher Barnes for their feedback, plot hole discoveries, and comma rehabilitation.

Chris - thank you for encouraging me, even when I quit writing about 30 times each book. I'm glad I married you and can't wait for the next adventure!

Of course, no acknowledgment section would be complete without mentioning my amazing daughter Liana. She's my regular coffeeshop writing companion, brainstorming partner, and graphic design consultant. Love you to the ends of the universe, then through a wormhole to a parallel universe. And back.

MAGIC & MAYHEM AT THE END OF THE WORLD

Amy Cissell is a USA Today Bestselling Author of urban fantasy and paranormal romance novels. She lives in Portland, OR with her husband, her haunted house-obsessed daughter, their two cats, and the murder of crows she's conspiring to turn into her vengeful army.

When she's not working or writing, she's sleeping because that's all she has time to do! There are few things Amy loves more than a well-timed pun, a good book, a glass of wine, and making calf eyes at Portugal when she thinks no one's looking.

Although she reads anything and everything, her first love has always been fantasy. Eleven-year-old Amy discovered fantasy when she 'borrowed' her father's copy of The Hobbit and an enduring love affair (mostly with dragons) was born.

facebook.com/acissellwrites

instagram.com/acissellwrites

bookbub.com/authors/amy-cissell

goodreads.com/acissellwrites

tiktok.com/@acissellwrites

patreon.com/ACissellWrites

ALSO BY AMY CISSELL

Contemporary/Urban Fantasy

Ghosts of Valhalla

Haunting the Route

Choosing the Slain (December 2023)

Calling the Blood (2024)

Waking the Fire (2024)

Waking the Fire (2025)

Raising the Dead (2025)

Seeking the Frost

Breaking the World

Drawing the Blade

Burning the Gods

Riding the Storm

An Eleanor Morgan Fantasy Adventure

(complete series)

The Cardinal Gate (February 2017)

The Waning Moon (June 2017)

The Ruby Blade (October 2017)

The Broken World (March 2018)

The Lost Child (June 2019)

The Iron River (May 2020)

The Dark Throne (February 2021)

Box Sets (ebook only)

Eleanor Morgan Books 1-4

Eleanor Morgan Books 5-7

Paranormal Women's Fiction

Vamps in the Vineyard

Stakes and Stems: A Prequel Novella (September 2022)

Here to Slay (September 2022)

Slay Bells Ring: A Holiday Novella (January 2023)

Midlife Magic in Eden Valley

(complete series)

Raising a Demon (June 2021)

Devil and the Deep, Blue Lake (September 2021)

Valley of Angels (November 2021)

Guardian of Eden (February 2022)

Eden Valley World Novellas (ebook only)

Match Made in Hell (June 2021)

Hell's Bells (December 2021)

Fall From Grace (January 2022)

Devil May Care (February 2022)

Box Sets (ebook only)

Midlife Magic in Eden Valley (Collection One)

Midlife Magic in Eden Valley (Collection Two)

Paranormal Romance

Psychics of Oracle Bay

Not in the Cards (October 2018)

First Hand Knowledge (November 2018)

Wing and a Prayer (January 2019)

Belle of the Ball (December 2019)

Hell and High Water (June 2022)

Tempest in a Teapot (April 2023)

Elements of Surprise (April 2023)

Dead Giveaway (2024)

Bad to the Bones

Shoot for the Stars

Fun and Prophet

Box Sets (ebook only)

Seeing is Believing in Oracle Bay (Books 1-4)